Praise for *Above Us Only Sky*

"These essays on a woman's wild ride through life give us Marion Winik's bracing tonic-of-truth voice in splendid form—her voice that is always brilliantly funny, intelligent, brave, haunting, and full of surprises, revelations, and wise, wild connections. At this point, I don't think I could live without it. If you don't know her yet, your life is about to get better." —NAOMI SHIHAB NYE, author of *The Tiny Journalist*

"NPR personality Winik mines the intertwined humor and poignancy of life's exigencies in this earthy essay collection, taking stock of moments from childhood to motherhood and reliving them with relish. By turns heartfelt and cutting, playful and contemplative, Winik's chatty narration and musings emerge as vivid brushstrokes on a crowded canvas, jottings of her thoughts at both pivotal moments and more introspective times." —*Publishers Weekly*

"Intrepid NPR commentator Winik's voice is as unique as her observations and as recognizable as her experiences. By turns pithy and poignant, outraged and outrageous, Winik . . . once again mines the rich veins of her personal life . . . and while the laughs are still there, there's also a tempered maturity that nicely balances Winik's self-deprecating, tongue-in-cheek approach. Middle age is upon her, a perfect time for reflection and prediction, appreciation and apprehension, making amends and making a difference." —CAROL HAGGAS, *Booklist*

ABOVE US ONLY SKY

ALSO BY MARION WINIK

The Big Book of the Dead
The Baltimore Book of the Dead
Highs in the Low Fifties
The Glen Rock Book of the Dead
Rules for the Unruly
The Lunch-Box Chronicles
First Comes Love
Telling
BoyCrazy
nonstop

Above Us

ESSAYS

Only Sky

MARION WINIK

COUNTERPOINT

Berkeley, California

Library of Congress Cataloging-in-Publication Data
Names: Winik, Marion, author.
Title: Above us only sky : essays / Marion Winik.
Description: Berkeley : Counterpoint Press, 2020. | First
    published: Emeryville, CA : Seal Press, c2005.
Identifiers: LCCN 2019047077 | ISBN 9781640093089 (paperback) |
    ISBN 9781640093096 (ebook)
Subjects: LCSH: Families—United States. | Friendship—United States.
    | Interpersonal relations. | Winik, Marion.
Classification: LCC HQ536 .W565 2020 | DDC 306.850973—dc23
LC record available at https://lccn.loc.gov/2019047077

Cover design by Sarah Brody
Book design by Jordan Koluch

COUNTERPOINT
2560 Ninth Street, Suite 318
Berkeley, CA 94710
www.counterpointpress.com

Printed in the United States of America

FOR SUZY DUNN

It would be an exaggeration to say that ours is a hostile relationship; I live, let myself go on living, so that Borges may contrive his literature, and this literature justifies me . . . Little by little, I am giving over everything to him, though I am quite aware of his perverse custom of falsifying and magnifying things.

—JORGE LUIS BORGES

There is a fine line between fiction and nonfiction, and I believe Jimmy Buffett and I snorted it in 1976.

—KINKY FRIEDMAN

CONTENTS

INTRODUCTION
(2005)

Among the ragtag facts still fluttering around my brain from the books I read in college is the four-stage plan for our lives outlined by the Hindu Vedas: student, householder, retiree, sage. I am now squarely in the second, and while on the plus side the householder is the only one encouraged to have sex, with this fringe benefit comes an intimidating job description. Householders are responsible for the care of their children, their parents, their friends and relations, their neighbors, their country, and their society.

And don't forget their pets, their plants, their cars, and the backed-up plumbing in the upstairs bathroom.

Back in my student phase, I wrote poetry, but my transition to householder corresponded almost exactly with a switch to personal essay writing. My first piece of creative nonfiction was called "How to Get Pregnant in the Modern World": as anyone whose popped-out belly button has preceded them into a room by several minutes can tell you, late pregnancy is an ideal time for navel-gazing. But while looking inward is obviously a key element of the personal essay or memoir, I think the narcissism of this genre is often overstated. Just as the householder begins taking care of the world by sweeping her porch (or at least planning to sweep her porch), the personal essayist looks for the truths that connect us all in the details of her own history, her experience of gender or loss or travel. The further paradox is that the more idiosyncratic these experiences seem, and the more specific the details of their telling, the more clearly they seem to strike a universal chord.

By the time I was the mother of a six-month-old, I had gone from complaining all the time about my lack of inspiration to having a notebook full of ideas for essays; twenty years later, I still have a couple left. I often joke that becoming a mother ruined my life. In some ways, it did. My social calendar, my cultural participation, my opportunities for drug and alcohol abuse—none of these has ever been the same. As a writer, however, it renewed me. Far from taking away the world, it handed it to me, demanding, squirming, and desperately needing a bath.

The subject matter of parenthood ranges from bedtime and discipline to birth and death. Even political issues, from reproductive choice to terrorism, and every philosophical problem, from the existence of God to the enigma of missing socks, are in the parental purview. As one responsible for explaining the world and transmitting values to the next generation, a parent is thrust daily into the position of expert. You have to figure out what you think, and you have to put it in words. So, really, you might as well write an essay.

If you belong to the first generation of women who grew up

expecting to have lives beyond motherhood, this project has particular poignancy, since what many of us have discovered boils down to this: there is no life beyond motherhood. Partly in the sense just described—because there is nothing so deep or so abstract that it does not somehow stand in the middle of family life; even physics, at the end of the day, is homework somebody needs help with. But it's also in the sense that, though your kids leave home, parenthood never ends. Its eternity is particularly apparent if, like me, you decided to have a baby in your forties.

These days, as I look at the world around me, I find my reaction is no longer the alienated what-the-hell-is-this of my younger years. I definitely still think, What the hell is this?—but I can't afford the luxury of alienation. I am in the same age group as the leaders of our world and its institutions, and like them I experience this place as my problem, my baby, mine. As a householder in the Vedic sense, I am responsible. At the same time, householding itself is the basis of my worldview, my understanding of politics, culture, and morality, my (pardon the expression) family values.

In the past six years, I have moved across the country from Texas to rural Pennsylvania and have adjusted to a new landscape, physically and emotionally. My children have grown, my skin and hair have betrayed me, people I love have died and been born. The news from outside has often been bad; I give my radio a don't-you-dare look before turning it on. What sustains me through these ups and downs is the abiding sense I have of watching stories unfold, my pleasure in the narrative itself. Some of the inevitable pain of living is alleviated by the joy I find in the arc of these works-in-progress, these farces and tragedies and morality plays, and the comfort I take in the certainty of their innumerable sequels. I find myself, too, going back over stories that seemingly ended years ago, the longings of a little girl in New Jersey, the adventures of a young woman in Austin, the challenges of a somewhat younger wife and mother than I am today—and finding messages there still waiting to be understood, still waiting to pollinate my thoughts with their sticky yellow motes of truth.

The following essays about family and friendship and faith (the title of this book refers to my deficit of the last) have been growing in my head for a while now. Some began as NPR commentaries that later merged with magazine pieces, one was a three-hundred-page novel that swallowed truth serum and went on a diet, some took decades to figure out how to tell, while others vaulted from my living room to my laptop overnight.

Now they finish their journey upon arrival in your hands. I've had so much help in this process that a list of acknowledgments might have to be published as a separate volume, raising the question of why I needed quite so much assistance. Instead, I will simply offer thanks to everyone. Well, actually, I couldn't sleep if I didn't mention the names Ingrid Emerick and Crispin Sartwell, perceptive editor and beloved pain in the ass, respectively.

POSTSCRIPT
(2019)

The new edition of this book comes at a time when my Vedic householding days are over, though I'm not exactly a retiree or a sage, and as I write this, my youngest child is coming home from her freshman year at college to spend the summer. Time to get out the twelve-cup coffeemaker and prepare for surprises.

To the essays in the original collection—Parts I through V, "Back" through "Around"—I've added a new section, Part VI, "Later." Almost all of these pieces were written for the Bohemian Rhapsody column I've contributed to *Baltimore Fishbowl* since 2011. A few come from the period when I was the "My Life as a Mom" columnist for *Ladies Home Journal,* and two were written for the Lives column of *The New York Times.* These essays move through the end of the householding years to the dawn of the empty nest. Altogether, it's twenty years of family life, documented in real time.

I find myself amused by the air of confidence projected in the first introduction to this book. In sorting through newer essays to choose which to include, I couldn't help but be struck by all the definitive pronouncements I've made that turned out to be incorrect. I was sure my second marriage was going to make it. I was sure that once I went gray, I would never dye my hair again. I thought Donald Trump could not be elected. More than once, I thought I had left all my bad habits behind, and made the mistake of announcing this. I thought that once I finally lost ten or fifteen pounds, I would surely never gain them back. I thought I would hate living alone after my children were gone, then I thought hell, no, I loved being by myself, then I realized every day is different and change never stops, which is why these pronouncements don't usually hold up. If there's anything I've learned since 2005, it is that there are endless opportunities to be wrong. Nonetheless, I keep seizing the opportunity.

The wisdom of age is that the wisdom of age only goes so far. As an essayist, all you can rely on is the act of paying attention. You keep noticing everything you can, you keep trying to put those observations into words, you keep trusting the words to bring the meaning. You accept that the meaning is a work in progress, which at least keeps it interesting.

Or that is my humble hope. May you be interested.

I

Back

WAITING FOR DADDY

The charismatic, high-spirited accountant Hyman Winik was rarely seen in his own home. Work was my father's blood, his food, and his breath. All day he slaved at his office in the city, all night at his desk at home, all weekend with ball games blaring on TV, the adding machine *kerchunk*ing, the phone ringing, the dishwasher running, the crazy dog barking nonstop in the yard, which begins to explain why the entire household was shouting all the time. Meanwhile, my father had partial hearing loss, reputedly from diving off the high board in his youth and from firing rifles in the Marines, though to us the deafness seemed suspiciously selective.

JANE. The Herzbergs want us for cocktails on Saturday.

HY. (Doesn't like the Herzbergs, doesn't look up
from his dinner.)

JANE. Hy!

HY. What?

JANE. The Herzbergs! Invited us for cocktails!
This Saturday!

HY. What about the Herzbergs?

JANE. Could you please wear your goddamn
hearing aid?

HY. What?

JANE. For God's sake, Hy. You're driving me nuts.

HY. If you think *I'm* driving you nuts, just wait till
we get to the Herzbergs.

Herzbergs or no, they would surely find something to do on
Saturday night. My parents were like movie stars to us: appearing
briefly, waving, drinking, yelling, getting dressed up in one costume or another, and leaving again. On summer weekends, they
would stop by the beach club to visit us and our babysitter. They
looked stunning in their emerald-green golf caps, their deeply
tanned legs and arms set off by one ethereally pale ungloved
hand. Then it would be home to change—Mommy standing in
front of her neat rows of labeled shoeboxes: Navy slingback? Black
backless sandal? Beige patent pump?—and back to the club for
some barn dance or twi-nite or clam bake.

We would do anything to get them to stop, to get their attention, especially his attention. Let's have a headstand race,
Daddy, please, we would beg as we lined up ready to go in the

froggie position he had taught us, knees balancing on our elbows. Daddy could stand on his head for twenty minutes, and that little skinny Olga Korbut sister of mine was just as good. It was almost scary, watching him, so big and heavy and upside down, his face reddening, his forearms trembling, and when he finally lowered his feet to the floor, it was as if the Chrysler Building had toppled—dishes rattling on the dinner table, tidal waves in the milk cup.

In my earliest memories of my father, he hardly makes an appearance. It's the memory of the buildup, the anticipation, like the memory of a place you spent years planning to visit, and then saw only during an airport layover. We moved from Manhattan to the Jersey shore when I was two; in those early days, Daddy commuted by train to his office at 1410 Broadway. In the evenings, we would pick him up at the Elberon station in our cavernous Renault, Nancy and me in the backseat, so small that our ankles stuck straight over the edge, Mommy two thousand miles away in the front, wearing a car coat and plastic rain kerchief over her perfectly smooth hair.

For what seemed like hours, we explored the limits of what two little girls can do in the backseat of a car without getting in trouble for "roughhousing." You could stick and unstick your legs from the vinyl, watch raindrops roll down the windshield, stare at a streetlight then close your eyes to see what color it made inside your eyelids, pester your mother, poke your sister—hey, no roughhousing!—pick your nose or a scab on your knee, sing *This old man, he played one* over and over under your breath, and then, after all that waiting, you might not even see the train arrive, and what a shock when the door swung open and he was there. Daddy! Yippee! Kiss me, Daddy, me. Oooh, you're all wet!

When our family got a second car, we female Winiks were somehow even more paralyzed by our anticipation. Instead of going to get him, which at least felt like involvement, we just stayed home and waited. And waited and waited and waited. Because little girls can't eat dinner at 7:30 at night (and his arrival would be greeted not immediately with dinner but with a relaxing cocktail and hors d'oeuvres—shiny circles of hard salami, stinky blue cheese and stinkier liverwurst, cut-up cubes of Swiss speared with toothpicks and arrayed around a shot glass of Colman's mustard), we girls were fed our dinner in advance.

We would be in our favorite smocked nightgowns, little red flowers printed on white flannel, thin and pilled from being washed a zillion times. Dinner would have been something like Shake 'n Bake pork chops with applesauce and canned corn, or one of many fine recipes using Lipton's Onion Soup Mix. To my mother, corn was a "starch," not a vegetable, so you could never have corn with rice, bread, noodles, or potatoes. In any case, this whole insidious food group was seen only rarely in our home, where weight-watching was a perennial concern.

If the maid wasn't there that day, Mommy would sit with us while we ate, supervising to make sure that I didn't exceed the recommended portions, and that my sister, Nancy, ate anything at all. Sipping her gin martini, smoking, Mommy would tell us jokes she had heard on the golf course, funny stories with priests and rabbis and lightning and three people jumping out of a plane.

I have a joke for you, Mommy, says Nancy. Knock knock.

Who's there?

Orange you glad I didn't say banana?

I roll my eyes. No! That's not how it goes. First you have to say, Banana banana banana banana banana. Like this . . .

I wanna tell it!

Girls, please. Eat your applesauce, Nancy. You love applesauce.

Can we watch TV after dinner?

Enough with the bread, Mar. Please. Slow down. (*Deep drag on cigarette.*) Nancy, eat.

Hours rolled by every minute as we waited for Daddy to come home and rescue us from our X chromosome swamp of lugubriousness. It was like sitting in the theater waiting for the curtain to rise. It was like waiting for the phone to ring or the mailman to show up. It was interminable and it was unavoidable and I think it used up every drop of patience I had available for the rest of my life.

Finally, finally, *finally*, the sound of the garage door, the rumbling rolling thunder roiling through the pork chop air, drowning out the constant low hum of our many home appliances. The garage door was manually operated, pre-electric-opener. It was he who forced it open with his own burly shoulder, his meaty palm, throwing his easy might against the corrugated metal to reenter his cave. Our ears pricked up, we shoved back our chairs, and we tore through the house like hockey players, elbowing in front of each other, stepping on the hems of our nightgowns, slipping on the beige faux-terrazzo linoleum. Just as we reached the foyer, the door to the garage would open and he would appear! We hurled ourselves against him, our whole weight into his arms, his coat, his scratchy face, Oowie, Daddy, you need to shave! He smelled like outside, cold air and New York and cigarettes in the car, and he dropped his heavy briefcase and picked us up, his big girls. Who lived only for this moment, for his return.

Who would you want to be in this little vignette? Would you want to be the waiter or the awaited? Would you want the car and the briefcase and the Second-Coming-of-Christ welcome, or would you choose the kitchen table, the pesky kids, and the Shake 'n Bake? I'm telling you, it doesn't matter what you want. If you're a woman, you can get the car, the briefcase, and the rest of it, and still nobody's going to cut the Swiss cheese into little cubes for you, no one will sit mesmerized waiting for you to appear. True, if you stay gone long enough, your children may grow impatient—but that's largely because they're waiting for you to come home and start the cheese-cubing. Nobody else can cube that cheese like you! No matter how far you go, you never become the thrilling, elusive master of the universe. You walk in the house and you're back in business, Queen of the Mundane. Whose fault is this?

Men's, genetics', the media's, the culture's—or yours, because you wouldn't have it any other way?

When it comes to the essential state of wanting, of waiting, of craving, and of obsessing, of living for the All-Important Thing That Is Coming Next, we women are trained professionals, waiting for the water to boil, the cheese to melt, the laundry to dry. On the other hand, who needs training? We're born for it, aren't we? Waiting for our bosoms to sprout, our periods to start, our babies to be conceived, gestated, delivered, weaned, then waiting for the babysitter to show up so we can get out of here. Waiting to be seen, to be noticed, to be chosen, to be asked. Waiting for someone to arrive and give us his undivided attention. Waiting to be kissed, to be loved, to be fucked, to be always the object, never the subject, except in our own confused minds. Until we go crazy from all the waiting, and rise up, seize the reins, take control, and become the convoluted freaks of nature you see all around you today, our femininity as full of holes as Swiss cheese, our macho dreams on the commuter train to hell.

Naturally, I wanted the briefcase. To grow up and be just like my dashing (yes, always dashing!) father. To sign my last name just the way he did, a slashing vertical scribble, the inverted triangles of the *W* followed by a hasty range of peaks for the *n* and the *k*. The vowels were left to your imagination: a waste of time, and he had no time to waste. I wanted to take up that much space at a table or in a room. I wanted to drive that aggressively, balancing a highball glass against the steering wheel on the way to the Burger Chef, to yell a lot and have everyone listen, to make everyone laugh at my hilarious jokes. I wanted to have lots of money and shower it on my adoring dependents, and a bottle of Stolichnaya vodka in the pull-out freezer drawer of the refrigerator, into which I would shave thin slivers of orange peel. (Such would be the extent of my domestic duties! Orange-peel shaving!)

Oh, Daddy, Daddy, Daddy, where are you? When are you coming home? When will we get to see you? When will you play with us, Daddy?

Daddy is busy. He's very busy! Run along, girls!

DEAR TEXAS,
GOODBYE

For six months I knew I would be leaving Texas. It was the first half of 1999; beginnings and endings loomed large for everyone. My personal Y2K–readiness program involved trying to live as if I were already gone. Friends called, but as the answering machine picked up, I sat motionless, picturing their plates of enchiladas Michoacán, their tall glasses of hibiscus tea, their lunch at Las Manitas without me. I saw Lamar Boulevard without my car, the Town Lake soccer fields without my sons, my front steps without my feet. People started greeting me by saying, Are you still here?

I had always thought of home as the place you left, the place you outgrew, the dull origin you made self-deprecating jokes about. Shot clean out of deepest New Jersey before the ink dried on my high school diploma, I embraced the interstate highway system like a cult religion, ricocheting between Providence and New York until I learned I could drive to Atlanta or Chicago overnight. But the day Interstate 35 led me into Austin, I slowed down, looked around, and parked for about twenty years, stone in love.

In my heart, the Texas capital remains as I first saw it in the tender green spring of 1976, before booms and busts, before sky-scrapers and silicon, before lattes and microbrews and national home delivery of *The New York Times*. Then, as now, it was a little city with a great big head. It was Texas, all right. Big drinks, big ideas, big university, big fat toast, big wide streets, and the biggest swimming pool you ever saw smack in the middle of town.

Milling around this supersize paradise was a motley crew of hippies, cowboys, hippie-cowboys, Mexican day laborers, sorority sisters, and UT exes in burnt-orange Caddies, every one of them so damn happy to be in Austin, they couldn't stop themselves from beaming and calling you "honey," couldn't wipe those big Texas grins off their faces, even standing in line outside the convenience store on the melting asphalt in the burning sun, apparently thrilled just to be waiting to pump their cheap Texas gas.

This contentment bordering on self-satisfaction bordering on arrogance got my attention, my curiosity, and finally my rent check. In this alien place, so beloved by its alien inhabitants, I had the compelling and life-changing desire to be home.

It took me a couple of tries to get my roots to take in the cali-che soil. One summer I drove for Roy's Taxi, shuttling my room-mates to jobs at the Stallion serving chicken-fried steak; later, I spent a few years in a crazy house over in Clarksville where we tried to stop the South Texas Nuclear Project and used a red ban-danna as a communal napkin to save money. IMPEACH REAGAN was silk-screened on our front door. More than once, New York and New Orleans lured me with their siren songs. But when it was time to at least entertain the notion of growing up, I went back to Austin to consider my prospects, and stayed.

So did a lot of people. I got to town in the seventies with a bunch like me in their twenties who had weird hair and wobbly bicycles and stayed up all night then recovered from hangovers with forty-nine-cent breakfast tacos on their way to business school or beauty school or Barton Springs. Two decades later, I left a group in their forties who wake up in the dark before the alarm goes off, who talk on cell phones from their SUVs, who are lawyers and motel owners and social workers, who have to leave the kids' baseball game early because of the book club. I think it was Austin that made that transition so painless.

All over the country, from the rain-soaked cities of the Suicide Belt to the Northeastern overdose metroplexes, people are trying desperately to relax. In Austin, you really don't have to try. In other places, if you work nights and weekends, people understand it. You're a go-getter. Gotta be. In Austin, adulthood isn't all that adult. Unless you're playing in a band or making jewelry out of Fimo clay on the side, your friends worry about you. They say, What's the matter? You're working too hard. Come to our dinner party.

These dinner parties once featured potato soup in mismatched bowls. Then they evolved to barbecues on the deck of somebody's first real house, where discussions of interest rates could be heard amid the usual scat of music and movies and various local celebrities' drug problems. Next, the parties moved indoors to a dining room with a dhurrie rug and halogen lights, or to the apartment after the divorce, where we ate baked blue corn chips and Thai noodles from the gourmet takeout. People who once drank Lone Star or jug wine developed a preference for Veuve Clicquot over Roederer—or for Stoli straight out of the bottle, and then found themselves at twelve-step meetings with those very people they used to talk about at barbecues.

By this time, of course, there was always a second party in progress in the background: a bunch of smaller guests playing with blocks in the bedroom, splashing in the inflatable pool outside, shooting hoops in the driveway, or coming to blows over Nintendo. Yes, the children. As if leading us to Narnia, they beckoned us through the darkness of bars and Sixth Street and places to buy a joint at 4 a.m. to an Austin we'd never seen: a prelapsarian garden of playscapes and baby pools, choo-choos and real canoes you can row. With parks full of peacocks and bridges full of bats and springs full of ducks, where every restaurant has crayons. We helped them color. We remembered then how much we loved to color.

In my case, Austin worked. To the surprise of none more than myself, I got out not just alive, but middle-aged, with hardly a self-destructive habit left to my name. Instead of burning my candle at both ends, I learned to light it only for special occasions. Came in a miniskirt, left in a minivan. That's the way it goes.

I left because of love, and love was in Pennsylvania. By the second time we saw each other, it seemed obvious how we should spend the rest of our lives. He had complications that prevented moving and I did not. Without even thinking, I was saying, Sure, of course I'll go. It took quite a while for this snap decision to sink in. Here's the problem: when you're totally obsessed with missing your lover in Pennsylvania, you can hardly worry about missing the place where you still live so intolerably without him.

"Intolerably," perhaps, is not enough to say about this.

From the day I met him in a bookstore outside of Baltimore, my attention was diverted as if by an electromagnet. Not that night, but the next time we were in the same state—ten days later—we slept together, and we did again every time we could after that.

It was not enough for me. After a few months, I had the calculator out: 140 nights since we met, 24 of them spent together. This was only 17 percent of the time, and our average seemed to be getting worse. I had not seen him in seven days, and I would not see him again for thirty more. This, I determined, was the longest separation so far, longer than our previous record by a whole week.

Most nights we slept more than 1,650 miles apart, and into that aching space I sent hundreds of emails, phone calls, voice mails, faxes, postcards, packages, poems, and even a drugstore "love" card or two, for which aesthetic collapse I cursed myself and him. But that was not the worst of it; soon I was writing affirmations in my notebook: It is okay for me to be here. Things work out on their own inevitable schedule. My love brings me joy.

My motherfucking love brings me joy! Some days it was true. Some days I was incandescent with ardor, lit from within, hot and bright and transparent as a kerosene lamp. Like a nun, burning with unconsummated passion, with holy fire. His golden curls, his stomach muscles, his blue blue gaze six inches from my face—like the Cheshire cat's smile, hovering in the distance, the last thing to go when he disappeared.

Some had lovers, I had a thesaurus: cornflower, Dresden, delft, daylight, sky.

Most of the time, I felt like a person whose body was rejecting an organ transplant. His absence was bigger than any presence. Soon, I could not eat or sleep or work. I could not even drink or smoke. All I could do was exercise and robotically take care of my children. Run, lift weights, eat macrobiotic takeout, turn on Nickelodeon, and stare into space. I was in exile, no longer home. What home? My house, my town, my life all felt surreal. They were exactly the same, and I could barely recognize them.

I said this to him: My home is where you are.

What? he said. Sometimes I moved kind of fast for him.

Well, you know, I backtracked quickly, I'm from New Jersey. Up there. Where you are.

Meanwhile, as I suffered so flamboyantly and copiously, many people told me my situation was not so bad, that they themselves liked this sort of thing. They found it exciting, romantic, tantric. Even he told me this! Dear God. Even now I never want to see the words "long distance" and "romance" in the same sentence again.

Finally, I stopped fooling around, said what I meant. My home is where you are.

Shortly before I moved north to be with him, he came down with his kids to visit, and I took them out to the Hill Country—the secret green bosom of the state, west from Austin on Highway 290 to 281 South, then on to Medina and Vanderpool. After crossing and recrossing the Sabinal along sunset ridges from Utopia to Lost Maples, we spent the night at the Foxfire Cabins. There, to the children's great delight, he pretended for hours to believe he was Britney Spears. In the morning, I loaded up Britney and her fans and headed north to the Willow City Loop, surely one of the most beautiful stretches of road anywhere in the world.

A mile of that narrow byway with its single barbecue shack and its many cattle guards is enough Hill Country to break your heart—one after another, spectacular vistas no outsider would dream exist in Texas. Knolls as green as Ireland, dramatic bluffs, rolling meadows, and terra-cotta river plains. The knotty live oaks shading winding creeks that run through valleys so thick with bluebonnets they seem, at first glance, to be lakes themselves. Then fields and fields of long-stemmed white prickly poppies lit long ways by the sun, hovering above the grass like tiny angels.

I could hardly bear to leave, but I couldn't stay.

Though I lived in the state for more than two decades, I never answered the question, Where are you from? by saying, Texas. I argued with other nonnatives over that. They would say, Sometimes people just want to know where you live. But I don't think you should say you're from Texas unless you are, and I was not. So much of my love for Texas has specifically to do with being an outsider, it's almost a point of honor to make that clear.

And so I left, and left nothing concrete behind, no family, no ancestral home, no rightful claim. How could I disappear without a trace from a place that left such a mark on me? Perhaps there is something, after all; perhaps the mirrors at Hyde Park Gym still contain my reflection, or library books are still checked out in my name. Someone sights a phantom Jeep Cherokee making illegal U-turns on the Drag, or swears they saw me in the cheese aisle at Whole Foods. My children's names echo faintly through our old neighborhood at dinnertime, my horrendous bellow resonating through the eons.

If part of me were still there, wouldn't I have to return some-day, like a character from a ghost story looking for her heart?

THE BIG PLAN

After my first husband, Tony, died in 1994, leaving me the single mother of boys aged four and six, I was lucky enough to have a damn fine boyfriend, a divorced guy who was a great cook and the father of two sweet daughters. We had been dating for almost five years when things started to get a little tense. I knew he thought that the next step was getting engaged or at least moving in together. But I was happy the way things were: him in his house, me in mine, each with our own two kids. Though I joked around, labeling my approach the Spare Me the Dirty Socks School of Romance Management, my reluctance was the result of real fear. I was afraid that more proximity would upset the balance; that we would risk putting our kids through a merger only to subject them to a painful loss. His had already been through a divorce; mine had lost their dad to terminal illness.

Or as I told him one night after a couple of drinks at the Rock 'n' Bowl in New Orleans: I'm so honored that you stick with this relationship despite the fact that I'm not doing what you want me to, and probably never will.

You know, you hear a lot about "don't drink and drive"; in my case, an equally important warning might be "don't drink and talk." My boyfriend seemed pensive after hearing this little speech. On the long drive home to Austin the next day, he told me it was over.

No! I shouted, but it was too late.

Oh, great, Marion, I said to myself. Are you happy now? My fortieth birthday was fast approaching, and now I'd be celebrating that milestone alone. I would have to go on blind dates, for God's sake. But first, I had to put on some lipstick and pull myself together, since my book about the joys of single motherhood was about to be published and I was leaving on a publicity tour.

The first stop on the tour was an overnighter to Bel Air, Maryland, a suburb of Baltimore, leaving on a Friday morning and returning home the next day. This sounded a little hectic, but the publicist explained that it would be well worth it. It was School Night at the bookstore, the school orchestra was playing, and "jillions" of parents were expected: a captive audience with credit cards in hand. Giddy, I bought a pair of glamorous Oriental lounging pajamas at the Nieman Marcus outlet for the occasion.

I knew something had gone wrong as soon as my driver pulled up in front of the store on the appointed evening. Jillions of parents were there indeed, but they were leaving, struggling to their cars with sleepy children and violin cases in hand. For at least five minutes, I couldn't even get in the place due to the throngs pouring out. And by the time I did, about the only people left were two bedraggled employees.

I'm sorry, one of them said. School Night ended at seven.

You're kidding, I said. That's terrible!

Wait, there is one guy here to see you, the clerk remembered, trying to shore up her rapidly disintegrating author. In fact, he's been here for hours. Go find him, Karen.

My lone visitor turned out to be a friend of some mutual friends, a philosophy professor/writer guy in a sport coat, running shoes, a blond ponytail, and a silver earring.

Thanks for coming, I said, fiddling with a button on what now seemed to be just what they were: bright-green fake-satin pajamas.

This must be kind of disappointing for you, he said with concern.

Oh, heck no, I replied bravely, and to prove it, I insisted on doing a reading for an audience of four: him, the bookstore gals, and my driver. My performance could not have been more gala if I'd been onstage at the Kennedy Center. And I'm sure it was that, and not just pity, that motivated all four audience members to buy my book—including the driver, who was from El Salvador and may not have read English.

After I had signed the last grueling autograph, the blue-eyed professor and I went out to dinner. He gave me a copy of his book, titled *Obscenity, Anarchy, Reality*. Quite a title. Quite a cover, too—it featured a shirtless, well-muscled male torso. Holding the book in my lap at the restaurant, I tried to figure out if the body was his. Meanwhile, it was turning out we had a lot in common: both writers, both about to turn forty, both single with kids the same ages. We had both been through personal tragedies in which drugs played a nefarious role. But it wasn't just the facts that matched up; it was something more. The click between us was practically audible.

Yet neither of us was thinking of this as the prelude to romance, evidenced by the fact that we spent most of the time bemoaning our recent breakups. Crispin told me about his new tattoo symbolizing his grief over his young, brilliant ex-fiancée. I would not call this a pickup line. Nonetheless, sometime during dinner, I realized that I was on a date.

At about one in the morning, he left me at my hotel, hugging me goodbye beside his car. And that was all. I was thinking, Wow. If there are guys like this in the world, I'm going to be all right. At least I hoped there were others, because I didn't know if I'd ever see him again.

But the next day when I got home, there was an email waiting. It said: The next time you're in the region, maybe we should sleep in the same bed.

I was dazzled by this directness. I typed back, But why didn't you even kiss me when I was sitting there last night five inches away from you?

Making up for lost time now, said the next message.

After lots of jittery emails and phone calls, I arranged to meet him in Philadelphia, another stop on the book tour. He picked me up at the airport—I felt like a mail-order bride getting off that plane—and though we were both almost too nervous to speak, we started to kiss in the parking garage, and it was soon clear that everything was going to be fine. (It was definitely him on the book jacket.) When we parted forty-eight hours later, neither of us could deny it: a totally unexpected chain of events had begun in our lives and in our heads. Already, all bets were off.

I next saw him about a month later, at my home in Texas. To both of us, Philadelphia seemed long ago. He was really anxious about meeting my kids. But our doubts dissolved when my sons reacted to him as if he were a hip, athletic Santa Claus. He paid so much attention to them I started to get jealous myself.

Six months later, we got engaged. It was a beautiful fall day in Seven Valleys, Pennsylvania. We took Emma and Sam to school in the morning and then drove back through the countryside. We were looking at houses, idly of course, and he was talking about how he needed to buy a house for tax reasons, and he needed a tax consultant, and—

I made a frustrated noise somewhere between a sigh and a giggle.

What? he said.

You don't need a tax consultant, baby, I said, unable to hold the words in check any longer. You need to marry me.

There, it was out. By the speed with which the conversation progressed, it was clear we had both been thinking about this for a while. Within twenty minutes, we were on wedding details and names for a baby. By then we were at his house, and he stopped the car and told me that thinking about marrying me was making him feel like crying and it was also giving him a hard-on.

Which really was the most romantic thing I had ever heard in my life.

Later that day, we went shopping and found a little diamond solitaire, exactly what I wanted. Nothing creative or original, please, just the international symbol for I'm Getting Married! Then we went out to dinner, and when we got home, he actually got down on one knee and asked me to marry him. I was so breathless, I could barely eke out a tiny "yeah."

Back home in Texas, people were a little taken aback. One minute I was sure marriage was not for me; the next I was planning a June wedding. I was running around lit up like a Christmas tree with all the loony, sexy new-love energy you can possibly imagine, leading some to conclude I was just crazed with infatuation and driven by impulse. But there were other forces at play, one of which was timing.

After my husband died, I surveyed the situation my young sons and I were in and decided consciously to spend the next five years shoring up and consolidating. I would not move, I would not remarry, I would make no major changes to further unsettle us. As it turned out, I predicted the duration of my emotional healing exactly. The Great Cook had been my rebound relationship, as I had probably been his; with Crispin, I was ready to plan a future.

The experience of true love is one that dazzles the eyes and opens the heart of even a pragmatist like me. I may not have sold many books that night in Bel Air, but when I consider that I might not have gone there at all, I catch my breath. What if our mutual friends hadn't told Crispin about the reading? What if Crispin hadn't taken their suggestion, hadn't waited that evening, or hadn't had the nerve to send that email?

Sitting here in my study in rural Pennsylvania with my six-month-old baby girl in my lap, I can only shake my head at the way the dominoes fell. When I think about the window of opportunity, which was so narrow, and the odds against it, which were so high, I have to wonder if, against all reason, there really is a Big Plan for Our Lives. I'm not the kind of person who believes in things like that. But the great thing about the Big Plan is that, if it did exist, it wouldn't care whether you believed in it or not.

BLOND MOMMY

Of course it was because his hair was blond. I had already given in to my chameleon girlfriend tendencies in the first months of dating Crispin by taking up weight lifting, getting a tattoo, going to AA meetings, and staying up late at night by myself to watch University of Maryland basketball games on TV. So the sudden change in my hair color couldn't have been much of a surprise to anyone at that point.

Though my hair went through a very colorful and creative period in the eighties when I was married to a hairdresser, it has been brown and long with bangs for most of my life. In recent years, I have dumped grocery store color on it every few months to hide the gray. But around the time of the chameleon-girlfriend episode, I read in Diane Johnson's book *Le Divorce* that all French women over forty have blond hair. Two days later, I ran into my very blond hairdresser friend, Ava, at the jogging track. Thanks to the incredible boost cell phones have given to impulse decision making, we right then and there scheduled an appointment with the receptionist at her salon.

Per Ava's instructions, I went out to buy magazines to find a picture of the shade I had in mind. I don't know what I thought I would find in the *New Yorker*. Here, can you make me look like Kathryn Harrison?

The day of the event I was a basket case. I stared beseechingly at Ava and her assistant as they painstakingly applied mixtures from five little plastic bowls. They seemed to be coloring each strand of hair individually, layering my head with innumerable squares of silver foil, creating a robotic orphan Annie look. Between that vision and the stir-craziness, I began to feel a little light-headed. Perhaps the chemicals were leaching IQ points right out of my head, releasing my inner bimbo. Ava noted my change in mood and smiled quizzically.

It's true what they say, I told her. I'm having more fun already.

After the multihour production came to a close, I rushed to pick up my sons at their friends' houses. Hayes, then ten, was the first to view the results. I wasn't too worried about his reaction. I'd read a composition he wrote for school in which his fictional hero's mother was a college professor named Julie, described as "thin and pretty, with blond hair and big lips." No bimbo she, however: she taught at a school he called "Hartford."

It's great, Hayes said, touching me to see if I was real. You should have always had blond hair, Mom.

His little brother was less enthusiastic, still being at the age where any change in Mom's appearance is bad. I don't like it, said Vince. You look weird.

Oh, but you're gonna change your mind, Vince, when you get to know Blond Mommy. Blond Mommy is nicer than Old Mommy. She's richer, too.

Really? He mused for a moment. Can we take Lunchables to school tomorrow? he asked.

Blond Mommy says yes! I shouted. She always says yes! And I swerved directly into the grocery store parking lot.

I hope they enjoyed Blond Mommy's largesse because she didn't last long; one of her final acts was to move her children across the country to start a new life. Apart from the tattoo, most of the other chameleon changes faded as well; by year two I had given up Maryland basketball and reinstituted the evening glass of wine. (By year six, Crispin was drinking too, but that's another story.) After several years of marriage, I went to a hairdresser and again asked to go blond. I noticed that she put in only golden-brown and sandy streaks.

I like it, but it's not very blond, I said, checking it out in the hand mirror she had given me.

Oh, she said, would you have wanted that? Very blond doesn't seem like you.

MY TYPEWRITER— A REQUIEM

When very small, my son was asked what his mother did for a living. He replied that I was a typewriter. I don't know how he knew. By the time he was born, I had begun to use a computer. Yet the aqua and white Smith Corona electric typewriter given to me as a present when I went off to college was for years the repository of my identity, by far my most treasured possession. Its obnoxious hum was the sound of my thoughts. Its filled-in *g*, muddy *x*, and slightly above-the-baseline *R* were my handwriting. Its swingy jam back to the margin when I pressed return—*rrrrrrm, hing!*—made each line I typed a public event. When the Smith Corona was on, I was on. We vibrated together. As it aged, its oscillations grew too powerful for its plastic frame: it would scoot toward me across the desk and I had to keep pushing it away like I would an overly affectionate pet. *Stay, baby, you stay.*

Oh, those garbage cans of yesteryear stuffed full of crumpled paper, no more than a word or a sentence typed on each sheet. You could root through them frantically if necessary, you could decipher the erasures, scrape away the correction fluid, read through the *x*'s typed over an offending sentence. Nothing was gone for good, the way it is now: one doubting moment and the delete key sends what were surely the best lines you ever wrote, the deepest insights you ever had, to the unrecoverable void. Undo, please. Not that, the one before. Come on, for God's sake, Undo!

Remember tabs and margins set manually with sliding stops? The twisting of the roller, the snugness of the bond against the platen? The goofy *j* key that couldn't find its way home in the fan of letters and left an inky kiss on your fingers when you untangled it from the *h* or the *k*?

Me and that Smith Corona, we were poets together; we were Marxist feminist hitchhikers. We lived in co-ops, we lived in sin, we stayed up all night unraveling the universe. We wrote love letters that would break your heart. Until one day in the mid-eighties, when its electronic replacement showed up and I stowed it in its battered, bumper-stickered case for the last time. After I moved, the new tenants called to say they'd found it in a closet. Oh, just keep it, I told them, I don't need it anymore.

Some years later, I heard Smith Corona had shut down its manufacturing plants. I felt awash in guilt, as if hearing a once-favorite restaurant I hadn't visited in years was closing. Oh God, did you hear? I'd say. But what did I expect? They certainly couldn't pay the bills with my nostalgia. No, we abandoned our electric typewriters and left Smith Corona and its products to languish. I hear they now import office equipment from Asia and Europe, but I doubt any of it makes the trademark jolly *bing*.

Easy for me to reminisce about the good old days as I sit here with my current wife, my sixth or seventh—a silver PowerBook, so svelte and modern, so quiet and intelligent. Of course, we have our problems, and when they arise, she can be rather unforgiving. You probably know what I mean; if not, spill a big glass of water on your keyboard, get an ant colony started in your monitor, or roll your swivel chair over the cord and yank the whole thing to the floor. You don't need seven trips to the altar to know that there is no relationship so perfect, it doesn't sometimes make you miss your exes—even those left gaily, without a look back.

MY OLD NEIGHBORHOOD

Mrs. Jo Yo was a very old lady with a small and terrible white dog named Snowflake. The dog seemed to be half Lhasa Apso, half pit bull, and could spring into the air as if released from a slingshot. If he didn't actually bite you, it wasn't because he didn't want to.

When my first husband, Tony, and I moved into the neighborhood, Mrs. Yo and Tony went to war about where we could park our car. She felt her side of the street was hers. Tony maintained it belonged to the public at large. This battle was conducted entirely via notes stuck under windshield wipers: her spidery right-leaning edicts on flowered notepaper, his balloony, back-slanting, unpunctuated diatribes on torn envelopes.

The way it was going, I thought they might end up shooting each other or at least taking each other to court. But amazingly they came to a complex agreement about exactly where the car would be placed, during what hours, and under which weather conditions, that satisfied them both. In fact, a few years later, I saw Tony lift a big cardboard box out of Mrs. Yo's trunk and take it into her house as she tottered along at his side.

Not long after that, I helped Tony, who was then in the last stages of his long struggle with AIDS, end his life. Better treatments for AIDS were about a half year away, but we didn't know that then, and nobody was giving Tony six months. Though his doctor and favorite nurse expressed sympathy with his desire to put a graceful, immediate end to the *danse macabre*, there was nothing either could do to help without endangering themselves. After weeks of arguments and difficulties (a pharmacist who caught wind of the plan actually called the authorities after I brought in a prescription for sedatives), Tony discharged himself from the hospital and came home to die on his own terms, in his own bed—the bed in which our son Vince had been born on Tony's birthday four years earlier. It almost felt like a victory. It was the first choice he had made about his fate in quite some time.

Though the nature of Tony's death was far from a secret and was exactly the kind of thing one's neighbors would begin discussing in whispered backyard conversations the minute the funeral home van pulled away, I nevertheless was surprised when, four years later, I had a series of strange messages on my answering machine. Marion, said a scratchy, ancient voice. This is Jo Yo. Come over and see me. I have to talk to you about something.

I had never spoken to Mrs. Yo, had never been in her house, and couldn't imagine what she wanted. Though I was a little afraid to find out, I crossed the street and rang her bell. Through the glass beside the door, I could see Snowflake launch himself into the air, yipping maniacally.

The scratchy voice emerged from the intercom. Is it Marion? Yes.

Let yourself in with the key under the planter.

Snowflake went mad as I entered the house, where I found Mrs. Yo in her bedroom, immobile, frail, and emaciated beyond belief. Her collarbone looked like a hanger on which her body was draped like wrinkled laundry. She motioned me to sit down on the edge of her quilted pink satin bedspread. I want you to help me the way you helped Tony, she said.

There weren't too many things she could mean by this. I knew she didn't want me to put her through beauty school, keep plenty of sugar in the house for her coffee, make holiday plans with her mother, or bear her children.

In what remained of her voice, she told me that she could no longer get out of bed, her son was living in England, and they were about to move her to a nursing home. With startling ferocity, she said she did not want to go. She wanted to die in her own bed. She had asked her doctor and her relatives to help her—no one would.

I was completely sympathetic to her situation, but as I told her, we really didn't know each other well enough. I was pretty sure I'd be charged with murder if I held the plastic grocery bag she proffered over her head. I did offer to help Snowflake, if she liked. I also proposed to read aloud to her or get her a drink from the kitchen, but she rolled her eyes in frustration and sent me home.

Not long after, I saw Mrs. Yo driven away by a young man in a Buick; across the street I was packing boxes myself. She probably went to the institution she dreaded. I went to Pennsylvania, and I don't know what happened to her dog. Maybe they helped him at the SPCA. Although I have offered my services to my second husband from time to time—for example, when he gets a little whiny about a lingering cold—no one has asked me since to assist in his or her suicide. This is a good thing, because I'd like to keep my amateur status. Which, as I explained to my kids during the last Olympics, is when you do something only for love.

MY FAMOUS
FAMILY

I was flipping through a copy of *Rolling Stone* one sultry New Jersey summer afternoon thirty-some years ago when my dear grandmother Gigi finally remembered to tell me that its founder and publisher, Jann Wenner, was my cousin. I stared at her in shock. My cousin? How? Gigi explained that Jann's mother, Sim Wenner, was first cousin to my grandfather. Papa? I looked over at my ancient relative, snoozing in a nearby lounge chair behind green-lensed sunglasses, gray hairs curling on his weathered chest. Papa—our blood connection to the Beautiful People. Who knew?

Up until that summer, I believed myself sprung from the loins of a stolid line of businessmen and accountants, a family of ever more assimilated Jews who had come to rest, by 1960, in various suburban outposts north and south of New York City. Mine was a nice, normal family, at least in my twelve-year-old view, and this disappointed me deeply. I wanted a gothic family, an extraordinary family, a family distinguished by personality and achievement. The fact that my mother was ladies' golf champion at her club several years running did not do it for me. My father, though a character in his own right, was not famous, fabulously wealthy, or in any way exotic. My doting grandparents, my pretty aunts and jokey uncles—all very gemütlich, thank you, but hardly the raw stuff of greatness.

Perhaps sensing that relatives with whom one has quotidian social contact are bound to remain depressingly life-size, I had begun to explore the family tree for towering, romantic relations beyond the members of the Winik and Fisch clans I knew personally. Endlessly pestering my elders with leading questions and half-baked suppositions (God forbid I should read in the newspaper about anyone whose last name had more than three letters matching ours), I repopulated, reorganized, and generally spruced up our kinfolk with a host of illustrious, if absentee, additions. As it turned out, the old genealogy offered some decent raw material for my embroidery project, and my overactive imagination supplied the shiny thread.

Shortly before the *Rolling Stone* incident, my sister and I had been up one night entertaining ourselves by watching old home movies on the wall of the den. The heavy iron projector roared and ticked as backyard birthday parties and seaside romps flickered by. Then, we found a film unlike the others: instead of a small plastic reel in a yellow Kodak box, it was at least a foot in diameter, stored in a cylindrical tin case labeled in spidery ink faded past legibility. When Nancy loaded it up, it turned out to be old-timey black-and-white footage in the classic silent-movie style, with title cards printed in curlicued serif type. "Mr. Winik and The Kid at the Palace," read one of them. Which Mr. Winik? Which Kid? It was set in London, that was for sure, and there were groups of men in bowlers posed in various postcard-style settings. There was a moustache that looked strangely familiar. I could hardly sleep that night.

I learned the next morning that my great-grandfather, Hyman Winik, had had business connections with the great Charlie Chaplin. (It was important to refer to him as the great Charlie Chaplin when conveying the story to preadolescent peers.) A carpenter who fled Latvia to escape Cossack pogroms, Hyman made his fortune by traveling the world in the wake of war and natural disaster, where the need to rebuild guaranteed plenty of work. Hyman wound up in San Francisco after the great earthquake at the start of this century, having by then acquired an Australian wife and sons born on four separate continents. He became fascinated by the newly invented nickelodeon and opened a little theater of his own.

Through a series of lucky breaks, Hyman obtained the rights to distribute Charlie Chaplin's films, and at this point, things became very glamorous: trips back and forth to London, a private screening for the queen herself, hobnobbing with the fashionable gents I had seen in the film. But the end of the story was tragic: Great-Grandpa fell out with Chaplin, who sued him for the unheard-of sum of a quarter of a million dollars, contributing to my ancestor's breakdown and death before the age of fifty. Too callow to see the heartbreak in this, I saw showbiz, globe-trotting, tabloid-level litigation—the sort of Winik I could proudly claim.

From then on, Spanish moss grew thick on our family tree. My great-grandfather was the great Charlie Chaplin's agent, I announced whenever possible, and my cousin owns *Rolling Stone* magazine. My audience was usually impressed more by the latter than the former, and I saw no need to clarify the fact that Jann—I still feel I can call him that—was my third cousin, twice removed, and that I had never laid eyes on or spoken to him in my life. I assumed I soon would, as a matter of course, once I began my career as a famous rock star and novelist.

Alas, Jann has proven to be much more useful as a conversation piece than a connection; the hopeful missives I addressed to him in my late teens and twenties were answered only once, rather gruffly. But by then I had realized I didn't need to meet Jann at all, just as I didn't have to actually know Charlie Chaplin, or even Oona or Geraldine. We're talking mythology here, not kaffeeklatsch.

With Jann and Charlie playing Zeus and Saturn, I went on to cast the supporting characters of Mount Olympus. In the entertainment world alone, our genetic cosmos fairly sparkled with stars. Gigi herself once dated Richard Rodgers (of Rodgers and Hammerstein), an older boy who wrote songs for her high school musicals. My great-aunt Ethel, Gigi's sister, sang on Broadway. My step-grandmother on my mother's side was a Rockette. And wasn't it entirely possible that my mother's grandmother Flora Arnstein was somehow related to Nicky Arnstein, the sexy gambler who married Fanny Brice? I was sure when I saw the movie *Funny Girl* that it had to be. Mom said no, but how could she know for sure? Even if the only evidence was the powerful identification I felt with the glamorous, tragic figures played by Barbra Streisand and Omar Sharif, it couldn't be ruled out entirely, could it? (I think in some versions of this story, I was distantly related, by the transitive property of celebrity, to Streisand and Sharif themselves.)

In the sphere of public service, I somehow gathered we were connected to the famous assassinated New York liberal Allard Lowenstein. My mother, always the skeptic, insisted I had confused him with Alan Lowenstein, our dentist's brother. It turns out, actually, it was Al Blumenthal that my father's first cousin had married, the one who was president of the New York State Assembly before he went into private practice. Lowenstein, Blumenthal, whatever. The fact is, during my college years, I was twice mistaken for Caroline Kennedy.

The unmet relative who is closest to me, both by bloodline and inclination, died shortly before my birth. I am named for her. My mother's mother, Marion Bachrach Fisch, may not have been famous, but lived her life on a passionate scale, defying social mores and giving all for love in a way I found mesmerizing. In the thirties, women didn't pursue romance to its tragic end, didn't leave their husbands for their lovers, didn't marry and divorce the same man twice, didn't conduct their personal affairs with reckless intensity and disregard for public opinion and even private feelings. Except for my grandmother.

As I uncovered the story of these long-dead grandparents, Roy and Marion, I realized I had a virtual F. Scott and Zelda on my hands. She, a stunning beauty with clear blue eyes and terrific cheekbones, fell in love with a family friend named Smith and left her husband and three girls to run off with him to Washington, DC. Furious, her husband and father conspired to prevent her from getting her hands on either her money or her daughters. But shortly after Marion married Smith and gave birth to a son, the man died. Distraught, she fell into the waiting arms of her ex-husband. Their second marriage to each other was brief. Soon she moved out again, and Roy began dating the aforementioned Rockette.

By this time, my mother was grown and about to marry my father. After the wedding, she spent two years trying not to get pregnant and the next four years trying to, as she ruefully explains. Desperate, she sought the advice of her elegant, worldly-wise mother, who escorted her around New York to the latest fertility experts. The day she finally went to Marion's apartment to announce the success of the endeavor, she found her mother dead on the floor of a heart attack. Seven months later, I was born.

At nineteen, I wrote a long narrative poem about Marion and Roy, adding just a few spurious dramatic effects and gratuitously saddling everyone with Fitzgerald-size drinking problems. When I read my poem to my mother and her sisters at a holiday gathering, they all burst into tears. I took this as a good sign.

Twenty years later, I no longer believe that suffering is glamorous, though I still think it's worth writing about, and the family which once seemed so impregnably, boringly happy to me has had its full share of domestic drama, bereavement, and pain. I have shed the illusion that famous people are automatically interesting, or vice versa, and do not tell new acquaintances I'm related to Fanny Brice. As for Marion, I now see her story is sad and even worrisome, though I can't help but take it as a compliment when my mother says I have her eyes exactly.

These days, my eyes are fixed on the road ahead, figuratively and literally: I spend a good deal of time ferrying carloads of children around the countryside. From the backseat, that cauldron of myth, I hear awesome tales of an aunt who played professional tennis, Herculean cousins, heroic pets, billionaire uncles. You probably already know that Marshall and Will Thompson's dad was the fifth Beatle. Because youth craves heroes, the stories continue, the apocrypha flourish. When they ask, I guess I'll dust off Chaplin, Wenner, Rodgers, and Blumenthal, and see if any of them still have what it takes.

As for me, I don't care about celebrities anymore as much as I do these kids; I confine my bragging to their soccer goals and art projects, their poems and spelling tests. Their future is more important to me than any past, glittering or otherwise, and I finally understand why grown-ups drink to health and security, not fame and fortune. Glamorous relatives and their lustrous achievements are dust to me: I don't need a claim to fame, but a chance at joy.

MOMMY AND ME

After my father died, when I was twenty-seven, I became a lot more appreciative of my mother. For about three months. Then things went back to normal. Her asking if I got my doorbell fixed, me snapping her head off. I like my damn doorbell the way it is, don't you get it? Broken! That's how I want it! My stance on the issue went far deeper than laziness: I was simply not the kind of person who got her doorbell fixed. I was busy! And even if I weren't so busy, I had bigger, less bourgeois things on my mind. Not like some people.

Don't even mention the doorbell again, okay?

Then one day last May, I got a call from her.

I was just picking up the phone to call you, I said, knowing she was anxious to hear the latest development in my work life, an interest I found somewhat more tolerable than the one in my d— b—. Anyway, I was supposed to call her the minute I knew anything, but I hadn't.

If by some chance you have experienced Failure To Call Mother When Supposed To Syndrome, then you, like me, probably had a plethora of excuses at hand. But putting all excuses aside, one always has to balance the pleasantness of one's mother's interest in the twists and turns of one's life with its faintly annoying aspect. Especially if she has the tendency to mistake a d— b— for a plot element.

Making up for my tardiness in calling her, I launched into the tale, and it wasn't until she broke in and said, Well, I have to go soon and . . .

I'm almost done, I said.

Yes, but I have some bad news.

I went rigid. What?

Well . . . it looks like I have a little cancer, she said. Then, in the five minutes remaining until her boyfriend, Ceddie, picked her up to go eat Chinese, and interrupted by my shrieks of what and how and when, she told me that she'd been diagnosed with non-Hodgkin's lymphoma, she had known for over a month, she was starting a course of chemotherapy and radiation on Friday, and she had a 50 percent chance of survival. Then Ceddie arrived and she had to run.

Oh, Mommy, I said helplessly.

No golf for me this summer, I guess, she said wanly.

Oh, Mommy, I repeated.

Well, she replied. I'm not going to fucking die.

I wanted to believe her. She certainly had not fucking died

before. Not from her two heart attacks, not from her bypass, not from her major intestinal surgery, not when my father died or her best friend died or just about everyone she ever loved died, and not when she caught robbers in her house or when the IRS post-humously audited my father's tax returns. As my nine-year-old son, Vince, said hopefully when told of her illness, Nana's a tough woman.

He's right. My mother has always been tough, never mushy or gushy, not exactly the maternal type, in fact. When I was a klutzy, messy little girl, the same age Vince is now, my mother was slightly terrifying. I would look at her and think, I came from that? That trimness and slimness and smoothness, those teeth that practically glowed in the dark?

Back then, she reigned over her country club as ladies' golf champion, not to mention her tennis and bridge game; and if there had been a championship for *The New York Times* Sunday crossword puzzle, Mrs. Hyman Winik (Jane), as her name occasionally appeared in the sports section of that very paper, would have won it as well, her hand moving across the page as though she were writing a letter. She had lots of energy, little patience, and was never less than utterly frank in expressing her opinions, in whatever words they might require and regardless of her audience. Martini drinker, athlete, sports fan, stock market expert, reader of guy-books, she was the mom who came in from the cold. Her politics were Republican all the way, with no sympathy for poor schleppers in this country or any other. Is the government in business to fix all the injustices of the world? Please.

When we were little, my sister and I used to play a pretend game where we put on bright coral lipstick and a pair of penny loafers, and stamped around the house exclaiming, Jesus Christ! Jesus Christ! Guess who? Though all the serious cooking and cleaning in our home was done by the maid, I did walk in on my mother ironing once, behind the closed door of her bedroom. On the television, the Mets were winning the '69 World Series. Can I try? I asked.

No, dear, she said, definitely not. Never learn to iron, that's my advice; and if by some fluke you do, never let anyone know you can. Shit! she then exclaimed, having kept the iron in one place too long while transfixed by a play. She set the appliance down and reached for a cigarette. Watch this game with me, honey! It's historic.

I curled up on her chaise longue and pretended to watch. Sports meant nothing to me, but throughout my childhood I listened to endless narratives of golf matches—we were behind coming off the front nine, but then I got out of the trap and birdied eleven, and went for the four wood to the green on twelve—these indecipherable phrases run through my head even today, like bits of the Latin Mass for someone raised Catholic. I watched games, took lessons, and attended clinics in various sports because, like sleepaway camp, these were things my mother had enjoyed and assumed vital to my development. I was terrible at all of it, and hated my mother for making me do it.

I had horrible, horrible fights with my mother in early adolescence. I vividly remember one drive up Ocean Avenue in her Pontiac Le Mans convertible, coming home from the orthodontist, or the diet-pill doctor, or maybe my psychiatrist, screaming, I hate you, Mommy, and I remember her pulling into the driveway and saying, I hate you, too. (If you ask her she will say this didn't happen, but it did; and when I think of how difficult I was back then, I hardly even blame her.)

It was important to me that I be nothing like my mother. Like my dashing hilarious libertine father, fine, but not like her. Even in my thirties, I made a little list of her character traits on a yellow Post-it note, just to prove to myself that I was the opposite in every way. She was cautious, negative, pessimistic, suspicious; I was none of these things. She made pot roast with onion soup mix and ketchup; I was a great cook. Even my coleslaw was imaginative. Once when my children were very small and she was visiting us in Texas, she watched me chop dill and watercress and do something arcane with *umeboshi* plums and asked if I really had to put so many ingredients in the coleslaw:

Damn right I did.

Over time, we have both changed. I've got the Inner Mommy now and often sound like her (You have a new boyfriend? What does he do?), think like her (A lawyer? That's good!), and even dress like her. Well, she keeps giving me all these blazers and pants and old evening dresses she can't use anymore, and I must say I wear them. I put on an emerald-green, floor-length Qiana tank dress—Qiana was one of those seventies synthetics that didn't quite make it—to wear to a wedding. I could just see her parading off to the golf club in it thirty years ago. So where were the sandals dyed to match? I called her and she sent them right out, UPS 2nd Day Air.

Oh, it gets worse. I watch both the NFL and the NBA on television. I have a cleaning lady, send my kids to camp, and inveigh frequently against credit card debt. You should see my hands—tan and veiny with her very same ridged fingernails.

I hardly ever make that coleslaw anymore.

She, on the other hand, has gone soft on us. Nana, as she is now known, often bakes cookies. She voted for Clinton. She's revealed some amazing stories of womanly passion. And nowadays she even pretends to need my help with the crossword puzzle. Though she first reacted to the news of my pregnancy at forty-two by saying, Jesus Christ, Marion, and shocked people who exclaimed she must be excited that both of her daughters were pregnant by saying, They're idiots, she came around fast. When we found out I was having a girl and decided to name her after my mother, as she had named me after her mother, she started knitting a baby blanket.

I called her every day after that Wednesday in May when she first told me the news of her lymphoma. I would tell her about my pregnancy, or about taking my car in for service, or about what I was going to wear to some wedding, suddenly not annoyed by her interest but acutely aware that absolutely no one else in the world would ever give a damn. She, in turn, would tell me about her wig, or the port in her chest, or her golf game. As it turned out, she did play right through chemo. Maybe only eleven holes, maybe in a cart, maybe bald and wearing a baseball cap, but playing nonetheless. And dining out, and going to Atlantic City, and watching *Jeopardy!* and *Wheel of Fortune* with even fiercer dedication and pleasure than usual.

In fact, my mother was getting unusual pleasure from many things. In one phone call, she launched into a detailed description of a lobster stuffed with crabmeat and vermouth she had eaten at a dinner party.

It was the best lobster I ever had in my life, she told me.

Well, I could believe that. But when she told me she got up the next morning and had the best bagel with egg and cheese she ever had in her life at McDonald's, I knew my New York Jew of a mother was having a profound response to her situation.

I had heard, of course, that some people respond to a diagnosis of terminal illness with renewed zest for life, and a sudden wealth of patience, love, and spirit. But I had never seen it happen. I watched my first husband die slowly of AIDS, and I have to say terminal illness really didn't do much for his personality, God bless him. But here was my mother, eating the best bagel of her life at McDonald's. And she was still talking about it. Remember how Daddy and I used to love those Egg McMuffins? This was so much better than that.

I miss Daddy, I said suddenly, because I did.

Me, too, she said emphatically. I was taken aback. It's not that I didn't think she missed him, but I never heard her say it in the sixteen years since his death.

From then on, I looked forward to our phone calls with secret hilarity, to see what she would come up with next. One day she told me about Diane and Leon Katz's fiftieth anniversary party, held at the golf club. She and a few other friends had worked hard to make it festive, planning a special menu, bringing in flowers and a cake and Diane's favorite candy, everything just right. They lost the candy, she said. And we had ordered the lobster steamed, but they stuffed it with some kind of thermidor. When they took Ceddie's order, he said I'll have the same, meaning the lobster, and then they misunderstood and brought him the salmon. I mean, everything went wrong that possibly could have gone wrong.

Oh my God, I said. I knew she must have been furious. Being furious at the management of the golf club dining room had been a major pastime of my parents since my earliest youth. I steeled myself for the firestorm.

It was the funniest thing I ever saw, she said.

It was?

Oh, you just had to laugh, she said.

You did?

I really could not believe my ears. My mother had become the freaking Buddha.

My mother continued doing incredibly well throughout her chemo. She wasn't nauseated, she wasn't tired; in fact, she was fine. When my little Jane was born in late June, she could no longer wait for the day my aunt was supposed to drive her to see us in Pennsylvania. Instead, she jumped in the car and drove the three hours herself.

After her nine weeks of chemo were over, she was to start radiation and go every day for a month. It wasn't easy; she really had trouble fitting radiation into her schedule. Morning appointments blew her golf dates, afternoons cut into bridge. We had come a long way from that first phone call, where she wasn't playing golf all summer (or, as I'm sure we both thought, ever).

Before she started radiation, she had a scan to check the progress of her treatment. She was injected with a dye that turned the lymphoma cells bright orange, and when they went to look at them the next day, there weren't any.

Can you believe it? she said.

No, I said, stunned, speechless, and really, really happy. But yes.

I am afraid to think of it as more than a temporary reprieve. But so far, it has been an amazing one. The very next day, my mother played in the finals of the Better Ball of Partners at her beloved club. It was an important tournament and there had been a large gallery, a brigade of senior citizens in golf carts following the match.

I was the Jane Winik of twenty years ago, she said, and gave me the hole-by-hole, just as the Jane Winik of my childhood would have done.

She parred three, four, ten, thirteen, fifteen, sixteen, and seventeen. She had a forty-one on the back nine. Her putting had been sensational; her partner, who had carried them through the first rounds of the tournament, was thrilled. And then there was eighteen, a par five. It all came back to me, she said. All the times I've stood on that tee, all those championships, all those memories.

She hit a good first shot, a good second shot. At that point, all four players had the same lie, and there was a big nasty trap between them and the hole. One after the next went into it. I hit a seven iron to the green and two-putted to win, she said.

I almost knew what she was talking about.

People were crying, she said.

I didn't blame them. I was crying myself. Are you celebrating? I asked.

Well, right now I'm just killing time until I go over for radiation, she said. I would be watching *Jeopardy!* but your sister's son messed up the programming on my VCR.

Oh no.

Ah, she said. So what. No big deal.

II

Underfoot

MY NEW NEIGHBORHOOD

I was on my way home from the locksmith when my car skidded on the lane leading to our house and lodged in a snowdrift. When I got out, the door somehow electronically sealed itself up behind me. I locked not one, not two, but three keys inside. I locked my cell phone inside. But worst of all, I locked in my six-month-old daughter, Jane, who already had been crying with hunger before we skidded. *No,* I screamed into the snow-covered cornfield, then composed a cheery smile and pressed it to the tinted window beside her car seat. She eyed me tearfully and somewhat accusingly and, when I failed to open the door, returned immediately to piteous wails.

My house was a quarter mile up the lane. So I ran back to the road, waving my arms and screaming for help. Not a car was in sight to witness my display. I scanned the few neighboring houses:

all deserted. Just then, a car came speeding over the hill and I threw my body in its path.

Do you have a cell phone? I shouted, shoving my head into the window they rolled down. There was cigarette smoke, two boys in knit ski caps, a blond girl with blue eye shadow, and a couple of toddlers, but no cell phone.

I told them what had happened and asked if they could go call a locksmith. They said the nearest one was thirty minutes away. So the police, then! I shouted. They'll just break your window, said the one who looked like Eminem. Not realizing this was an offer to enter by other means, I begged them to go and they headed back into town.

By the time they got back, I had pried the electronic window open about a quarter inch with my bare hands. Jane was hysterical and I was seriously considering throwing a rock through the windshield. Eminem got out of the car and said the motherfucking police would be there when they got around to it, if I wanted to wait. He came down to take a look. Well, it just figures I don't have my jimmy on me today, he said, but I can open this car in a couple of minutes.

Do you think so? I wondered. It's so cold out, and you have those kids in your car, too.

They're mine and my buddy's, he said proudly.

As Eminem worked a broken-off car antenna into the crack I had made and steered it to the door-lock switch, his buddy was out in the street directing traffic. When one driver didn't take kindly to veering around our motorcade, he began to jump up and down screaming, You wanna fight? Bring it on, mofo! The car slowed and began to back up. Eminem looked up from his work.

No, boys, no! I cried. Remember, you just called the police!

By the time the official emissaries showed up, my boys (as I had begun to think of them) had freed the baby and the car, the latter by kicking away heaps of impacted snow with their giant jackboots. And before I could offer these good Samaritans money, or candy for their kids, or even address a simple thanks to the patient girlfriend who had been sitting there the whole time, they were gone, like publicity-shy superheroes or thieves in the night, or some very fortuitous cross between the two.

THE CASE
OF THE
DISAPPEARING
BABY

Yesterday, while we were horsing around on the floor, my eighteen-month-old daughter accidentally banged her head into my jaw. When she saw the look on my face, her blue eyes grew round and she covered my cheeks with baby kisses. Utterly undone, I closed my eyes and tried to imprint those kisses into my memory: the softness of her skin, the lightness of her touch, the little kissing sound her lips made, the smell of pear baby shampoo and milk breath.

If you have ever loved someone who was going away, someone you were bound to lose, you will know how I felt, how I feel every day when I look at her, my precious baby girl.

Let me hasten to say that neither of us is ill, nor am I about to start a long sentence in the federal penitentiary. She is a normal, healthy child, growing and developing at the breakneck pace toddlers are famous for—and that's the problem.

Jane the infant is already gone. She has been replaced by Jane the tyke, and Jane the two-year-old is on the way. Just beyond her is Jane the elementary schooler, and soon after, I'll have a young soccer player or poet or pianist. Someday, God willing, my grown daughter will stand as tall as I do. And when that happens, the tiny person I love so passionately will live only in photographs, home videos, and in my mind.

I don't disagree with the notion that you can see lifelong personality traits in a baby early on: a strong will, a placid soul, a hatred of stupid hats are sometimes noticeable in the delivery room. But even given certain consistent characteristics, I would still say the baby disappears.

The continuity of growth is deceptive. Though each phase of Jane's development flows smoothly from the one before it, and today never seems that far from yesterday, with each new level she attains, part of her younger self is left behind forever. We focus on the skill gained, but there is always something lost too. Some sound will never be made again. Some facial expression or funny way of addressing the cat has vanished. The little hands, the little feet—remember them well. Because that body in the bathtub is turning into a bigger body that will very soon only shower behind a locked door.

I have a couple of those—sons aged fourteen and eleven— which is how I know what I'm talking about. Fourteen-year-old Hayes, currently five feet nine and 160 pounds. Our relationship is close and often warm: we spend lots of time together, do algebra problems, drive around laughing, and also get furious with each other because we have very different rhythms and approaches to life and for God's sake, he's an adolescent boy and I'm his mother.

All that goes double or possibly triple for Vince, who seems to be growing up even faster.

So my question is this: the little guys I nursed and potty-trained and took baths with, the one who had such a hard time giving up his pacifier, the one who said "butcept" and "prentzel," my boys who were so close they still felt like a part of my body for years after I delivered them—where are they?

I remember when Vince was little; I wrote a poem for him called "Little Guru from Outer Space." The little guru's gone back to his home planet now. My baby Vince is a memory—a memory I have when I look into his eyes, or into my heart. He is a memory of mine, not even of the boy he is today.

The other day I pulled up in front of the house to give Hayes a ride to school and saw something that gave me a start: a good-looking young man in a shirt and tie carrying a little blond baby on his hip. It was Hayes and Jane; he dressed for an away basketball game, she coming along for the ride. To see the tender side of one's adolescent son—the father growing inside him—is a sweet shock.

I tried to imprint that picture, as I did Jane's baby kisses. One day soon this will be all I have left.

CODE

The other night as I watched Hayes sleep, resting my gaze for some minutes on the contours of his nose and lips, I had the sensation that I was looking at his father, that sleeping inside that draped scaffolding of bone and flesh was not the boy but the man who died almost nine years ago. It seemed for a moment that Tony, not Hayes, would awaken.

I spent a great deal of time watching Tony sleep during the eleven years of our life together, especially in the early days when I was simply too excited to close my eyes. His sleeping face became a code for what I loved about him: his beauty, his sensuality, his boyishness. In the last chaotic years of a marriage caught in a hurricane of misfortune and mistakes, I could still watch him sleep, on a deck chair in our backyard or on a hospice pillow, and those peaceful, classical contours would still touch the source of it all in me.

Now those same facial angles are code for something else: for genetic code, the echoes and imprints of Tony in his sons. He died when Hayes was six and Vince four. But it is so clear that his mark goes deeper than their accessible memories or even their subconscious, preverbal ones. They say now that there are genes that control thrill-seeking, impatience, various aspects of sexuality. I also believe there is a gene that inclines one to favor clothing with designer labels, a gene that controls the rearranging of hair in bathroom mirrors, a gene that can make one almost sphinxlike in social settings, yet warm and easy around babies. I expect to discover many other specialized genes over the years, and as many mixed blessings. The code I see in Hayes's face is his complex inheritance from his father, and the tenderness and trepidation that inspires in me. It is code now for loving this boy.

It is astonishing how gone a person is who dies, and part of the adjustment to loss really comes down to making yourself believe this unimaginable departure has occurred. But once you accomplish that, once you believe they will not be pulling up in the car or sitting down for dinner or leaving a message on the answering machine, once you believe they truly are gone, you have a new challenge. You have to deal with how present they are.

What I saw the other night is that the angles of Tony's face are not lost to me, nor are they only inside me. They are actually here. This may be as much afterlife as we have, certainly as much as I can let myself believe in. Like so much of our human reality, it is a simple physical thing, embroidered in a thousand layers by our consciousness, our wishes, and our dreams.

JUST SAY NO
TO SPORTS

〜

Jane's preschool offers tumbling classes—a fact that I have been trying to conceal from her. It's not the extra $15 per month. It's not that she's too young. After all, Tiger Woods began playing golf at three, Serena Williams entered her first tennis tournament at four, and if you haven't started figure skating by six, you might as well forget the whole thing.

No, it's not her age. It's mine. I have already raised two children to adolescence—one now a testosterone-oozing varsity football player, the other a disaffected punk rock snowboarder. It's been many laps around the track since I took two excited little fellas out to buy their first pairs of soccer shin guards. But now, with the T-ball sign-up sheet soon to appear in their little sister's lunch box, I find myself remembering all those happy yet incredibly boring and expensive years.

What parent would deprive their growing child of fresh air, exercise, friendships, healthy competition, and the many other benefits of sport? Few, probably, would have the courage. But nobody can stop us from complaining about it either. Consider this:

They can't play. The relationship of kiddie sports to the adult versions of these games is hypothetical, represented more by the outfit worn than by actual moves and plays. Baseball is an endless slog of walks and steals. You don't see a passing game in junior football; sadly, you don't see a running game either. Soccer features gaggles of kids chasing the ball in groups while the less motivated wander aimlessly around the field. For real laughs, check out the peewee golf clinic. It would be funny; and it is, for the first ten minutes. Which brings us to the second problem.

You can't leave. Most sports for the primary school set require parents to remain at practices, and of course you have to go to the games. Bring a book. Bring a cooler. Bring a cell phone. Bring your briefcase. I remember sitting in the bleachers with some weary parents watching our kids lose the thirteenth game on their baseball schedule. This is starting to feel like Vietnam, said the dad beside me. Some prefer periodonture.

You can't drink. I once almost got ejected from a West Austin Youth Association soccer tournament for having a six-pack. I'll say no more.

Ka-ching. You probably know enough about skiing to realize what you're getting into if you take your tykes to the slopes. But have you ever priced a skateboard? Over $100, easy. A lacrosse stick (needed even to play one game and then decide they hate it) is $30. If they lose enough knee socks, even soccer can be a financial sinkhole. You might think of swimming as a low-cost sport. What does it take—a bathing suit, right? Well, one of my friends is the mother of two high-school-age swimmers. It began a decade ago when one of them was in first grade and brought home a flyer for two weeks of free lessons at the Y. Free! Soon, swimming took over their lives, their weekends, their bank account. In the past four years alone, the bill has come to $20,000, one $75 single-use competition bathing suit at a time. Of course my friend says she has no regrets—but who does, after they've been inhaling chlorine fumes for fifteen years.

The outfits. I mentioned the importance of outfits in signaling which sport is being played. But these outfits are neither cheap, nor easy to keep track of (have you seen a green-striped knee sock at your house, maybe?), nor easy to put on. I suggest you try getting a sweaty fourth grader ready for football practice on a warm September afternoon. If you are not an athlete yourself, you may not be aware that ordinary sneakers are used only for hopscotch and poker. Depending on your children's interests, you will be acquiring baseball, football, soccer, basketball, track, skateboarding, and cross-training shoes. These are outgrown and discarded every few months, and if you think the younger sibling is going to take those mud-covered hand-me-downs, you've got another think coming. Speaking of mud, stock up now on Tide, Clorox, Spray 'n Wash, Shout, OxiClean, OxyContin, and white spray paint.

Actually, it is whether you win or lose. You'll be charmed to learn that score is not kept in the pint-size leagues. As they tell the kids, We're just here to have fun! Everybody's a winner. Everybody gets a trophy at the end of the season. And while the kids are out there having said fun, you'll find the parents in the stands arguing over whether it's 3–2 or 3–all. (That's a basketball score.) I don't know how long the kids believe this crap, but recently even I got a rude awakening. When my son's high school football team went 1 and 9 last season, they fired the entire coaching staff. This is high school we're talking about, not the NFL. But it's also Pennsylvania, where anything relating to football is definitely worst-case scenario.

And yet. And yet, I just this month signed little Janie up for tumbling. And I suspect my husband has his eye on the job of kindergarten girls' T-ball coach. Why? Come on, you know why. Because there is no I in *t-e-a-m*! Go, kids, go!

DYSFUNCTIONAL FAMILIES AT SEA

When my sister, her family, and our mom finally joined us at the dock, they seemed slightly out of sorts. Aside from a disagreement about the directions to Cape Liberty, New Jersey, my mother—set to sail in a lemon-yellow pantsuit—didn't approve of the overalls and tank top my sister had selected for the first evening on board our cruise ship. Upon sighting me, the two must have felt simultaneous twinges of disappointment (Mom) and glee (Nancy). Getting dressed that morning two hundred and fifty miles away in Pennsylvania, I had put on the exact same thing as my sister.

You have to admit it's kind of funny, I said to my mother that night as I sat beside her at dinner beneath the glittering chandeliers of the plushy La Bohème dining room, in my overalls.

My mother hadn't reached the amusing-hindsight phase of things. Is anybody else dressed like this in this place? she said, gesturing around the three-tiered, opera-themed hall (downstairs was Carmen, upstairs the Magic Flute). I don't know what's wrong with you girls.

I found myself enjoying this conversation quite a bit. I am forty-six and my sister is forty-four, and being chastised by our mother about our sloppy clothes was taking me right back to the 1970s.

At least your sister didn't have a giant tattoo on her arm back then, my mother said, as she turned her attention to the real work of the cruise vacation. I'll have the Vidalia onion tart, then the prime rib, she told the waiter. Rare.

How come there are no prices on the menu? asked one of my teenage sons, sotto voce.

'Cause it's free, the other one told him.

Not free, I explained. Included.

My sons and my sister's two younger boys soon fully comprehended that Nana's lovely gift to us came with all the food you could eat, available from the ship's various restaurants, cafés, and snack bars twenty-two hours a day. And they were just the people to take advantage of it.

Judging from the size of the tables in the dining room and the tenor of conversations overheard in the elevator and the hot tub, the *Voyager of the Seas* was full of extended families like ours, enjoying themselves despite the inevitable emotional mechanics of such groups. At first I didn't mean to eavesdrop, but soon I was hanging around the elevators and hot tubs, collecting lines I would later quote over dinner. From the Archives of Nautical Family Life:

Outside the Johnny Rockets takeout window, a tall man to a small boy: She gets upset because she's sacrificing for the rest of us and she thinks we don't appreciate it.

On side-by-side treadmills in a gym with a panoramic view; teenage girl to her mom: Every time we see her, she showers us with money and you get mad!

Four men with beers in the adults-only solarium hot tub: Where is everybody, anyway—bingo? . . . Your mom and them are . . . What about Mike? . . . Probably trying to find out if you can get divorced at sea. Around them, the steam from the hot water rose into the mists of the North Atlantic and the piped-in reggae music was interrupted at intervals by the ship's foghorn.

On our five-day cruise from New Jersey to Saint John, New Brunswick, and Halifax, Nova Scotia, the sun almost never came out. At least for the first few days, we hardly minded, since we had never been on a cruise before and the sight of the vast Atlantic was enough to amaze us. Through the large porthole of our compact stateroom, we saw the white wake in the black water as our ship sped through the night. We saw rays of moonlight hit the waves like a spray of diamonds. We saw ethereal shades of gray layered horizontally—water/mist/far-off land/sky—as we played shuffleboard with our preschoolers outside the casino.

Inside that casino was my mother, who at that moment and many others was hunkered down at the blackjack table. A devoted blackjack player, she follows a strict system from which she never deviates. It works pretty well. Honestly, my mother probably could have had a perfectly good time on this cruise without dragging the other ten of us along. But she really is a very nice mommy and grandma, and even if that thought had occurred to her, I'm sure she dismissed it immediately.

On the way back to the room, I noticed a family of four at a table outside the Pig and Whistle, the English pub on the mall-like Royal Promenade. For their midafternoon snack, the parents each had a line of martini glasses in front of them, Junior and Sis had enormous sodas, and everybody was sharing a can of Pringles.

On our third day at sea, my husband announced that he was going to check his email. I was against this.

Yes, there were a half-dozen computers in the ship's wood-paneled library (where, overlooking the bustling promenade but separated from it by four stories and a wall of glass, non-gambling older people lounged in easy chairs, hiding from their families), and yes, you could connect for a mere fifty cents a minute. But I felt that he was violating the principles of cruise living, which I had dubbed "vacation jail." No phone, no cell, no email, no newspapers other than the flyer that was stuck beneath our door every morning. "Day Two," the headline read, "Pick Up Tickets for Ice Jammers!"

While my traitor husband was visiting reality via the internet, I did just what I'd been told—got in line for ice show tickets. Eager to miss nothing, or nothing of interest, anyway, I made a practice of carrying the daily schedule around with me at all times so I could decide whether to go to Pilates class or the Family Disco or just settle for French fries in the Windjammer Grill. I probably would not be attending the class in napkin folding in Cleopatra's

Needle or the art auction at the Aquarium Bar, but I liked knowing about them all the same.

I also carried around the schedules for the Adventure Ocean kids' program, which ran all day and most of the night and had separate agendas of activities for ages 3–5, 6–8, 9–11, 12–14, and 15–17. We had representatives of each of these groups in our contingent, though their enthusiasm for organized fun decreased in reverse proportion to their ages. My teenage sons were certain they could meet up with other kids and plan their own activities, and in fact, I hardly saw them the whole trip—they roomed with my mother on the other side of the ship, slept until midafternoon, were first seen at dinner, then disappeared to find their new friends, and did not come back to the room, my mother reported, until 4 a.m.

And what were they doing all that time? Drinking "mocktails" in the teen disco, Optix, as suggested on the activity schedule? I don't think so. Not my little six-foot-tall darlings. They were hot-tubbing with the ladies, eating, roaming the ship from bow to stern, trying to slip quarters into the slot machines before anybody could catch them, and snatching half-drunk drinks off tables and smoking cigarettes on the poop deck. Or the crow's nest. Or something. If they got in trouble, I never heard about it, which was good enough for me.

My sister's nine-, eight-, and three-year-olds were lukewarm about the unlimited babysitting, but lucky for me, my little Jane took to it enthusiastically. Energetic young staff, a mini-rock-climbing wall, and a steady diet of activities like face painting, pirate parades, and pajama parties overcame most of her usual resistance to anything that looks like daycare. In fact, she burst into tears when I picked up her up just before 9 p.m. one night to go to the ice show. She had just decorated her guitar and was going to the rock and roll dance. You picked me up too early, Mommy, she wept.

It was a really good ice show, though, with internationally ranked skaters from Russia, Canada, the United States, and Sweden, and a pair of brothers from Italy who threw each other around the ice while juggling one set of balls between them. I had really wanted my sons to come, since their dad skated with a touring company of Holiday on Ice in his own youth. Vince never showed and Hayes disappeared as we went in.

But as the lights came up at the end, I realized they were there after all, standing close behind me in the back aisle. They waved and vanished again before I could say a word.

One night, as we sped over the inky ocean and my husband, daughter, and niece slept peacefully in their bunk beds (we were a little taken aback, at first, by just how compact the staterooms were), I climbed down the ladder and wandered out into Party Central. People were pouring out of a late show at La Scala, the theater, and streaming into a nightclub across the way. I found my mother at the blackjack table with a drained glass of iced tea beside her. My mother drinks gin, but not while she's playing blackjack.

Your son took my key because he locked his in the room and said he would be right back, she told me grimly. That was an hour ago. And now I'm losing and I want to go back to the room but I can't. And even if I could, I couldn't get from the door to my bed because the boys have thrown all their clothes on the floor.

By this time, Hayes had lost three keys—which were called Sea-Passes and doubled as credit cards for drinks, arcade games, and other things that cost money. I felt it was not a good idea for her to have entrusted him with her key for even a minute, and I promised to go find him.

Finding someone on a fourteen-deck ship with three thousand passengers and fifteen hundred crew members (from sixty-three countries, as was frequently pointed out) can be something of a challenge. Most of these people, along with their children, seemed to be awake at this late hour. The family of four, or another one just like it, was still at the Pig and Whistle. Hundreds of seekers from the "scientific spirituality" seminar being held in the conference center milled around. I sped from the snack bar on Deck 5 to the miniature golf course on Deck 14, running into the same five people I kept seeing over and over—the woman who looked like someone who works out at my gym, the group of ladies in saris, the sturdy-looking fellow with lush gray hair and one short leg—but no Hayes.

Finally, one of the two dozen times I called the room on the house phone, he answered—he had just gotten there.

How did it take you an hour to get to the room? Nana's ready to kill you!

Really? he said in his usual dopey sixteen-year-old way. I stopped to talk to some girl on the way up.

Get down there and give Nana back her key! She's losing and it's your fault!

Okay, Mom. Stop going ballistic.

I got back to my room, where I found everyone now awake,

and mad at me too, since Jane had woken up and was crying piteously for Mommy.

Because we were eating major meals about every two hours it seemed, I tried to balance it out with exercise. One afternoon, my sister and I did a few turns on the jogging track on the top deck, where there were always a few brave souls slogging through the mist and rain. I used the time to tell her how much antidepressants had helped me in dealing with my stress and urged her to go on them as well. I also suggested medication for some of the other members of our family.

Another day, when Nancy passed up jogging to ice skate with her kids, I noticed a friendly-looking, white-haired guy in a windbreaker puttering along at the same pace I was. I turned and joined him. Pete Wickersham was the guitar player from the Pig and Whistle, and he had been on this ship for months. After they dropped us off in New Jersey, the ship was heading down to the Bahamas. And I should stay, too, he told me. The Canada route is often a little dodgy weather-wise, but down in the Caribbean, he said, it's Margaritaville.

Just after Pete and I finished our jog, I got a tiny taste of what he was talking about. The sun came out—and everything changed. All the grays were gone, replaced with glittering turquoise and sparkling white and sapphire blue. Daiquiris started pouring out of the Sky Bar, and people filled in the tiers of pool lounges so fast it seemed they had been waiting in the wings for this moment. Pool boys appeared with towels, and waiters circulated with trays of refreshments. I rushed to the casino to find my mother and tell her, but by the time we got back to Deck 13, the foghorn was blasting again. Oh well.

That night was formal night in the dining room and we all passed muster with Mommy: my husband in a tux, all the boys in ties, the little girls in frilly dresses, my sister in red with a chiffon wrap draped artfully over her tattoo. We had a family picture taken by the ship's photographer and we looked terrific. Well, there wasn't one photo where we all looked terrific, actually, because in the one where my little niece Molly didn't appear to be contemplating suicide, my mother had her eyes closed. As my sister and I debated which proof to buy, I overheard a conversation.

Your brother looks drunk, said a woman at the next display stand, scrutinizing an eight-by-ten.

He *was* drunk, the man explained.

But Mildred looks terrible in this one.

I'm just gonna go back to the room, the man sighed. Come get me when you're done.

A few minutes later, we got in line behind his wife to purchase our glossy, not-quite-perfect image of family bliss at sea. Clearly we were all in the same boat.

VINCE'S FOOTBALL CAREER

My son Vince had been practicing football in the rain, so I expected him to be a little wet when I picked him up. But I didn't expect to find him standing behind the equipment building in a dripping T-shirt—no helmet, no pads, no jersey—crying.

I quit, he informed me. I quit the team.

What? I said. God, Vince, get in the car.

I went to find the coaches on the dark field. If he wants to quit that's fine with me, the head coach said before I could open my mouth, thrusting the wet equipment at me. He can't get frustrated like that. That's not football. He sounded just like Vince.

What should I do? I said.

You? Nothing. I might give him a second chance, but he's got to learn to control himself.

I was floored. Vince, who had never been much of a sportsman, was having a pretty good year with football. A big nine-year-old, he was greeted with gruff, manly-man enthusiasm when he joined the team, and was made a starter. He had risen to the challenge of putting on the many-layered uniform and getting out there every day. Football had become a big part of our lives. I had already ordered my FOOTBALL MOM shirt.

As I tossed the equipment into the car, Vince launched into a long, tearful story about a little guy from the B team who had been harassing him on the line, illegally pulling his face mask and jersey. When Vince's short supply of stoicism ran out, he threatened to punch the kid. The coach came down on Vince; Vince lost it and chucked his helmet and pads on the ground.

I'm afraid Vince comes by his quick temper genetically, and standing in the cold rain for an hour running football drills probably didn't help. But not having witnessed the incident, I didn't know whether he was right or wrong, and didn't know what to tell him to do. That's a hard place for a mom and her kid to be, because if I don't know what to do, who does? Knowing what to do is my job. So I let him go on and barely said a word. As it turned out, the force was with me.

Why do you have my equipment? Vince asked when we got home. I quit, I don't need it.

Well, the coach said he might give you a second chance, I explained.

Vince narrowed his eyes. I'm not playing stupid football. I hate those coaches. They're mean. They never give comments. They just yell.

I knew he meant compliments, not comments, and I knew it wasn't true, but I kept my mouth shut.

I might give them a second chance, he said after changing

clothes, showing an equally hereditary tendency to cool off even faster than he'd heated up. I might go back.

Vince, I said. You acted pretty crazy over there. It might not be that simple. Maybe you should call the coach and talk it over.

Minutes later, I found him with the portable phone and the football roster. I listened, surprised and impressed, as he choked out, I'm sorry I blew up but can I tell you my side of the story? He repeated his tale and listened to a long reply. Okay—okay, he said, then hung up.

I'm back on the team, he told me. The coach knows there's a lot of fouls that don't get caught and come get him next time and he 'cepts my apology and I won't do it again. He grabbed a piece of pizza and curled up with his brother to watch television.

Vince finished the season rather grudgingly, and as of this writing, five years later, he has never again gone anywhere near a team sport. While his teammates are now using those blocks and tackles to play high school football, Vince learned something even more important from his season on the gridiron. If you're a kid with a bad temper who hates being told what to do, your reconciliation skills are critical.

VINCE'S FIRE

If you can look out your window and see a blade of unscorched grass or a building left standing, count yourself lucky. Since my son set the fire that burned fifteen acres of hayfields here in Glen Rock, I have learned that just about every self-respecting adult male has a conflagration in his past. We're lucky there's a world left.

So the other day I got a call from the girl who lives on the farm down the hill saying there was a fire out back and she just saw Vince and Ian running away.

How big is the fire, Sophie?

Well, I can hear it crackling from inside the house, she said with amazing calm.

She could hear it crackling, and I could see red flames over the treetops. Minutes after I called 911, the two arsonists, ages eleven and thirteen, came struggling up the hill. They were rending their garments, clawing their breasts, and wailing for help from God. And they got it, in fact. While the fire burned and burned and burned and three separate fire departments arrived to help put it out, and after more than an hour, the firemen ran out of water and had to wait for more trucks as flames raced to the woods, somehow in the end *nothing bad had happened.* The hay in the fields had already been cut. Not a single building or living creature was hurt. While we were thanking God, we thanked Sophie too.

When all that was left of the operation was a single truck soaking down the smoking fields, the stern but kind fire marshal took Vince and Ian on a tour of the damage, sending me to call Sophie's mother, the owner of the property, to see if she wanted to reserve the right to press charges. She already had received several calls at work about the fire, but I couldn't help reprising the story from my own stressed-out, panting point of view. So what do you think? Do you want to at least wait till you come home and see it?

You know what I really think? she said.

What?

I'm so relieved this is finally happening to someone else.

She and her husband are the parents of a son in his early twenties who'd been a bit of a trial; they were not going to press charges. She thought *I'd* had a rough day and should go home and have a beer. I did.

The state police and the fire chief declared it an accident. It *was* an accident. But from what I've heard since, it's an accident that happens a little too often. Vince told me there was a moment about ten minutes into their little bonfire when he got a bad feeling. He even said it: I've got a bad feeling about this. Ah, it'll be fine, Ian replied, and Vince agreed, and soon they were dropping armloads of dried grass into the inferno.

I'm pretty sure Vince has learned not to play with fire. But what I really hope is that he's learned to listen to that bad feeling. Because that's it. One tiny little Jiminy Cricket intuition is all we ever get before we light the match or run the red light or stick the needle in our arm or say, See you tomorrow, to someone who's just said he or she is thinking of doing something awful. And all the fire safety classes and DARE programs and driver's ed horror movies in the world can't teach you what ignoring that bad feeling one time will do.

Let's try to make it once, Vince, okay? Because God is busy, Mommy is powerless, and nothing says "oops" like a wall of flame.

VINCE'S CAR WRECK

One of the hardest things about being a parent is being so invested in the fate of a person whose actions you have no control over, I remarked to Vince one morning. (It has been two and half years since the fire; he is now thirteen and nearly six feet tall. But I think you will still recognize him.)

The occasion for my comment was the unfolding of yet another episode in the series of bad decisions and misfortunes that tends to dog the child with a defiant streak and an impulse-management problem. Recently, because of bad behavior and outbursts in his health class, Vince was suspended from school. And because of his suspension, he lost the right to go on the overnight trip the eighth grade takes every year to Williamsburg, Virginia.

Here's how it happened. The health teacher told Vince to take his seat. Vince would not. So the teacher sent Vince to the office, saying, Now you're going to miss sex ed. Vince replied, That's okay, I already know how to rape people. Though Vince meant this as a joke, having seen "rape" on the list of topics they would cover in class, unsurprisingly it didn't go over. And then he never showed up in the office.

Vince had known for months that if he got in trouble again, he would be kicked off the field trip, and that had kept him on the straight and narrow until this moment. But from the day I got the notice informing me that he'd be booted from the trip after one more incident, I was filled with apprehension. Be good, Vince, I called every morning as he got out of the car.

Then a few days ago my phone rang. Mrs. Winik, said a familiar voice, this is the vice principal from the middle school.

Oh, no, I wept.

Did I mention that the already slender Vince had gone on a diet so he wouldn't feel embarrassed to go in the hotel swimming pool in front of the girls? Probably you think I shouldn't feel so sorry for Vince since he was clearly completely at fault here (though he would be happy to explain to you that, on the contrary, he didn't do anything). But it is practically unbearable for me to watch my son make mistakes, and compound them, and suffer for it. In the last few months, he's wrecked my car, quit his band, lost his job, been forced to give up summer camp, been kicked off the field trip, and been falsely turned in at school as a drug dealer. That may not be everything, but I'll stop there.

Some of what happens is not his fault, and this recent spate of disasters started with an incident that was actually my fault. For example, you may be wondering how it is that a thirteen-year-old wrecked my car. Well, people out here in farm country sometimes let their kids drive the car to do errands on their own property. So I started letting Vince take the trash cans down our half-mile driveway to the street. Gradually, he started driving up and down for fun. And then one icy day he decided to load up a few friends and show them how fast he could make the circle on the driveway. He lost control and skidded into an apple tree. The kids were fine, thank God, but the car did have a little owie.

As I watched Vince deal with the fallout from that situation, which included his withdrawal from skateboarding camp as a start toward reimbursing me for the damage, I knew I was partly responsible for his error. I said he could do it! Obviously bad judgment is also hereditary.

This morning I was telling Jane why Vince is in trouble at school—for her, I boiled it down to him not going to his seat when the teacher asked him to and then he was rude. She understood perfectly. Steven and T. J. at her preschool get in trouble for the exact same thing every day. Vince may be tall and have the mouth and habits of an adult (albeit an annoying, inarticulate adult), but somewhere in him he is still four years old. That seems to be the problem for adolescent boys in general, and they certainly aren't the only ones.

Last night, after having spent the day in in-school suspension, he went to start his homework—at which point, he found he had lost the stack of one hundred and fifty note cards for his research paper on the early history of California. As he searched his backpack to no avail, his eyes filled with tears. This can't be happening, he moaned.

Come on, I said, and rushed him over to the school, which luckily was open for a night game in the gym. We went down to the basement, where the "alternative education room" is nestled between metal shop and drafting.

He put his hand on the door of the classroom; unbelievably it was unlocked.

And even more unbelievably, in the carrel where he had been working sat the thick stack of rubber-banded cards.

Our luck has changed, he cried, high-fiving me, his whole face blossoming with relief and joy at the gift of being able to do his homework.

I hope he's right. I hope we can change more than just his luck. He's got to change his attitude, and his way of dealing with anger, and all those other qualities that make the lives of boys, and adolescents in general, so difficult. I'm going to try to help him, and I'm going to try to enlist others in his cause as well. And whether it helps or not, I am going to worry myself half-sick and half-crazy in the process.

I write these words with circles under my eyes and a cup of coffee beside me; already my normal waking hours no longer provide enough time for my anxieties. Perhaps it serves me right. I could never sympathize with the sleep problems so many of my friends went through when our babies were young. As infants, my kids were easy; they never kept me up all night, every night, until 3:18 seemed just another time of day.

Well, hello, 4:41. My teenagers, it seems, are another story.

MRS. PORTNOY'S
COMPLAINT

She was so deeply imbedded in my consciousness that for the first year of school I seem to have believed that each of my teachers was my mother in disguise. As soon as the last bell had sounded, I would rush off for home, wondering as I ran if I could possibly make it to our apartment before she had succeeded in transforming herself. Invariably, she was already in the kitchen by the time I arrived, setting out my milk and cookies. Instead of causing me to give up my delusions, however, the feat merely intensified my respect for her powers.

—PHILIP ROTH, *Portnoy's Complaint*

Everybody knows what a monstrous emotional burden it is to have a mother. Whether the mommy in question is angelic, asphyxiating, absent, or just annoying, it is the task of the child to endure her, escape her, then explain her, to unload her like containerized cargo, perhaps in therapy. In our child-centric culture, we see the relationship from one direction, as if the child were the living thing and the mother something tremendously powerful yet insensate, like the ocean or the weather.

But this high-pressure system I'm in right now is hardly barometric. As the mother of two teenagers from my first marriage and a toddler from my current one, I am experiencing simultaneously two phases that really should be separated by a decent interval: the wild tumble of falling in love with a baby and the bewildering pain of living with adolescents. As I respond to my daughter's dependence on me with passion that is no less fearsome for being evolutionarily ordained, I'm also coping with my sons' break for the fence. Sure, growing up is tough. But check out this bad love affair from my point of view, and you tell me who's being scarred for life.

To my three-year-old, I am the world, I am God, and I am love incarnate. Jane can barely stand to let me out of her sight. She cries my name as soon as she wakes up and any time we are separated. She lights up like Las Vegas at my reappearance, often leaping into the air with joy. There is almost nothing I cannot fix with my embrace, very little she prefers to my attention—sorry, Dora the Explorer, but you're not even close—and she showers me with positive reinforcement at regular intervals. You're such a good helper, Mommy, she tells me when I hand her the toilet paper. That's beautiful, she says when I put on a pink shirt. I lub you, she reminds me every hour or so, in case I've forgotten, sometimes racing into the room and shouting it as she flies past me, sturdy legs churning, dark blond tresses flying, urgent in her errand as a medieval messenger.

I am not the only person to bask in the love light of this little love machine. She adores her father, whom she calls "Honey" with imperial confidence. She responds to her older brothers and sister (my husband has two kids from a previous marriage who live with us on weekends) with pure delight. But I am Mommy, and I am number one. What do you expect? The germ of her was stored inside me since my own birth, she waxed like the moon in my belly, for eighteen months she took her food from my body. To say I am her favorite means little in such a rigged competition, I know, but I am.

It's not like this is the first time this has happened to me. I remember the infancy of my son Hayes, now sixteen, as one long, golden afternoon, a swoon of nursing and cuddling and staring into his big dark eyes, the ceiling fan spinning overhead and the Dream Academy playing in the background. I had lost a baby, a full-term stillbirth, less than a year before he was born. Hayes washed over me like morphine for a person mangled, lying in the woods, waiting for medical assistance for quite a while. Then, a couple of years later, Vince came, so charismatic and radiant we called him the baby messiah.

But Jane is the last, and I know she's the last, and I thought I would never do this again, I thought I would have sons but never a daughter. My sweet little girl, my beauty, my nooza pooza, my fountain of love. Even as struggle and irritation find their way into my responses—even as she learns to say No and Get my shoes! and to whine and hound Mommy this Mommy that Mommy Mommy *Mommy!*—I am stunned to realize how connected, how consumed, how converted to a tool for her use I have become. (Again!) If anything were to happen to her, I think once or twice a day, and stop myself right there.

And something *is* going to happen to her, even if none of my worst fears comes to pass and she grows normally to adolescence. At that point, I can expect to have precisely the inverse experience of the festival of love I now enjoy. Toppled from my pedestal like a statue of Saddam Hussein, I will be rejected as powerfully as I was once embraced. For just as a toddler is devoted to cathecting you, a twelve-year-old uses all the force of his particular being to tear free.

With emotionally muffled Hayes, it was a quiet junta, a revolution of rocky sullenness. He responded to less than a quarter of the conversation I directed to him, and to that fraction with icy rebuff or curled-lip scorn. The idea, it seemed, was that I would wait on him hand and foot while staying entirely out of his way, requiring nothing of him, and completely avoiding all public and private displays of affection. The summer he was twelve, I remember, my mother asked him why he was being so mean to me. He replied simply, Because I hate her.

With the more passionate Vince, things have been livelier. At late eleven, it began when he seemed about to literally explode with rage because I asked him to put the ketchup on the table (a few dozen times), then accidentally bumped into him in front of the fridge while he was finally complying. This past year, seventh grade—watch out, my friends, for seventh grade—it got much worse. He cursed at me, he screamed at me, he ordered me to shut up and leave him alone; I was without question the worst thing that happened to him on any given day.

In the preposterously rainy spring of this benighted year, it came to pass that Vince was not doing his homework, his grades were dropping, and thus a scheme was inaugurated where the guidance counselor and I were both to sign off on an assignment sheet he completed every day. One afternoon, I asked him several times to see the sheet, and instead of answering me, he left the kitchen and went to his room. A bit later, I was knocking on his door, asking him to show me the sheet—little Jane was right beside me, I was on my way to take her to the bathroom, I think— and finally he responded: Go away! Just go away! Stubbornly, I did not. So he came out on the landing and stuck his face in my face and put his hand on my chest and shoved me, and he said, Fuck you, you dirty bitch.

My response to this was more profound and less coherent than anger. I struggled to breathe. For three days, I would find tears welling up in my eyes on and off, every time I thought of it. I could barely speak to him. Yet, the infraction seemed virtually past punishment. When, the previous summer, he and a friend had semi-accidentally set fire to a neighbor's hayfield, I grounded him for a month. But what to do about this? Take away his screen name?

Talk to him, I asked his stepfather, and I believe he tried. Finally, there was an apology of some sort, followed by a conversation about what it is that makes him blow up like that, about how his explosiveness hurts and even frightens me (though I know what it's like to have a bad temper, actually), about how we could do it better next time. This first, halting conversation was followed by others, and eventually, after he had a contretemps with a teacher at school, I took him to a counselor to talk about dealing with anger. But the fact is, I don't know how to be one of those parents whose child would never dare talk to them this way, and if he did, make sure he would never do it again. I know this is a weakness of my parenting, and it is also a strength.

Whatever I did about this incident, what I could not do was turn back the clock. For a few terrifying moments, my baby messiah had turned into a demon-child from hell, and he was determined to drive me off.

He has to, right? He has to separate, to break the bonds of my milky mothering, my cloying care. I did it too, so I know. I remember how it was, remember how I treated my mother—though I believe I stopped somewhere short of Fuck you, you dirty bitch. Adolescence is poison, it is torture, it is unbelievable frustration, I didn't just hate her, I hated everything, which was her, and to escape her, I wanted to molt my life like snakeskin and wriggle free to some unimaginable other world.

Even if I know this separation is necessary, it breaks my heart. And even if my heart is broken, I can't just skulk off and lick my wounds, because the little infidels still need me to love them, still want that tiny dot in the distance that used to be the whole world to receive them warmly on their occasional visits. All I can do is find some cooler place to stand, some way to let go but not leave, so I can continue the task of caring about people who are conducting a vigorous multiyear exorcism of me.

But for God's sake, do I have to go through both of these things at the same time, the toddler and the adolescents? It is truly insane. It forces me to remember that this boy who cannot tolerate me standing next to him once sucked me in as if I were oxygen. It makes me envision the day my darling lover-girl will see me as the toxic cloud that blocks the sun. I know I'm supposed to accept this as perfectly normal, part of the job and the process, and know that it too will pass. But imagine the indignity: the people you once took baths with, whose very tushies you tenderly cared for, *will not even answer you when you speak.* And nature, that dirty bitch, doesn't make you fall out of love with them the way it does them with you. They see your embrace as a chokehold; to you, it is still an embrace. They see your curiosity as a vile invasion; for you, it is still a natural act of care. And so I teach Jane to cut her food, to ride a bike, to say her phone number and address, knowing full well what I am pushing her toward.

Of course, every day is not the same. Just last week, I spent over an hour chatting amiably with Vince as we bodysurfed together at the beach. Not long from now, they will leave adolescence behind and become fresh-minted grown-ups, and I will fall in love all over again with these friendly, busy people who carry my whole beating heart in that jeans pocket sagging below their asses. Then they will move on into their lives and patronize me, remind themselves to call me, brush aside my queries about their classes, their careers, their marriages. They will dread my death, but they will also dread the sound of my voice on the phone, like an old flame who won't go away.

And like a billion mothers before me, I will make my peace with it. I will play cards, read novels, and make the favorite pie when asked. I will take my crumbs and hide my scars. I will smile a serene and knowing smile when they hand me my grandchildren.

III

In the Mirror

THE MAD NAKED SUMMER NIGHT

Shall I compare thee to a summer's night? Thou art more lovely and more temperate but I'm afraid that's not saying much. These nights are thick and heavy as black velour, hot and formfitting against our bodies, over our faces. A humid landscape through which we plod like testy zombies, arms outstretched, eyes blank, returning slowly and inexorably to our air-conditioned tombs. We have sacrificed our last calorie of energy on the altar of daytime. We have burned the skin off our thighs getting into the car. We have permanent ruts between our eyes from the weight of our sunglasses. Exhausted drag queens in melted makeup, we have worked our last nerve.

Motorcycles thunder, jet planes roar, a distant procession of sirens *woo-woos* for hours, as if people for blocks around us are dropping like flies. The cicadas drone the same annoying phrase over and over, a garage band of four-year-olds with sitars. Then the monotony is cracked: shattered glass, a shot, a bomb, a fire-cracker, maybe just a boom car throbbing down the street. To-ward midnight, the fabric of the sky is torn by heat lightning; even the atmosphere cannot take it anymore.

Somewhere, a serial killer's air-conditioning conks out, and he leaves his home.

What is the half-life of a snow cone? But a millisecond com-pared to the sticky mess into which it devolves. And what of the scent of honeysuckle? No match for the sweetness of ripening dumpster rot. Ah, the perfume of summer. Chlorine, tar, sun-screen, burned meat, and ketchup, yes, ketchup, red and viscous, dripping from refrigerator shelves, down every picnic table, every T-shirt, from the Formica of every takeout window to the hot as-phalt. Ketchup, the blood of summer, oozing from our food, our food which is fast and salty and greasy, our food which is like our sex, only with more ketchup.

Don't start with me about fireflies, drive-in movies, hide-and-go-seek, skinny legs swinging from the fire escape, the sound of a radio drifting through the open windows of the house next door. I've had my good times, like Walt Whitman, my mad naked sum-mer nights. I've had frozen drinks so cold I lost two years' worth of memory. I've danced so hard and long I had to throw away those clothes. I've climbed over the fence at the city pool for a midnight swim and gotten busted. I've eaten ice cream till I puked, I've drunk until I puked, I've stayed all night in bars that smelled like puke. I've waited and waited for the fireworks and I've waited for you to kiss me and I've waited for someone to get back with the goddamn beer.

Sure, if I still had a bedtime, I'd be happy to stay up past it.

If I still went to school, I'd be glad it was closed. If I still fell in love with lifeguards, I'd be delighted to screw one. But those days are over. Now our kids are in bed, our cockroaches in their cupboards, our empty beer cans nestled in the recycling bin. We're avoiding an argument. You want to set the AC on sixty-five and sleep with five quilts, that's fine with me. I've had it with showers and ceiling fans and it's almost time to get up anyway. Let's kill this night and call it morning while there's still time to make coffee before the burning starts.

SNAP

I recently watched from the sidelines as dear friends went through the process of buying a house in Washington, DC. Purchasing real estate in the nation's capital would be an ordeal for anyone—little is available and what is, is unbelievably expensive. It's an accepted practice to offer much more than the asking price, and the whole operation is more like an auction of a Picasso sketch than what normally passes for home buying.

For my friends, the situation was exacerbated by the husband's affinity for getting all the facts about any decision he has to make. As each serious possibility emerged, he researched it with methodical thoroughness, shining the bright light of his will to know into every dim corner of the property. He talked to the neighbors. He investigated the schools. He timed the commutes, assessed the shopping, and discussed with appropriate professionals the soundproof qualities of the basement that might house his son's rock band.

When they finally became the owners of an excellent house, meeting almost all his criteria, my friend was miserable. His sorrow may have been caused by the fact that they spent much more money than they initially meant to, or because the family had to leave DC proper for Maryland. But another pal of ours, a PhD in marketing, proposed a third possibility.

According to the latest research, she explained, the more time you spend evaluating your options, the worse you feel about your decision. In the process of carefully considering these options, of rolling them around in your mind, you become so attached to the choices you reject that you can't help pining for them when they are gone.

I have to say this was welcome news for me, a person with a lifelong history of making snap decisions about everything from houses to husbands, from cheese to childbirth. I rarely consider more than one option. Two is a lot, a real lot. If I do any research, I pay attention to only those pieces of information that support my already-formed instant choice. Though I know it makes me less than a woman and less than an American, and constitutes a miscarriage of my suburban Jewish upbringing, the fact is that I am a failure as a consumer. Not to say that I fail to consume. Alas, that is false to the tune of thousands of dollars per month. But I fail to take pleasure in consumption. I fail to consume with passion, intelligence, and style. I fail to find zest or fulfillment in the prospect of acquiring the perfect object. In short, I hate to shop.

To begin with, I do not like stores. Most are too big, too confusing, and offer too many choices. They are nefariously designed to make you waste time and money. Even grocery stores, especially the new theme-park-style grocery stores, fill me with a fear of being swallowed up, never to emerge, trapped in an infinite decision loop involving twelve varieties of tomato or chicken wing. As for department stores and shopping malls, these I really don't understand. How is this recreation? What is the fun part? Wandering lost through miles of walkways? Flipping through racks and racks of items that would probably be a great addition to your wardrobe if you had a wardrobe to begin with? Being ignored by salespeople? Viewing your cellulite in a three-way mirror? Waiting in line? Forgetting your packages? Or, the grand finale, loading your purchases into the trunk, fully aware that everything you bought will go on sale next week for half of what you just paid for it?

As we all know, to pay too much for something is to be a bad person, a person who has forsaken the bedrock American value of thrift. This person does not clip coupons, neglects to read advertising circulars, has no patience for comparison shopping, and does not subscribe to *Consumer Reports*. She buys tampons at 7-Eleven, clothes at whatever store has the most accessible parking, refrigerators over the telephone. When her car breaks down irreparably on New Year's Day, she heads out to purchase another, finding only a single dealership open on the holiday. You sell cars? Great. Could I have one? (And yet schizophrenic frugality shipwrecks this same person in the yogurt aisle, as if Yoplait and Dannon and their enticing cents-off promotions were the Sirens themselves.)

I am a kamikaze shopper, my emotional and financial stability at risk every time I leave the house in search of provisions, every time I descend into the vast and terrible maw of plenty with its dazzling plate-glass teeth. And as for regrets—well, this research interests me. Because I've always thought if I spent more time studying my options, I might be happier with my decisions. I might not have spent the first day at my own new house crying because it had no air-conditioning or water heater, or the first winter going crazy over the horrific (and completely obvious) snow-removal problems. I would have had better marriages and fewer children and wiser investments. But now it turns out, even if I'd done my homework, I might have felt worse than I do. What a relief.

GREEN ACRES

Let me tell you about my driveway. It is a quarter mile long, it is hilly, and it has some rather dramatic potholes and ruts. If you drive its curving length from the street to my house, you will surely feel you are visiting someone who lives in the country, or even that you are embarking on an adventure.

That's how I felt when I wound along it the first time with my husband-to-be and the real estate agent—it seemed like something in a fairy tale. At its end, a brick house with a bell tower rose from a glade of towering oaks. The house had reddish-gold wood-plank floors, huge fireplaces, and views of red barns and surrounding hillsides. It was located on a two-acre piece of land in the middle of a large farm that the owners planned to retain. This was a good thing. Even my husband, who loves everything country including country music (and back then, George Jones and Patty Loveless just seemed like part of his charm, the exotic blend of Søren Kierkegaard and Merle Haggard that was the man I loved), even he didn't actually want to become a farmer.

And so our new blended family cruised up the enchanted driveway in June of 1999, and for a few months none of us had much of anything to do but play board games and explore our new terrain. At dusk, we watched the sun set behind the hills as the alfalfa field became a carpet of fireflies. I didn't even notice that the movie theaters were so far away or that there was no-where to have a margarita or that I'd left all my friends back in Texas because deep down I didn't believe I was staying here.

Anyway, to give me a completely false impression of what my new life was going to be like, the first thing we did in the house was have our wedding, right out in the clearing in the woods. My new stepdaughter, Emma, was my maid of honor, Hayes was Crispin's best man, and Vince and my stepson, Sam, walked us down the aisle. Crispin played the wedding march on a Cajun accordion. In one of the few similarities to my first wedding, a mayor was on hand to officiate.

Combining two fully operational households, we hardly needed gifts. Instead of registering, we informed our guests we would be interning them as servants. The thirty-five adults and children who attended not only witnessed the event but also put it on: they cleaned, decorated, and arranged flowers, hauled rocks and rental equipment, prepared food. They brought in the crawfish feast from New Orleans for the rehearsal dinner and the tomato pies from Philly for the wedding lunch; my late first husband's mother baked our wedding cake and drove down with it from the Poconos. The highlight of the whole event was a talent show in the cornfields that went on into the evening with music, poetry, lip-synch dance routines, and trampoline demonstrations.

In the afterglow of these festivities, I was so elated, I had the illusion that my adjustment to my new home was already accomplished. I felt sorry for people in the city with their draining social lives and many commitments. Who needs home delivery of *The New York Times*? An old friend wrote and said she remembered my announcing long ago that my dream in life was to live on a farm and write a novel. I had no recollection of saying this or even thinking it, but I was glad to hear it. I would probably start my novel any minute.

That fall, however, when both my kids and my professor husband went back to school and I stayed home all by myself, my spirits plummeted. I became extremely lonely, then extremely sad, and then, extremely pregnant. Right about when I hit my second trimester, the snow started to fall. I watched it from my new permanent position on the living room couch. Soon I couldn't sit up long enough to write an email, much less a novel.

Now I could see what this driveway was really all about. It was about isolation. During that winter, snow drifted so deeply that there were times we could not get in or out—even in our new Dodge Durango. We acquired the four-wheel-drive Durango specifically for navigating the driveway after I upended its predecessor in a creek while trying to cut across the field because I couldn't make it up the slippery hill.

This was the winter of Jesse Garver, a man with a piece of heavy equipment called a front-loader. When the snow got too deep for plowing, the front-loader could remove it a bucket at a time. It took hours and cost $150. I had a kind of love-hate relationship with Jesse: until he came, we were stranded; but once he left, we were broke.

What am I doing here? I wondered. I had made only one friend—a running partner, actually, and though she still forged bravely on through snow and ice, I did not. I had met other people, too, people who lived on or near old farm roads named after their families. The stones in the cemetery bore those names. By these standards, I could be a newcomer for a couple of centuries.

In other places I'd lived, people were eager to show off their hometown and its highlights. But showing off of any kind is frowned upon in Central Pennsylvania. No one's going to rush up and tell you about the place they go for sour-cherry pudding or the spot on the road into Glen Rock where the view of snowy hills and deep red barns is right out of an Andrew Wyeth. It's not because they don't enjoy these things, or because they're trying to protect their secrets, but because they don't brag. They don't make a big deal out of anything. They've been here a long time; they've eaten a lot of cherry puddings and seen a lot of snowy hills. You'll figure it out in a couple of generations. Or else you'll leave, and nobody'll miss you much.

That February, I sadly noted the passing of Mardi Gras, a holiday I had grown to love on visits to New Orleans over the years. Actually, I learned, this pre-Lenten festival did indeed have a traditional celebration here in Pennsylvania Dutch country. Not with parades, or beads, or alcoholic Hurricanes, but with something called fastnachts: fat, yellow, sugar-drenched potato doughnuts.

Not bad, I conceded, after I had my first dozen or so.

Spring came, the snow melted, and soon it was the hottest

May in memory. I wrote a check to retrofit my castle with central air-conditioning and talked to my ob-gyn about Zoloft. How do you like the country? people would ask me. Oh, it's very beautiful, I would say.

"Beautiful" had become a code word for all my sad alienated urban Jewish thoughts about this place, the church-supper capital of the world. It's not even the country, I thought meanly. It's the ru-burbs. Sure, it looks rural—the patchwork quilt of gold and green, the deer and turkey milling around the satellite dish, but just a mile or so up the road, there're six fast-food places and three dollar stores. You show me Walden, I'll show you Walmart. Soccer moms and Taco Bells dot the manure-scented pastures; Mennonite fruit stands are attached to miniature golf courses; kids ride lawn tractors to the Pokémon swap meet.

Part of my attitude problem must have been the pregnancy, because once my little York County native was born on the summer solstice of the millennium, I gradually began to feel differently. My body and heart lightened and my days filled with the sweet rituals of new motherhood. By the time my baby girl toddled over to look at the horses and sheep that live next door, I had come to associate a sunny freedom of movement with my environment. And when winter came round again, my husband built a bonfire and took the kids midnight sledding on the hill out back. Little Jane threw her first snowball and had her first cup of hot chocolate.

By this time, Jane's older brothers had become a part of the community: they had friends and social lives; they ate meals in other homes and went along on family trips to Ocean City, Maryland. They started to adopt York County speech patterns, saying My snowboard needs waxed, Let my room the way it is, and calling adults "Miss Kris" and "Mr. Tom." They picked up the local habit of asking questions without the usual lift in tone at the end of the sentence, as if the answer were implicit in the question. This interrogative style was one of the first things I noticed about folks around here. Did you like that potpie, someone would ask me. Or, Is the school road plowed then. I would pause awkwardly before replying, not sure for a moment that I'd been asked a question.

It was the boys, with their sports events and carpools and telephone trees, who led me into our new world, and it was when a tragedy occurred in their circle that I realized my relationship to this place had changed. Did he shoot himself in the driveway, I heard Hayes say on the phone one day, and I froze on the kitchen steps, my arms full of bottles for recycling.

Two days later, we were among those present at the funeral of a man named Jack Allison. I didn't know Jack very well: a tall, affable guy pulling up in my driveway in a pickup to get his boy; another dad at the game. His wife, a pretty, sassy neonatal nurse, I knew a little better, but still, I wasn't sure whether it was my place to go to the funeral. But then the whole basketball team decided to attend together, and it fell to me to pick the boys up at school in my big Durango, a bunch of thirteen- and fourteen-year-olds wriggling in suits and leather shoes. I stood with them and their parents in the cemetery on the hill where headstones bore names of Allisons since the early nineteenth century, veterans of wars, couples and their children, a baby who lived only three months a hundred years ago. In the midst of it, a minister tried to make some sense of what had happened to Jack, how things turn so dark so suddenly, how a community can become a shelter to keep a family from blowing apart.

I left the funeral chauffeuring even more boys than I'd arrived with, one of them Tait, the younger of Jack's sons. On our way to Tait's grandma's house, my baby began to cry in her car seat, as eighteen-month-olds in car seats often do. There was only one solution to this problem, and it was for everyone in the car to sing *There was a farmer had a dog and Bingo was his name-oh* immediately, no matter how inappropriate it seemed. So we did, and we did it with gusto, coming over the hill through the cornfields singing as loud as we could. Tait didn't sing, but his face relaxed for the first time that day. There was a simplicity and a silliness to that moment, a sudden light and air I think all of us will keep in some mental scrapbook, all those boys who grow up and raise children here, who bury more loved ones in that cemetery, who, long years from now, are buried there themselves.

As we pulled into the grandmother's driveway, the place where Jack died, you could see that life was slowly taking over again. Kids were going to see the bike ramps and the tree fort. People were saying the pretzel salad was delicious. It was an odd-looking concoction, but after one big bite, I agreed with them. Is this Jell-O in the salad, I asked. I was starting to get it. With a question like that you may not be looking for information. You want reassurance.

In the summer, the corn grows so high on both sides of my driveway, it feels like a leafy emerald tunnel. These days I wait through

June and July for the stalks to get that tall, so I can crawl between them invisibly as an ant in the grass. Like all the York County cognoscenti, I shop for fruit at Brown's Orchards, homemade ice cream at Carman's, and beef from women in long skirts and white snoods at a Brethren butcher shop called Godfreys. Weekends often pass without social invitations, but our basement is always full of kids, and there are several kitchens where I stop in for a cup of coffee or a glass of wine when I drop off a kid at home. I learned to drive too fast on country roads, the way many people around here do, but then I learned to slow down again after I killed a cat named Doc who lived on a farm with horses about a quarter mile from my house.

Though I still complain quite a bit about York County, its red barns and fenced hillsides are no longer just decoration to me.

This past year I read Vladimir Nabokov's *Speak, Memory* with the students I teach at a local college. I was quite taken by his account of meeting up, much later in life, with two women who had been his childhood governesses in Russia. Though the ladies had hardly been on speaking terms when both lived under his roof, they were bosom friends in old age. "One is always at home in one's past," he writes, "which partly explains those pathetic ladies' posthumous love for a remote and, to be perfectly frank, rather appalling country, which they had never really known and in which none of them had ever been very content."

This will be my seventh summer in Glen Rock and there are no signs of our departure. I seem to have gotten a head start on the posthumous love.

JUST READ THIS ESSAY TO LOOK AND FEEL TEN YEARS YOUNGER

From a distance you can't see it, the surface of the skin, the crumply crosshatched creases where it once stretched smooth. Close up, I catch it in the mirror: beneath my eye, a slight pouch demarcated by a parabola engraved tangent to the cheekbone. Immediately I flick my gaze away. My invisible face, the face of my consciousness, is still the smooth one. If I look too long, this new one will stick. (How long is too long? After being a varsity lacrosse player, my father-in-law was paralyzed by polio at twenty-two. I always meant to ask him, before he died at seventy-nine, if he could still run in his dreams.)

The first time I thought of aging I was twenty-two. I know, because I wrote a poem about it. Did I find one gray hair? Spy one pucker above my lip from the kisses I gave my cigarettes? I don't remember what started it, how I heard the gong within me saying youth is over, something else is beginning, come to me, my precious. That's how I thought of it then: aging was my dark prince, my demon lover, my secret husband, taking me on a bridal journey of ten thousand nights to our true home.

Perhaps I was already tired, already willing to lay it down. Already it seemed simpler to conceive a love contract with death than negotiate the reality of a woman's life:

First, the tuning fork of beauty always ringing in your ears. At best you are flat or sharp, more likely off by octaves.

Second, and in fact no matter what you look like—graceful Lassie or pop-eyed half beagle—the awesome and awful effect of your bitch-body on men, and all the social arrangements, artistic endeavors, high crimes and low thus engendered, the vast conceptual kingdoms and tiny backyard corrals built to contain the desire and the fear.

Third—optional but recommended—children, borne and suckled and tended and cosseted and lost and mourned, on, in, with, from, and by your body, your body which is their very ground, the beloved home they struggle to leave like tortured expatriates, discussing you over drinks in a bar in Guadalajara.

And these are just the most salient gifts that come with the Amazing Female Body. We could talk about Hormones, Cycles, and Sanitary Products. We could bring up Housework or Centuries of Oppression. We might mention Personal Responsibility for the Emotional State of Everyone. But we would probably be preaching to the choir.

So one possibility is that when it's over, when your rear sags like an empty hammock and nobody gives a hoot what you look like and your children have taken off in their lime-green Volkswagen Beetles for Guadalajara, you feel liberated. A crone, feminism tells us, is not a shriveled witch, but a sorceress-monk, a bodhi-sattva being who crawls out of the milkweed cocoon of female sexuality. Fragile-boned, gnarl-fingered, breasts long in retirement, her eyes sparkle in her crinkly face. She floats free. The root of her wizening is wise.

Does that sound good? Not sure? Okay, think of it this way. Imagine there's a mandatory worldwide beauty contest for all females between twelve and fifty-some. The cutoff used to be a couple of decades earlier, but between age-defying moisturizer and gray-covering hair dye, between Botox and Premarin and pricier alternatives provided by plastic surgeons, between Pilates teachers and day spas, fifty is the new thirty. Unless you're an actual Oscar nominee or a trophy wife, in which case sixty is.

So there's this contest, and every time we leave the house (the house? the bathroom, really) we're crossing the pageant stage in front of the judges. And every day just about every one of us loses. Loses abysmally. Doesn't make the first cut. Clings to some one-time special-category award—Pretty Face for a Chubby Girl; Most Delicate Ankles of All the Sisters; Wow That's Some Red Hair; Nice Rack. Then she trudges wearily on, leading with her dog-eared "assets," her consolation prizes, until aging takes them too.

People my age talk a lot about age. One of the things they sometimes say, after mourning the decline of their skin, hair, energy level, etc., much as I have here, is Inside, I don't feel any different than I did when I was twelve—or nineteen, or twenty-five. Wherever they pinpoint the archetypal moment of youth, the idea is that they feel like a young person in an aging body, an unchanging self in a changing vessel.

Well, I don't. I don't feel at all like I did at any of those ages. As far as I'm concerned, this is a good thing. To me, the idea that I might someday feel like a twelve-year-old in an eighty-year-old body sounds like the worst of both worlds.

I was actually pretty happy about it when I turned forty-five one May day early in the century. I had the sense that I was at the beginning of something—as if I had metamorphosed into a very young old person, instead of becoming an older and older young person, as I'd felt for quite a while. In the same way world-weary eighth graders turn into wide-eyed high school freshmen, I seemed to have crossed the boundary on my forty-fifth birthday into a new demographic.

Someday, I thought, I'll go to my son's graduation or choose a mother-of-the-bride dress. I'll sit in a rocker and whisper to a sleepy grandchild. My husband and I will lock up our empty nest and board a plane for Bangkok. By that time, not only will I have an AARP card and get discounts at the movies, but I'll actually be able to go to the movies whenever I please, without weeks of strategizing and arranging babysitting, rides, and sleepovers. I told you so, I said to myself the other day when I read that researchers at Brandeis reported that the majority of women find aging is much better than they expected. But get this: those over eighty gave the most positive report of all on their emotional and mental health. Over eighty. Hell, yeah. Of course, this is probably because they have a better idea of what illness and trouble really are. Or at least are more familiar with the alternative.

In any case, I was glad to hear it, because I know when I'm eighty, I'm going to feel exactly like I'm eighty.

So. The mirror. The crow's feet. The thinning lid-skin, drooping a bit. The darkish crescent under the eye. The pale-etched curves lapping the cheek like salt lines left by waves on the shore. Well, of course. I never wore sunscreen as a kid, though I grew up on the beach. Smoked a lot of cigarettes before I knew any better. Smoked some more after I knew. Was told at forty by a facialist there was still time to repair this damage; didn't listen. Have found the time perhaps twice in the last ten years to put on eye cream before bed.

One day my mother-in-law—the one who was married to the varsity lacrosse player who spent so much of his life in a wheelchair—showed me a picture of a suntanned, clear-eyed woman about my age, her ginger hair swept back from her forehead. Who is that? I said.

It's me, she replied ruefully. And every time I look in the mirror, I'm shocked to find out I don't look like this anymore.

I looked at her again, looked into the blue eyes behind her glasses, the very eyes of the woman in the photo, her gaze still frank and curious, yet somehow slightly inward, as if still trying to figure out something sad that happened a long time ago.

For everything time takes away from us, this is what it leaves.

SILLY RABBI, TRIX ARE FOR YIDS

Hayes has gotten to the age of filling out applications, and he often has questions for me. Some are silly (What's my zip code?), some are understandable (What's my congressional district?), and some are a bit confounding. Last night it was, What's my ethnicity? I leaned over his shoulder to peer at the choices on the online form and told him to click None. None of the options listed by the U.S. Naval Academy's summer seminar for high school juniors applied to us. Yet I cannot help but feel we do have an ethnicity, sort of.

I am the daughter of Jews; Hayes is the son of a Jewish mother. Though we represent the dreaded result of generations of American assimilation, for my sons' father was Catholic and barely a smidgen of Jewish religious faith survives in our household, I have little doubt that I am an ethnic Jew. It may not be a category that exists in the world of college applications, but it is not one I can escape, nor would want to. My children may feel otherwise, perhaps already do. Because of how I have raised them and because there's nothing in their environment either encouraging it or forcing it on them, the idea that they are "Jewish" must seem slightly unreal.

I was brought up by Jews among Jews. Though my parents seem to have had as little personal attraction to religion as I now have, they had no doubt they were Jewish, nor that they should join a temple and send me and my sister off to Hebrew and Sunday school. Surely they chose this course without much consideration, because what sense did it make to drive us there three times a week to learn a foreign language and dozens of inscrutable songs—*Dahveed! Melech Isroel! Chai chai vechai-aa-am!*—that decades later I still can't get out of my head, not to mention the *berachah*, the old-timey stories about soldiers and sages, and the cockamamie rituals (did we really parade around that little grape-trellis sukkah thing waving bananas?). None of it, not a single syllable or gesture, had any connection to Jewish life as it was lived in our household, which involved a certain kind of self-deprecating humor, a set of unquestioned doctrines regarding good grades and homework, and a predilection for smoked fish.

At Hebrew school, however, we learned otherwise. Being a Jew was definitely not just eating bagels and giggling over Allan Sherman records. Our teacher, a very serious and intense young woman whose dark stringy hair hung over the edges of her owl-round glasses, enlightened us as to the true meaning of being a Jew, which seemed to be more like being a Martian than being a Presbyterian or a Hindu. Evelyn Rosenblatt wanted each and every one of us to feel personally the legacy of two thousand years of Jewish persecution, and most important to understand that we were the Chosen People. To be the Chosen People was very, very good and also very, very dangerous, but most of all it was irrevocable.

Once Chosen, we could never be Unchosen, Miss Rosenblatt explained. No matter where we went or what we did or how we acted, no matter what color we dyed our hair or whom we made friends with or what our profession, no matter if we worshipped another god in some alien church, no matter if we became Christian missionaries or went native in the Congo, no matter *what*, we would always be Jewish. When push came to shove, at the end of the day, when all was said and done and the shit hit the fan, "they" would find us and we would still be Jews. So don't try to run, don't try to hide—you are a Jew like you're a boy or a girl, like you're black or white. It's that deep. It's not a choice, not a voluntary matter of faith or culture—it's an intrinsic property, an essence, something you can never lose.

Old Testament, pogrom, Holocaust, QED.

This spiel definitely made an impression on me, but seeing as we weren't being pursued by Gestapo agents or the pharaoh's army at that very moment, being Jewish seemed more like being in a club than wearing the irrevocable brand of doom. You had your club passwords, club songs, club rituals, and, of course, your secret clubhouse, the temple itself with its holy holies and velvet curtains and dusty books. And, for a brief moment, I loved it all, the edifices, the paraphernalia, the tchotchkes. What's more, the idea that there was a path of righteousness and I could follow it appealed to me. A mitzvah a day keeps the doctor away, and gets you off the hook in case God doesn't approve of little girls who are addicted to bouncing around in bed all night with their stuffed bunnies between their legs. Well, who knew what God really thought about such things?

My parents were mystified by my vigorous Judaism. After all, my mother served bacon for breakfast and shoved live lobsters into boiling water with her own two hands, while my father not only didn't go regularly to services but also connived to skip the religious portions of bar mitzvahs and weddings.

Not me. I went for the whole megillah. I wanted to be the first woman rabbi, make aliyah, and raise my children on a kibbutz in Israel. What's my Hebrew name? I asked my mother, and when I learned I hadn't been given one, I chose Rachael, which had that satisfying gargling *ccchhh* sound while it also conjured up the world-famous shiksa Raquel Welch. I began using a great deal of Yiddish in my ordinary speech, which my sister copied, until at one point my mother heard one "oy gevalt" too many and told us, It wasn't our background, an assimilationist distinction lost on me at the time. She said the same thing later on when we started calling her "Mamacita."

Little Marion Winik, queen of the Jews. I dressed as Vashti for Halloween, lit the big patchouli-scented candle in my bedroom on Friday nights whenever I remembered, and wrote poems using all fifteen words I knew in Hebrew. These I showed to our rabbi, a short, round, bald man in black robes who is confused in my memory with my father's friend the Cadillac dealer.

My sudden religious devotion and my passionate social idealism combined to make me something of a joke in my extended family, easy to bait and even easier to flummox totally. But it's just *wrong*! Don't you see? I would wail, so upset by my uncle Phillip's defense of the United States' role in Southeast Asia that I ended

up running out to the backyard in tears. Then Daddy would come
out and find me, smushed up against the side of the house with my
knees shoved underneath my sweater.

You know Mommy doesn't like it when you stretch your
sweaters out like that.

So.

Marion, get up. Stop being a baby. You almost had him this
time, and then you let him get to you! Don't take it personally! He
only resorts to teasing you because he's losing the argument.

He's an asshole.

Well, no doubt about that, but it's not the point. What you
were saying about the Vietcong was absolutely right.

I hate Uncle Phillip!

You don't hate him, you just hate being backed into a corner.
You're talking about moral issues and he's talking about politics.

How can politics be different than moral issues! You're as bad
as he is!

What the hell was wrong with these grown-ups? But once I
started to see through their insane hypocrisies and illogical prem-
ises, I couldn't stop, and before long the faith of Abraham was
dust to me. My disillusionment was pretty classic, composed of the
same thoughts that occur to many adolescents. First of all, organized religion in general was ridiculous. How could the God that
made the Catholics do all their stuff be the same as the one who
set up the Jewish deal and the Hindu and the others? God would
never be so multifarious and so silly. These things could not all be
true at once; therefore, to me it was only reasonable and fair that
none of them were true. (Apparently, I believed that a just God
would not treat the peoples of the world any differently than my

mother treated me and my sister—one could not have something the other did not, especially not something like universal truth.)

Furthermore, God could not possibly be as involved in human affairs as everyone said, because no God would get behind the Vietnam War, or the Holocaust, for that matter. It was clear to me that everything about religion, not just ours, but all the religions—particularly the ones that had elaborate magical views on the afterlife, as appealing as they might be—was invented by human beings, not by God. What fool couldn't see that! No one knew a damn thing about God! And I was not going to be part of this pretext anymore!

I drafted an ardent essay explaining my new views and the inescapable logic behind them, and made handwritten copies for my parents and Rabbi Shulman. This I delivered as notice of my intention to become a Hebrew-school dropout. My parents, I'm sure, privately agreed with me. Theology was not their long suit and the Bible was no history book to them either. If anything, it was my religiosity that had been the conundrum; agnosticism was a hereditary trend. But considering all the work I had put into it, and all the carpools they had driven, and Israeli tree-plantings they had funded, it was a surprise how quickly they caved in, and they never made my sister Nancy go again either.

Soon I would be involved in Eastern religions, and after that, none at all. I loved Jewish humor, Jewish literature, Jewish food, and—after living a long time in places with very few of them— other Jewish people too. In fact, I started getting an instant home-girl feeling whenever I ran into one. After listening to gentiles say "schlep" and "schmuck" it was a relief to hear the authoritative pronunciation.

Give me the latest Philip Roth and a toasted bialy, hold the Torah.

But so simple it isn't. After a thirty-year hiatus, I started lighting Hanukkah candles again when my boys were small. It was partly because their father and paternal grandparents were such Yule-aholics that I felt the need to put in a word for my own heritage, distant as it may have been. Tellingly, after their father died, I flip-flopped and put what little holiday energy I had back into the Christmas side of the operation. More recently, I weakly swung back the other way, after having instilled in my little daughter a belief in Santa Claus (I can't help it, I love Santa Claus and the Tooth Fairy and even the Easter Bunny, and the capacity of a four-year-old to believe in almost anything), sweeping her off her feet with a red-and-green tide of Christmaphagoria. This was all very fun and in keeping with my own upbringing, but gradually I began to understand that she could have even less connection to her Jewish ancestry than her brothers, if that's possible.

So, I dragged out my grandmother's menorah and since no Hanukkah candle of any kind is available here in the rural part of York County—you should have seen the look on the face of the lady at the Hallmark store—I put in a call to my husband's ex-wife, who lives in a section of Baltimore that has more kosher restaurants than downtown Tel Aviv. Guess what, her name is Rachael. It really is. She is an actual Jew, raised by observant parents, and she has raised my two stepchildren with menorahs, Hebrew day school when they were small, and bar and bat mitzvahs when it came time. She was happy to get me a couple of boxes of candles. We lit them, on the nights we remembered to, and what Jane made of the situation, I have no idea. Hayes and Vince looked slightly nostalgic, I believe, as they wandered past.

This whole situation is a conundrum and a burden to me. I am no more excited by the story of the Maccabees than by the story of Christ's birth. I do love repeating the joyous present-giving ritual of my childhood and driving around to see Christmas lights and singing "Rudolph the Red-Nosed Reindeer"; otherwise I would just say no to the whole schmear. I've already said no to Passover, supposedly a celebration of liberation, but to me an annual festival of scab-picking and vengefulness. I almost said no to bar mitzvahs recently when the rabbi at my young cousin's prayed for the demise of then-comatose Yasser Arafat. Damn it, I thought, I have got to stop entering these houses of worship for good. Like I did when I was a kid, I have to stand up for what I believe. Nothing!

But the hard part is that though I am an atheist, though I feel queasy about Zionism, I have such tenderness for being Jewish. I still want to take that long-postponed trip to Israel and see the place for myself. The Hebrew schoolteachers were right: this is who I am. But I cannot pass on more than I have truly received— so I give my kids the social values, the sense of humor, the flavors. Here kids, read *Portnoy's Complaint*. Have some sturgeon. What, not hungry? I'll wrap it up and you can take it with you to the Naval Academy.

To be the diluted, distilled person at the end of a traditional culture is sad: in a way, I am only as Jewish as the anti-Semites can make me. On the other hand, I'm an atheist only Jews could create. As the Fiddler on the Roof might say, *L'chaim*.

REGARDING MY
DIAGNOSIS

I yell at my kids too much, like I used to yell at my mother too much. But it was when I started yelling at my friends that I really got worried. I made an appointment with a psychiatrist, expecting a long drawn-out production: a couch, a box of Kleenex, a weekly monologue. But psychiatry has changed since I last took the cure. I was out of there in a jiffy with a diagnosis and a prescription.

I told the doctor what I thought my problems were, but he had other ideas. We filled out what he called an inventory. Do I hate waiting in line? Am I impulsive? Irritable? Distractible? Do I fidget, doodle, and pace? Do I blurt non sequiturs, break rules, butt in, and boss everybody around? Do I often feel that a sign that reads NO PARKING ANY TIME actually means THIS SPOT RESERVED FOR MARION WINIK?

If this was an inventory, I was certainly fully stocked. Ah yes, said the doctor, you have adult attention-deficit disorder.

What? I said. I wasn't listening.

ADD, he said, you have ADD, and if you'll just go on this stimulant called Ritalin, you'll be fine.

Oh *really*, I said. Listen, buddy, if taking speed was going to do anything good for me, it would have done it a long time ago.

Whaddya know. I go to the doctor about my anger, and he just pisses me off. But that night, when I almost threw a chair across the room because my children wouldn't carry their plates to the sink, my nine-year-old asked if there wasn't some medication I was supposed to be on. He knows all about it from school, where kids line up outside the office every day at lunch to get their pills.

I'm glad Ritalin works for them, but I think I'm too old to be cured. Let's assume for a moment that I do have ADD. The question becomes, Who would I be without it? Not this me, that's for sure. A whole other person, I guess, who drives in the right-hand lane and chews her food. Who doesn't walk away from a frying egg to look for a sock. Who doesn't spend one hour a week searching through the garbage for crucial items.

At least if I have to have ADD, the culture has it with me. I recently read how they've eliminated the split second of black between the television show and the commercial to keep us from losing interest, saving us as a result fifteen seconds of boredom per day. Which is about what I save by cutting in front of slow-moving people at the grocery store. Fast cash, headline news, instant prints, drive-through Starbucks, microwave dinners—it's probably people who *don't* have ADD who are suffering here. Unfortunately, the shrinks don't have time to talk to them. Surely there's some drug they can take that will help.

Though I don't want to take medication, it's made me feel

better to have the label, to know that I am suffering from a syndrome, rather than just being a scatterbrained rage-monger. This comforting news may be less help to those around me. I still don't know people's names after meeting them a dozen times, I still space out completely in mid-conversation, and my second most frequent utterance to my kids after I love you is Hurry! Hurry!

They may not sound like words to live by, but they've gotten me this far.

16,409 EASY
STEPS TO
LATE-LIFE
FITNESS

Do you have what it takes to run a marathon? Consider this. Mbarak Hussein of Kenya, who won the 2002 Honolulu Marathon, finished in two hours, twelve minutes. Marion Winik of Pennsylvania came in 16,409th, just shy of four hours later. (Yeah, what of it? Another ten thousand finishers moseyed in after me.) While the more competitive Boston Marathon closes its course before I would have crossed the finish line, Honolulu and many other races let you take as long as you want.

That is, if you want to do it at all. I know what you're thinking. I, too, once had as much interest in long-distance running as I had in other ancient arts, such as washing clothes with stones in a river. So what happened? How does a perfectly sane food-, wine-, and booklover turn into one of the nearly half million people who finished a U.S. marathon in 2002?

I was closing in on forty when I first started exercising: a little walking, a little running, a little weight lifting—just your basic fend-off-death-with-thinner-thighs type thing. Then a few years later, at a 5K race I ran right after I moved to Pennsylvania, I met a group of middle-aged women who were marathon runners.

Vicki, a Jewish mother and lawyer with a touch of asthma, ran her first marathon on her fiftieth birthday. Marsha, a gentle librarian from Kentucky, began training when her son was diagnosed with leukemia and she started to worry about her own health (he's been in remission for years, and she's run four marathons). Theresa, market researcher and recovered alcoholic, refocused her hard-core compulsive tendencies on the goal of doing a marathon in each of the fifty states. And Nancy, and Katherine, and Paulette . . . as I heard their unlikely stories of athletic accomplishment, I was sure I would never become one of them.

Theresa, who became my regular running partner, knew just what to say to that. It's like when you first hear about sex when you're a little kid, she commented one day on the trail. You think, Ick! People actually do that? Not me! Never! Then the years go by, and you get more and more curious. Finally, you do it, and once you do, you're never the same.

If you don't want to run a marathon, make sure you don't meet this woman. She breaks you down. I just thank God I met her when she was into exercise rather than booze and drugs.

Over the next few years, Theresa and her friends trained for the Steamtown Marathon in the Poconos, the Marine Corps Marathon in DC, and the Disney in Florida, but I kept my distance. Run in a good state and I'll come with you, I said. What's a good state? she asked. Hawaii, I told her.

Less than a year later, we were buying our tickets for the pre-race luau.

My four-month training program started in September and ran according to a schedule Theresa gave me: two runs each week ranging from four to eight miles, plus a weekend long run, increasing a mile every Sunday to a twenty-miler a few weeks before the race.

But as it turned out, my longest training run was twenty-one miles, not twenty, because it was so dark when I started out that freezing, rainy morning I couldn't even see the mile markers. I finished more than five hours later, hobbling, soaked, maniacally chanting Car! Car! Car! Car! as I caught sight of my vehicle. I was sure the marathon could not be more of a challenge.

That is the kind of thought you should never have. For not long after we passed the giant lit-up Polynesian Santa Claus at Honolulu city hall, at about mile three of the marathon, I got a very bad cramp in my right calf. I had experienced this cramp in the last few weeks of training, and when it showed up that morning in Honolulu, I knew I wouldn't be able to wait it out or stretch it out—I would run the race with it, or I would not run.

So I kept going. After all, I hadn't come all the way to Hawaii, leaving my husband in a midwinter snowstorm babysitting all five of our children, to give up. I certainly couldn't imagine telling my teenage sons I hadn't done it. Didn't Theresa say I was golden, trained to go the distance, sure to finish? I could do it stamina-wise if I could stand the pain. I knew from childbirth that I could go quite a distance with quite a lot of pain, and that the joy at the end of the road can erase the memory of the hurt.

And there were some excellent distractions along the way. There were packs of Japanese participants, chanting, carrying flags, and running in coordinated costumes. There was a man so old and delicate he looked like an ancient sage; he had a private nurse striding beside him in a white uniform and cap. There were Santas of every nationality, there was a barefoot man in a grass skirt, and there were thousands of runners and walkers raising money for leukemia, arthritis, diabetes, AIDS, and other charities, often with coaches herding them along. At mile twenty-three, there were people handing out little paper cups of beer. If there had only been Percocet at mile twenty-four, everything would have been perfect.

As it turns out, all any neurotic layabout needs to do to achieve radiant physical fitness is refocus her God-given obsessive tendencies on exercise. Forget your eyebrows, your pie crust, your children's social lives, your career, or whatever compulsions you're wasting your time on now, and get crazy about working out. In my case, for example, there was a little drug problem, some alcohol issues, an eating disorder, the usual slow cooker of self-destruction simmering between the ears . . . but now that I have finally filled the gaping hole left in my life by eliminating those behaviors with exercise fetishism, I'm so rehabilitated I can't believe it. Instead of being such a dreadful burden to myself, my family, and my friends, I am the envy of all those people who finished after me in the Honolulu Marathon, as well as the three who followed me in the York County Ten-Miler (cerebral palsy, car accident, wheelchair).

If you think you hate exercise, you may be focusing too much on the idea that it is good for you. Forget virtue. Forget social acceptability. To discover your inner Sick Jock, you may need to take a different approach. Perhaps the following tips will make no sense to you. On the other hand, you don't have to tell anyone if they do.

1. Make exercise a habit (like a heroin habit). Do it because it hurts, and you can't stop. Find the exact mix of guilt and desire that gets you going, and go. When you force your lace down to the evil nipple of pain, you don't do it because someone else said you should. You do it because you are mentally ill. Be as ill as you can be.

Theresa, who as I mentioned shares my passing acquaintance with substance abuse, calls people like us "adult-onset" runners, as if we had a disease. Perhaps we do. Because we like that it exhausts us utterly and makes us smell bad. When it almost makes us puke, we like that too. We like the obsessive rituals required, the narcissistic routines that make our heads feel different inside. We do it because it is not working, it is not raising children, it is not being nice and helpful to other people. It is that other thing we so very much love: It is flight. It is escape. It is going going gone. We could just as well be at the crack house as on the hike and bike trail; who would know?

2. It is okay to think you suck. Though you probably have heard you need a positive attitude and an inspiring vision of your goal as you set out on your exercise regime, you may find you can't quite swing it. Don't worry. It's actually perfectly fine to believe that, no matter what you do, you will never be a sleek, buff, well-coordinated, and cellulite-free athlete. Especially if, as in my case, it is so, so true. And it's exactly my poor self-image that keeps me from comparing myself to people so much more gifted than I that they might as well be from a different species. I'm not one of them. This is not discouraging; it's just genetic. I gaily smile and wave as ten or eleven thousand of them run past.

When you have already lost the race, you are in a place of total liberation. You do it only for the head rush.

3. Shop. Buy expensive running shoes and cute tights and moisture-wicking socks and high-tech support undergarments. This is the trick they used to use in transcendental meditation classes when you had to pay $1,000 to get your mantra so that you would be in too deep to quit. Similarly, to discover your inner artist, as any would-be creative thinker knows, you begin by stocking up on fancy pens with purple ink and hand-bound journals from Florence. To become a runner—just like the bodhisattvas and the poets—you need gear.

(Honestly, for the first year or two, I ran in vintage housedresses and blue jeans, but true addiction has proved to require lucky socks and magic arch supports and the jog bra from hell. And now that I have them, I've damn well got to use them.)

To be all that you can be, buy all that you can buy.

4. Pray. There are no atheists at mile twenty-six. I would know.

5. Make friends. As with other habits, peer pressure is helpful, at least when you're a beginner. So buddy up with people to walk with, run with, kickbox with, take turns on the incline bench. It's even better if these new chums are slightly ahead of you in the progress of their addiction and can turn you on to new shopping opportunities or compulsive behaviors.

Finally, however, just as with drugs and alcohol, when you're really sucked in, you don't need company anymore. You may pretend you're still a social exerciser, but the truth is isolation works too.

6. Don't improve—at least not consciously. Rather than setting goals for time and speed and reps, rather than going on six-week ramp-up plans from fitness magazines, just forget about getting better at it and work on getting more comfortable with it. To me, the point of aerobic exercise is to hit the zone where you don't even know you're moving: where your head lifts out of it and you are as free as you thought you were when you did your first line. You don't find this by brutally pushing yourself. You find it by letting your body be. Even if you are a social exerciser, make sure you do it by yourself once in a while so you can connect with your natural gait or pace. This will change over time, but it is your deepest and most essential groove.

7. Lift weights. If you have never tried this, you cannot imagine how much fun it is to make horrific grunting noises and hideous faces in public. Being macho and strong is such an excellent way to occupy space compared to constantly trying to make yourself disappear. Weightlifting changes the outlines of your body faster than anything I have ever tried, and I've tried a thing or two.

8. If it doesn't get you high, you won't do it. So don't do anything or think anything that ruins your high. Protect your pleasure in the way you would protect your drugs or your chosen mate. Crave it, move toward it, get flushed, breathe hard, drip with sweat from head to toe, get in the shower under the hot water, then cold. Do nothing that doesn't support your rush. If you are the kind of person who thinks drugs are good, but medication is bad, you must make exercise your drug, not your medication.

9., 10., etc. Let nothing stop you. Grab it like somebody's trying to take it away from you, which is true: time and age and death and your own limiting voices and all the many more important and less selfish things you have to do today. Fuck 'em. Let your inner Sick Jock drive you to sit-ups on the cold tile floor of a hotel bathroom. To swim at dawn. To run twenty-three miles with a leg cramp.

Exercise turns out to be a mental challenge more than a physical one. It is all about what you have decided you can do. The muscle you stretch most thoroughly is your will, and just as the physical rewards you receive spill over into other areas of life, so will the tough-mindedness. So remember: The obstacles are in your head. The finish line is in your head. Even your thighs are in your head. If you have a will of steel, you can have abs of steel. If you have a will of marshmallow, you can make s'mores. Get out of the fat, into the fire, and burn, baby, burn till you scream like Jane Fonda on MDA.

I offer these tips in the spirit of passing the bong. Just try it this once. You'll like it. It's really good shit.

LOSING

⁓

I guess when you marry a guy with six tattoos and a wide-gauge silver barbell through his earlobe, you should know what you're getting into. But over the years when my husband suggested he might pierce his eyebrow, I thought my expressions of revulsion had discouraged him. I thought my suggestion that there was something pathetic about a middle-aged man trying so hard to be hip had sunk in. I thought he loved me.

I can't believe you think a little piece of metal in my eyebrow means I don't love you, he said, in the third day of tears and recriminations.

I can't believe you think it's just a little piece of metal.

Sometimes a man's got to do what a man's got to do. Sometimes a man's got to leave the engine running while he runs into the drugstore even though his wife thinks ten minutes is too long.

Sometimes a man has to set the timer on the dryer to a full sixty minutes even though his wife thinks the automatic settings are better. Sometimes a man's got to get his head shaved even though his wife loves his curly blond hair. Sometimes a man's got to duck into a makeshift stall on St. Mark's Place in the East Village and let a Filipino lady impale his eyebrow on a thick needle, then slide in a barbell, even though his wife is across the street pitching a fit. Henpecked? Pussy-whipped? On a leash? Sometimes a man's got to prove that's what he's not.

How do you expect me to respect you when you show me by your actions you don't want my respect? That was our eighth grader, the preppy one. Well, when Dad turns eighteen, somebody's got to be forty.

Not everyone ganged up on Daddy, though. The teenage daughter was present at the event and cheered him on. The skateboarder son is still begging to get one just like it. And even Daddy's mommy, who initially voiced despair at her son's prolonged adolescence, now says it's not so bad. A lot of people are saying it's not so bad.

No, it's bad. For a few years in the early seventies, my father owned a discotheque. During this period, he grew his gray hair down to his shoulders and wore flowered velvet bell-bottoms. It drove my mother crazy. I heard her on the phone talking to her friends: He's a forty-three-year-old man, for Christ's sake.

Well, the other day, I heard myself say the exact same words. Now that's bad. It's bad when you've become the most flagrant caricature of your own mother. It's bad when you're no longer hip, and you no longer care. But what's really bad is when you fight hard and you lose. And when the victory flag is planted in your husband's eyebrow, well, that's losing.

PS. If only as testimony to the power of the personal essay, I am compelled to add that the offending jewel lasted only about another two weeks.

THE STEPMOTHER'S TALE

Once upon a time there was a little boy with hazel eyes, a dimpled chin, and freckles scattered across his wide cheeks. His parents split up when he was three and his dad went to live on a farm in Seven Valleys, Pennsylvania, where the boy and his sister got to visit him on weekends. The sister, four years older with wild dark brown hair, thick eyebrows, and a very high IQ, constantly teased the boy, making fun of his chipmunk cheeks. Yet he was her slave nonetheless.

The farm had no cows or sheep, but it did have a flock of awkward, flightless birds with spiky, ashen feathers and round, rust-colored eyes. The emus pranced in slow circles around their pen, making a thrumming drumming sound, a sound you would not expect to come out of a bird at all. Just down the hill there was a creek you could fish in, and an old-fashioned train went by in the evenings. The train was always full of fancy people leaning out the windows, laughing and pointing at the emus. It moved so slowly that if you were close enough you could see the tables with their white cloths, the trays of sparkling glasses, the jacketed waiters.

Maybe, the father replied vaguely when the boy asked if they could go on the train, maybe someday. It wasn't that it was expensive, though indeed it was. While the father was not a wealthy man, he was not averse to credit card debt. He was simply not the ye-olde-dinner-train type. He was the bowling type, the Frisbee type, the nature-hike and homemade-tree-swing type, and he had never heard of the misconception common among grown-ups that you can watch too much television. At his house children ate oatmeal with candy dinosaur eggs for almost any meal and went to Walmart to buy a toy almost anytime. He read stories to them every night for as long as they could stay awake, and let them sleep in his bed when they nodded off.

Then the father got a new wife who came from Texas with two big stepbrothers and two cats and they moved to a house where you couldn't see the train. To the boy, the best thing about this new situation was the brothers (though they proved to be rather violent—the older one liked to play a game he called "Which Hurts Worse?"). But the bad part was that it was now much, much harder to get his father's attention. Often the boy had to ask many times. Can you read to me? Can you read to me now? Can you read to me? He couldn't sleep in the bed with his father and stepmother. Sometimes at night he would call his own mother secretly. Hearing her voice would make him cry and then he might be allowed to go home.

The big sister thought everything about her new stepmother

was just fine. She took one look at her wild brown hair and intense gaze and saw one of her own kind. Before long, the two of them were involved in an endless round of Scrabble, learning arcane two-letter words and ways to use *q* without *u*. Across the playing board they would roll their eyes at each other about the little boy and his obsession with his father. Any time he lost track of him for a couple of minutes he would wander through the house saying, Where's Dad? Where's Dad? And five minutes later, Where's Dad?

Once upon a time there was a stepmother who was not evil or murderous or mad, though at times a little jealous and impatient. She had a problem with messy houses and improperly balanced meals and purchasing toys on every Walmart visit. Nonetheless, she planned to be a magnanimous, bountiful stepmother, a pal to all, and in the new home of her blended family, there were kittens and video game systems and a giant trampoline in the backyard.

One of the first birthdays they celebrated together was the little boy's eighth, and she bought everyone tickets for the dinner train, where it turned out neither the food nor the entertainment was very good by big-city standards, but no one seemed to mind. Look at the emus! The little boy seemed amazed to have this dream finally come true. After dinner, the grown-ups made out in the disco and the children ran up and down till they found the double-decker observation car at the end. Up a spiral staircase with a neon banister they went. They lay down on plushy forties banquettes under an arched glass roof as a crescent moon and the Big Dipper floated above them.

However, life was not always a birthday party. Every weekend, the little boy would come and take up all the time and space and every drop of his father's attention; then when it got dark out, he'd have a nervous breakdown and need to leave. If he's going to cry all the time to go home, maybe he shouldn't come in the first place, the stepmother would say to her husband. Then she would hear herself, shudder, and go to the kitchen to make the boy a quarter pound of bacon and a tray of cinnamon rolls.

The stepmother had not fully appreciated the complexities of stepparenting before she got into the business. She could see that there were many adults in the world whose love for children exceeded the biological imperatives. Actually both of her husbands had been raised by stepfathers whom they adored, and she knew many people who had adopted kids, who had foster kids, people who would take any kid to Disney World. Her own mother had not been this type, though. She was very devoted to the two girls she had borne, but her enthusiasm for childcare did not extend beyond them, and she did not seem to have a lot of unused capacity in the family department.

The stepmother could see she fell somewhere between these two poles.

Also living in the kingdom was the real mother of the boy and girl. She was nervous from the start. Who would not have been nervous about a stranger in her children's lives? But one day the mother and stepmother met for coffee and bagels and saw how easily they could be friends, and soon they were the ones on the phone figuring out how to divide the camp fees and fight the insurance companies and plan the weekend visits. Soon the stepmother realized she was no longer resisting the secret urge to unplan the visits. Around this time the boy began to laugh at her jokes.

Then one day he said, Where's Dad?

I don't know, the stepmother replied wearily, why?

I wanted to go to the video store, he said.

I'll take you, she replied, certain he would say Nah, that's okay.

Great, he said.

On the way, they talked about a program he liked on MTV, which she could not quite believe was called *Pimp My Ride*, and at the store she did all the things she normally frowned upon, such as renting more movies than could possibly be seen in the time allotted and purchasing candy at inflated movie-store prices.

Things were changing; the kids were growing up. The stepmother and the girl took trips to New York and to Texas, and they went jogging and to yoga classes together and told each other secrets. The boy turned eleven, and then twelve. His palate began to broaden dramatically. Now he loved the stepmother's cooking and brought her gifts for her kitchen that she used every day—a Japanese rice steamer, a banana hanger, a retractable vegetable peeler that shot out like a switchblade. Because no one else in his family was interested in the culinary arts, she knew it was because of her that he started to want to make soups and bread and pies.

Fortunately, the boy was already a teenager by the time his mother remarried and became a stepmother herself.

Today when the stepmother is asked, she says she has five kids—four teenagers and a four-year-old. Though there doesn't seem to be any other correct answer, she still feels awkward about saying this. She has come to believe that ordinary life offers few varieties of moral education more potent, and more underrated, than stepparenting, and she admits to being a little inconsistent in rising to the challenge. The fact is, she simply does not feel like a mother to her stepchildren. They already have a mother. And she already has children.

Perhaps her stepchildren's mother pinpointed it last summer. The mother had accidentally discovered her daughter's online diary and read a few sentences before she stopped herself. From these few sentences she gleaned that the girl had many secrets and that the stepmother knew them all. She was able to forgive the stepmother for this appalling situation by remembering an aunt she had been close to when she was young. How fortunate it was that she had had her to talk to because there were some things a girl was not going to discuss with her mother.

Friend, aunt, mentor: some combination of those things might be it. In any case, the stepmother will tell you that the wry, tolerant, uncrazy relationships she has forged with these children, one easily, one not, bear no resemblance to the mother-child relationship as she knows it. Ask her other three.

And yet when the girl plays a seven-letter word to come from behind and beat her at Scrabble, when the boy spends all of Thanksgiving in the kitchen helping her with dinner, she feels something that can only be described as filial pride. It has a surprising sweetness, perhaps like love found in an arranged marriage, or faith in a religious conversion: in any true thing that is made, not born.

DOWN THE TUBES: A REPRODUCTIVE MEMOIR

I got my tubes tied last fall, at age forty-five. It was a coup d'etat, essentially. I was taking over. For thirty-three years or so, I struggled to gain control of my reproductive potential and its power over my destiny. Finally, instead of letting nature continue to screw around with me, at least in this one regard, I engineered a preemptive strike.

Out of the approximately 354 eggs fired by my ovaries into the slippery dark of my fallopian tubes, out of 354 tumbles to the crimson divan where they lay, awaiting the arrival of suitors, six met Mr. Right. Right for them, anyway. Unfortunately, it didn't always pan out for me.

1. I wasn't ready for the baby whose beginnings appeared in my uterus when I was just sixteen, so good thing about *Roe v. Wade*, which was just two years old.

2. Still not mommy material at twenty, but having trouble getting birth control devices to work as advertised.

3. Eight years later, the baby my husband and I had spent nine months glowing about was born dead, with no explanation.

4. I was two weeks from turning thirty when my son Hayes arrived to turn on the lights again.

5. Vince slid in behind him two years later, born at home with a midwife.

6. I was supposedly all done, except my husband died and I eventually remarried a baby-loving type with two kids of his own and gave birth at forty-two to darling Jane.

When I finished nursing Jane and my period started up and I had to once again think about birth control, I found little energy for the tedious matter. I'd had enough. Enough of IUDs and diaphragms and pills and condoms. Enough of calendars and pregnancy test kits. I knew that getting my tubes tied wouldn't end my periods, wouldn't end PMS, wouldn't even end my stupid pimples, but just not being able to get pregnant again was good enough for me.

As my husband sat with me in the day surgery center, I reflected aloud on the apparent oddness of my decision. When I'd told my friends I was doing this, no one else had gone through the same procedure. Instead, some of their husbands "got snipped," as they put it—reportedly a much simpler operation. One friend with four kids, the last two being twins, suggested that her husband felt it was the least he could do.

I thought my husband didn't want to do it because he was squeamish about the operation, but when I alluded to this, he told me that wasn't it.

Well what is it?

Well, I'm not sure I'm done having children, he said.

In the back of my mind I guess I knew that. I guess maybe that's part of why I was there in the first place, a way of heading off an argument I couldn't bear to have. But what I blurted out instead was, Oh, you mean like if I get killed and you're stuck raising the five kids we already have, you want to be sure you can still have a few more with your new wife?

He smiled.

At that point, there was a total power failure in the building, which was a good thing, because it distracted me from my intention to locate a divorce lawyer who could visit me on my stretcher. And when I woke up after the operation and my husband was all kindly and brought me a Balance Bar, I decided to forgive him. It was kind of a thoughtless comment to make to someone about to undergo general anesthesia. But he was entitled to his own vision of the future. I, on the other hand, felt that if the entire human race were wiped out and it were up to me to start the new breed, well, tough.

Recently I marched with hundreds of thousands of women in Washington to keep those reproductive rights that have stood me in such good stead. I had mixed feelings on that day; the issue of abortion makes me feel both fierce and sad. I smiled though when I saw a lady in a big sunhat carrying a sign that read MENOPAUSAL WOMEN NOSTALGIC FOR CHOICE. Choice makes it sound so much simpler than it ever is or was. And that's why I want my nostalgia now.

HOME BIRTH, HOME DEATH, NURSING, AND THE TALIBAN

In July of 1990, I delivered my son Vince at home with the help of a midwife, a dear woman named G.B. who ran the mothers' support group I belonged to, one devoted to cotton diapers, home-made baby food, and breastfeeding. A mother of four and a prac-ticing Sikh, G.B. had the boyish figure and waist-length blond hair of a teenager, combined with the gentleness and insight of a tribal elder. Part of the attraction of having a home birth was hanging out with her for twenty-four hours.

Most of the women in my mothers' group had already experi-enced this most natural of natural childbirths, but I had delivered twice in the hospital. The first was a tragedy, a full-term, unex-plained stillbirth; the second, the blissful arrival of my son Hayes less than a year later. My obstetrician, with whom I'd become close during the roller coaster ride of back-to-back pregnancies, and who had lost a baby herself, was uncomfortable about my decision to deliver at home. But after attending a friend's home birth, after seeing life's beginning demedicalized and deinstitutionalized, I was determined to do it myself. Realizing I was beyond convincing otherwise (and probably also because I lived a few blocks from the hospital), my doctor agreed to help with my prenatal care, and to back me up if I should need it.

The stars were on my side this time. Vince was born on the sunny afternoon of his father's thirty-third birthday with hardly a hitch.

The experience of giving birth in our own house, in our own bed, without the entire hospital superstructure on top of us, was a revelation. No rules, no paperwork, no Big Nurse. I had experienced the nightmare of delivering a dead baby in a maternity ward. I had returned to the swanky alternative birth suite of the same hospital to have Hayes. But now, I was going to get through the contractions hanging on to a pole in my crooked carport with its peeling pink and blue paint, breathing my own free air. Just to be outside and not cooped up walking sterile, linoleum halls seemed like a miracle.

Tony and I actually strolled over to the neighborhood 7-Eleven just before dawn for a carton of orange juice and a pack of Newports for him.

I'm in labor, I told the clerk giddily.

What? Get outta here, she said. Don't you have somewhere you need to be?

Despite her concern that I might give birth in the convenience store, labor inched along through the morning until we all got bored and G.B. gave me an herbal remedy to speed things up. Shortly after, the chitchatting phase was over and oh, yeah, now I remember this goddamn thing! *Shit! Why didn't someone remind that I said I would never do this again?* I climbed into the giant bed I had bought after enduring two pregnancies on a futon. G.B. had made it up with some old sheets on top, a rubber sheet in the middle, and beautiful new sky-blue, tie-dyed cotton sheets underneath, ready to be revealed in all their glory when the bloody mess was over and the top layers stripped away. She had pushed the bed into a corner so I wouldn't fall off in my writhings and piled it with pillows onto which I threw myself, hollering like a madwoman. It was two in the afternoon; I guess no one was home in the neighborhood or surely somebody would have called the police.

Can I push?

Not yet.

Can I push?

Not yet. Remember your breathing.

Fuck my breathing.

Okay, okay, you're doing great. Now you can push. That's right. Push as hard as you can. Come on, push. Wait, wait. Don't push.

Push, don't push, make up your goddamn mind!

Now! Push! Come on! You can do it! Push!

I'm motherfucking pushing for Christ's sake I can't take this anymore how many times do I have to tell you?

You're doing great. It's almost over. Oh, come here you guys, the baby's crowning, you can see his head, okay, wait, great, now a big push.

Go to hell.

And there was Vince all slimy and beautiful and Tony cut the cord and everybody was laughing and crying and I demanded my baby and a glass of champagne. I pushed out the placenta, but then I was sort of falling asleep.

Marion! Marion! Do you feel all right?

Yeah, I feel okay, just a minute, just give me a minute. I just need to rest.

Keep talking to us, said G.B. nervously, wrapping my arm in the blood-pressure cuff. Your blood pressure is low. You're going into shock. I'm going to give you some oxygen.

She whipped out her handy tank and put the mask over my face. The oxygen perked me up a little but not enough. Then she said she was going to give me a shot to make me have another big contraction so I would expel whatever was left in there.

No fucking way.

Okay, then I'll just stick my hand in there and pull it out, said G.B.

You'll do what? I said.

Keep your feet up, ordered G.B. She and the other midwife who had come at the end to help her began to discuss "transport-ing" me—i.e., taking me to the hospital.

Just give me five minutes, I said. Five minutes. Just let me rest.

Well, it took a little more than five minutes, but my blood pressure went back up and I expelled the clot and was so glad I hadn't gone to the hospital. I could just imagine what it would be like, turning up at the emergency room at the tail end of your botched home birth. I figured they'd whisk the baby away and stick me in a cubicle with an IV and that would be the end of having any say over anything. If I wasn't in a life-threatening situation—and if I was, G.B. wouldn't have bothered getting my opinion—I was going to do it my way.

Later on we didn't know what to do with the clot and my sister was so grossed out she made G.B. come pick it up. She was cheerful about it. It's part of my job, she said.

Thirteen years later, I think of my home birth as one of the few times in my life when I've been off the grid, free from the control of the institutions and customs that regulate everything from the way we eat and dress, to the way we raise and teach our children, to the way we die. The other most significant time happened four years later in that same bed where Vince was born. There his father Tony died of an overdose of sleeping pills and a shot of potassium chloride, defying those who would have prevented his choosing how and when to end his death-match with AIDS.

But then the funeral home van came, the blanketed gurney, the crematorium, and the box of ashes. It wouldn't have occurred to me that a home death could go beyond the moment of farewell, and it didn't until almost a decade later, when my second husband, Crispin, lost his stepfather, Richard.

Despite his hopes of dying at home, Richard was in a hospital for what turned out to be his final illness. Thus his family was determined to honor his other wish, that he be buried on his own farm in a pine coffin he had built himself, next to two of his sons whom he had already buried there. Unsurprisingly, there was quite a flurry of resistance and confusion at the hospital around the notion of simply handing the body over to the kinfolk. But there is no law against it in the state of Virginia, so when Crispin and his stepbrother Jim pulled up to the hospital's loading dock in a pickup, the staff huffed and puffed and finally gave them what they had come for. And then he and Jim dug a grave and buried their father with their own hands. Their cousin came and built a marker from the hunks of granite they had wrenched out of the hole.

To some, it may sound odd that my mother-in-law lives with the bones of her men in her backyard, but since I have a husband and a baby in red ceramic urns on my bookshelf, it seems just fine to me.

To live from conviction requires constant vigilance and effort. Even in our free country we have to work hard to be free. It takes energy and courage to buck the system, whether you want to home-school your children or grow your own food or marry a person of the same gender or die when you are ready rather than being kept alive by technology.

For example, when I was still nursing Jane at almost two, I started to wonder when, and if, I was going to stop. I had weaned her older brothers when they were each about a year and a half; I was ready, but I also knew that society thought it was high time. (If you've ever nursed in a public place a child who can walk, you know the look.) With Jane, I started to fear I would never be ready, that I would be one of those mothers who has her breastfeeding middle-schooler removed from her care.

And why was I finding it hard to wean her? Partly I blamed my age. Partly I blamed her gender. And partly I blamed the Taliban.

I was forty-two when Jane was born, and without a doubt having one last chance to nurse a baby was one of the carrots that dangled in front of me during that rather tedious pregnancy. I already knew: if labor and delivery were the most excruciating physical experiences I had ever had, nursing was one of the sweetest. As amazing as the transfer of immunities and other benefits may be, it was the feeling of my little baby beside me, curled into my body, tiny feet kneading my stomach, face at my breast, that really blew my mind. Having weaned two already, I knew what I was giving up: the last concrete form of the physical bond you have with a being who came from an egg that was inside your own body at birth. When it's over, something is gone forever.

So that's the wisdom of age, the flip side of which is the exhaustion of age. I just don't enforce my will the way I used to. While my other kids didn't have sugar until they were well into preschool, Jane sometimes preferred to nurse with a Tootsie Pop in hand; today, at four, she determines her own television schedule and bedtime. I pick the positions I have the strength to uphold. In any case, I was far too ambivalent about weaning to work up the energy for it.

And to top it all off, she was a girl! My own sweet little lassie, complete with curly blond hair, a bow-shaped mouth, and what seemed to be feminine wiles. When her brothers, at eighteen months, would barrel up, knock me over, pull up my shirt, and demand to nurse, I didn't have that hard a time saying no. Nobody wants to nurse Attila the Hun. But when Jane gave me the big blue eyes and the "Peeze, mama?" I found I couldn't resist.

As it turned out, I didn't have to for very long. In a tactful yet definite way, Jane revealed her decision to stop breastfeeding before we had celebrated her second birthday; when she gave up diapers shortly afterward, I understood that, for better or worse, her babyhood wasn't going to be extended for my benefit.

The last few weeks I nursed my only daughter, I happened to be reading two memoirs by young Afghani women who spent most of their girlhoods living under Taliban rule. I read about the day the Talibs outlawed kites, pets, dolls, photographs, music, and even school; the day childhood ended just like that. I tried to imagine raising my daughter in a situation of such severe institutionalized misogyny, where the sound of a woman's voice or the sight of her face is considered virtually pornographic. I tried to imagine the despair those mothers felt as they lost in an instant all control over the lives their children would have. I read these books with Jane in my lap, her trusting gaze fixed on my face, tears of outrage forming in my eyes.

Drink it down, Jane, I thought. Grow tall and strong and free. To raise my daughter in comfort, in safety, with hope, in a society that will value her: that is my good fortune. To bring her up according to my principles and tendencies, even when they differ from those of that society: that is my challenge. But the challenge, too, is a blessing. If we have the strength, we can live and die in a way that is personal, right, and real.

Like the midwife said, it's time to push.

IV

Back Again

ABOVE US
ONLY SKY

In the spring of 1981, when I was twenty-two years old, I fell in love with a girl named Anne and a boy named Mark. She was my good friend, and he was her boyfriend, and they hardly needed me to complicate their delicate situation, but they got me anyway.

For about twenty years, I avoided thinking about this episode, and when I finally did, first tentatively, then obsessively, big chunks of the story seemed to be missing. Like a temple at a Mayan ruin, it had to be reconstructed from what was still lying around. I went back and checked my datebook from that year, a lemon-yellow, spiral-bound *women's calendar* with Lady Liberty on the front and feminist quotes inside. Scribbled among them were lists and appointments, plans to see Joe Ely and Grace Jones, names of forgotten movies like Robert Altman's *Popeye*.

On Saturday, January 17, an entry says *Dinner with Anne Nodotties*, and *Nodotties* is scrawled on many Saturdays following.

Sideways on the margin of a week in April are the ingredients for Anne's black-bean recipe, set down in her elongated, slightly whimsical printing: *Black beans, basil, garlic, oregano, onion, comino, Pace's, mustard, molasses.*

There are a few hexagrams from the *I Ching* copied down along the way, sometimes accompanied by lines of advice, resplendent in its ancient impracticality. *It furthers one to cross the great water. The superior man is yellow and moderate. Thus he makes his influence felt in the outer world through reason.* But the violent disruptions of that May get no Chinese deep thoughts, just two words: *Leave Austin.*

Just reading the words of those hexagrams brought back the flavor of that time to me, so I dug up another yellow book acquired that year, my copy of the *I Ching.* It contains a few more lines of Anne's handwriting, her inscription to me, dated May 7, 1981. It had been years since I used it; the last time I did I could no longer remember how to throw the pennies or figure out the yins and yangs.

So why open it now, do you think, and let it recommence its portentous yammering? It could be the students at the art institute where I teach, almost the same age as we were then, and as supercharged emotionally, though now they take Paxil or Zoloft for it. Hearing about their lives—watching helplessly from the sidelines of their melodramas—may have been what sent me back into the wilds of my own.

When I was about halfway through my attempt to write a novel based on what memories I could dredge up from the two yellow books, I whisked off a jaunty letter to Anne, my first communication with her in many years. I told her about my project and said that of course I wanted her to be the first reader.

It seems she was surprised to hear from me. "Marion," she wrote back a week later, on a piece of hemp-colored stationery in her famous handwriting, "I kinda liked you when I met you, and then I learned to love you, but now you're just the skank that fucked my man when I was struggling to make a family."

If there were a museum of angry correspondence, this letter would deserve a special exhibit. I was shaky for days from the emotional sucker punch, alternately avoiding the sheet of paper as if it were growling at me, then grabbing it to make sure it still said what it had before. As soon as I could gather my thoughts, I sent her a reply saying how floored I was by her response, how I didn't think we had left things this way. She answered again, still angry, and again I replied by return mail.

"Yesterday I received your third letter," Anne wrote back. I felt like Tommy in *Goodfellas: I thought I told you to go fuck your mother.* But I knew she wouldn't keep answering me if she didn't want to reconnect; I had the feeling she was about to conclude that I was too stupid to be so mad at. I was right—in her next letter, she put down the rifle and agreed to help me, sending me some of her journal entries from that time, then agreeing to spend an afternoon with me on a trip up north.

That afternoon in Baltimore as we pushed my daughter around the Inner Harbor in her stroller, talking about who we are now and who we were then, I was chagrined to realize how many of my recollections had been distorted and self-serving. I had things mixed up in such a way that all of my bad ideas and actions were less bad, and less mine. I had told myself, and had come to believe, that I was just a bystander swept up in the action, Woman #2, Townsperson in a Red Dress.

Well, Anne pointed out, it's true you were swept up.

Swept up like a person who runs into the yard as the funnel cloud approaches, arms spread wide.

I first met Anne when she was hired to help me at the *Texas Natural Resources Reporter*, a regulatory reference guide cloaked in a sludge-colored three-ring binder, used by the legal representatives of big polluters and coastline rapists. Parts of my job, writing ad copy and harassing nonrenewers, I was pretty good at; but anything mechanical, like pasteup, xeroxing, or collating, I regularly screwed up, to the great irritation of our subscribers, not to mention our boss.

Lots of interesting people interviewed for the job of saving my ass. A Mexican American muralist, a former museum administrator, a sad man with a PhD in geology—the usual Austin applicants for a part-time position doing pasteup.

They hired Anne, a graphic artist and painter who roared up in a vintage red Volvo. She was twenty-nine, which seemed a lot older than me at the time. With her long curly hair and wide-set, gray-blue eyes, she looked something like Janis Joplin, though prettier and less squinty, but with that same oh-yeah, what-is-it-to-you expression. Like Janis, she never wore a bra or makeup, and had a proclivity for frankness in all things, including nonfiltered Camels and Scotch neat.

She took over pasteup, and from then on it was all ninety-degree angles and consecutive page numbers. It was also her good fortune to come in nights to erox and collate the three hundred sets of replacement pages we sent out every month using our gigantic, hideously noisy photocopier. Yet it was that machine and the sleek IBM Selectric typewriter in our office, and the prospect of long nights alone with them to work on her journals, plays, and artwork, that made this bad job seem like a good deal to Anne. She preferred to work nights anyway, because it gave her time during the day with her baby girl, an eighteen-month-old named Rose. Anne was the first friend I had who was a mother.

There we were, the two of us in that sterile, windowless office, the copier grinding away in the background, or in the parking lot that overlooked the Arby's next door, smoking and watching people rush in and out with their sacks of sandwiches and Jamocha milkshakes. Anne had a musical voice, a *Gone with the Wind* accent, and a history I loved to hear about, though parts of it were so painful she avoided talking about them. Her mother, Ruby, was a lounge singer and party girl who had abandoned her husband and five children when Anne was nine to run away to the big city and pursue her career.

I pictured a little girl with pigtails walking into the house after school, lunch box in hand. Mom? No answer. Mom?

I had a version of my family for her, too: my mother the golf champion, my father the workaholic, a whole clan of wisecracking Woody Allen types, shouting witticisms at each other over the Sunday *Times*.

Anne had had some affairs with women, and this impressed and intrigued me, but she had something else that triggered my second-chakra energy even more. At that point in my life, all you had to do was put a deeply depressed, closed-off guy in my path, and my antenna would start twitching. If he was also attractive and talented and seemed to light up just a little at the sight of me, I might soon become so interested, so hooked, so filled with lust that I'd hardly be able to see anything else.

I first remember meeting Mark at a gathering he and Anne had after the murder of John Lennon. On December 8, 1980, forty-year-old Lennon was shot getting out of a taxi in front of the Dakota, the apartment building where he lived with Yoko Ono on Central Park West. The gun was fired by a disturbed fan named Mark David Chapman, who said he had been receiving messages not only from J. D. Salinger, that perennial favorite of psychopaths, but also from more unusual sources like Todd Rundgren and Willa Cather. After releasing the fatal bullets, he sat down on the sidewalk and continued reading *The Catcher in the Rye*.

Lennon's death was a tragedy felt worldwide, and the inhabitants of Austin, Texas, freethinking potheads, latter-day flower children, slacker musicians, long-haired grant writers, rock 'n' roll cowboys, and guitar-playing lawyers, were on the front lines of the bereaved. Coming as it did just a month after the election of Ronald Reagan, Lennon's passing seemed to many the end of an era. The country had turned its back on any shred of idealism and now it was just every man for himself and his bank account. Nuclear plants were exploding, South Africa and Central America were vicious pits of oppression, and there was a paint-haired puppet of the right sitting atop it all. Imagine.

Mark was devastated by Lennon's death, Anne had told me.

John was his hero. And though she hadn't felt as strongly about Lennon as he did, something odd happened the night of his death. More than ever before, she felt the actual presence of another soul.

This was very Anne. Half the things she said made perfect, rock-hard sense, and the rest were as exotic and intoxicating as opium smoke. She and Mark were definitely not your ordinary residents of South Austin, a neighborhood known at the time for beer-swilling Bubbas with cars on blocks in their driveways. Hidden in the trees, their house was an ivy-covered castle, a pink granite edifice with a loggia, turrets, and a widow's walk. The night of the Lennon vigil, it seemed like some underground club in Amsterdam, full of life and music, with carloads of tie-dyed and bandanna-ed mourners arriving after the public memorial in Zilker Park, now moving in clusters from the house to the porch to the tepee in the backyard.

I found Anne and her friends in the kitchen, smoking joints and drinking wine; the radio's daylong tribute played in the background. *I read the news today oh boy.* Anne fondled the massive head of her gentle Great Dane, Jude.

Like me, she had a lot of housemates: her best friend, a seamstress named Susie; a fifty-something Bolshevik-looking man from Philly; a bicyclist couple who had ridden down from Minnesota. Sallie, a dancer from England, knew Yoko Ono, had done a performance piece with her in the glass-fronted windows of a department store for a few weeks. We were listening to her story about this when Mark walked into the room.

Who has an extra cigarette? he said, pushing his hair out of his face with one arm, holding their blond baby on his hip with the other. I looked up to offer my pack and registered his compact form, his thin white T-shirt. Anne had told me that he was a mime and a clown and you could see from his smooth, elastic face and body, his pale skin and button-dark eyes, he would be perfect for it.

He walked toward me with an ironic smile and I gave him one of my Merits. His face was close as he bent over the match I lit, and he flicked his gaze from the tip of his cigarette into my eyes. Everything with cigarettes was incredibly important and rich back then; my poems were full of them. *Cigarette, smoke, light, flame,* even *ash,* these were my favorite words.

Someone asked whether Mark's clown troupe, the Great No-dotties, would be doing their scheduled gig that week, and he sighed. The show must go on, he intoned gloomily. Death with acrobatics and penis jokes.

I made a mental note to check this out. Maybe I could go with Anne. I watched the three of them together as the night wore on, Anne's steady gray gaze on Mark's face; their gentle attentions to Rose; later, his hands beneath Anne's hair, unknotting her neck and shoulders. Though Mark said little, at one point he abruptly commented that it was obvious that Lennon's death was all about who can survive in our twisted, fucked-up world. He quoted some lines from the *I Ching,* a hexagram he had thrown earlier that evening. Though the implications of the weak line in the third place didn't make much sense to me, I was deeply intrigued. Anne and Mark were completely at ease in a world of tantalizing connections and synchronicities. As they saw it, any seeming coincidence, puzzling occurrence, or persistent dream was nothing less than a message from the collective unconscious. Their fates were mythic, their intuitions prophetic, and their marijuana very strong.

One of the clearest images I retain from that night comes not from the ethereal realm but the earthier one I was to prove hopelessly stuck in. It is jalapeños. Like it was yesterday, I can see Mark Hutchison bending over to take a mason jar full of gleaming pickled chilies out of a smallish white refrigerator. He plucked them from their greenish juice, laid them in a line on a cutting board, and sliced them with a knife. My mouth was watering.

Even during the twenty years when I hardly thought of Mark and Anne, I still whispered his name in my head every time I put a jalapeño on a tuna fish sandwich, an excess he taught me.

The inauguration of Ronald Reagan as the fortieth president of the United States six weeks later caused a gnashing of teeth in my household about equal to the tizzy over the Lennon death at Anne and Mark's. Of no help in moderating the bombast and glee that reigned in the nation at that moment was the timing of the release of the fifty-two hostages in Iran. After a year in captivity, they somehow managed to board planes bound for West Germany minutes before the new president took his oath of office.

My housemates and I gathered round the television, looking on in utter alienation at the gargantuan American flags, the marine band playing "Yankee Doodle," and the evil geezer making his speech before the stirring vista of monuments. This was not our America.

Our America had its capitol in a ramshackle house in a little neighborhood called Clarksville on the edge of downtown Austin. Originally a community of freed black slaves, the shanty part of Clarksville was now surrounded by small houses, and in places these were giving way to upscale residences. Still a decade from complete gentrification, it was a half-funky, half-bourgeois neighborhood with an old mini-mart, a yuppie wine and cheese shop, and a taco stand side by side.

604 Pressler Street, or the 604 Club, as we called it, was a typical Austin bungalow, a term widely abused in the local real-estate market. These bungalows had been built in the forties and fifties on the premise that the town's relatively temperate climate (relative to Juneau or Libya) would make up for the utter structural flimsiness of most of its dwellings. Central air and heat? What for? Hotter than the outdoors in the summer, miserably cold and wet in winter, beloved by bugs, leaky of roof, tiny of bathroom, shabby of kitchen, but, hey, it had hardwood floors, stained and scratched as they may have been, and we loved it, right down to the last shallow, inadequate closet and mildewed shower tile.

I had originally rented the house with my sister, Nancy, her boyfriend Steve, and my college friend Jennifer, an antinuclear activist and soup-kitchen Catholic who had brought me down to Austin four years earlier. Jennifer's investment-banker dad and garden-club mom watched in dismay as she funneled the distributions from her trust fund to refugee efforts in El Salvador.

Next we added Kathy and Tim, a British couple whose Austin visit lasted several years longer than expected (Tim is still there). Shortly after, Bill arrived, a tall, sardonic fellow of dotty WASP stock who was getting his MBA at UT. You might think a business school student out of place in our enclave, but Bill had responded to a notice we'd put up in the neighborhood Laundromat. I had cut out a picture of a white horse flying through the sky and printed A DREAMY SITUATION underneath it, followed by some specifics on our four bedroom/one bath vegetarian household. My housemates referred to the poster as Come ride the white pony, claiming that it looked like an ad for a junkie youth hostel.

The population of the household was constantly in flux, with new people always arriving: people picked up hitchhiking, people met on a bus, total strangers who heard we had room. There was no bouncer at this club and little in the way of a selection process, like a bar in town that had a phone book dangling from the ceiling on a string. In black Magic Marker on the cover was scrawled "Charlie Sexton's Guest List."

Domestic life at our house was governed by a fierce combination of politics and penury. We eschewed kitchen paper products on both financial and ecological grounds, and passed a bandanna around the table as a communal napkin. We took turns grocery shopping, where we supposedly applied the same strict standards, but in truth, verboten items like name-brand ketchup moved through the house on a kind of underground railroad, shifting between various hiding places and bedrooms. We took turns cooking as well, which meant that many nights we ate white rice with vinegar, an entree Bill had grown to love while in an international service program in Micronesia. Among us, few had the patience required for vegetarian cooking; it was common to find hunks of onion and squash as big as a toddler's shoe in your stir-fry.

Yet despite the beloved eccentricities of the 604 Club and the general excellence of life in Austin, I had other plans. I was going to stay until my chapbook of poetry was published that spring—I had won a contest sponsored by a small press in the nearby town of New Braunfels—and then I was moving up to New York with my sister and best friend, where I was going to enroll in graduate school and get an MFA. As the writer of such poetic works as "Sunbathing at the North Pole" and "The Tampon Poem," I had outgrown Austin and its provincial poetry scene; New York was a much more appropriate setting for the fabulous literary career that awaited me, a slot somewhere between Susan Sontag and Patti Smith.

Mark, too, was a performer with serious ambitions, and this became the basis of our developing friendship. From the first time I saw the Great Nodotties, I admired their humor, their physical grace and energy, and their combination of traditional mime and clown routines with themes ranging from the political to the spiritual to the hilariously inane. *Nodottie knows, nodottie sees, nodottie cares but me,* the boys would sing in barbershop harmony to open the show.

The Nodotties—both of the other guys were named Mike, but one spelled it Myke—had a regular gig on Saturday nights at Scottie's Barbecue, a sliver of a place wedged into a seedy block of bars downtown, an unmarked brown door leading to two concrete-floored, cinder-block-walled rooms. One room contained a barbecue pit and a counter, the other the Nodotties' theater—some tables and chairs.

From the first time I saw the Nodotties that Saturday in January with Anne, I wanted to be part of them. After the show, I made haste to the little room off Scottie's kitchen where the Nodotties were packing up. Mark had taken off his whiteface and his hair was wet; he shook his head like a puppy and rubbed his eyes. In makeup or not, his brown eyes were what drew my attention:

sometimes sparkly and deep; sometimes darting and anxious; or, when he had withdrawn into himself, flat and murky, like cold coffee.

Now they were encouraging; he and the others were enthusiastic about the idea of my performing with them. We planned for me to come to some of their rehearsals and to make my debut on Valentine's Day.

There was another regular Austin gig I attended with Anne in those months, sometimes heading over after the Nodotties: her good friend, the well-known local musician Dan Del Santo, with his band, the Professors of Pleasure, at the Hole in the Wall. The club was on the Drag, a strip of shops and sidewalk vendors on Guadalupe Street right across from UT, kept busy by the school's forty-five thousand students. The Hole in the Wall had two salient qualities: The cover charge was low and the sandwiches were huge. During the day it was mainly a restaurant, though how people could take that stale beer and cigarette smell with their lunch I don't know.

Dan Del Santo was a volcano of a man whose mountainous exterior, usually clothed in a dashiki, concealed a molten mass of anger, talent, and arrogance. He had voluptuous Italian features, many chins, and thick black hair, with a handful of silver on either side of his part that he said had appeared suddenly after an automobile accident. His preternaturally deep bass voice, as deep as the voice of God, made a seductive presence on his weekly world music show on the public radio station. The Professors of Pleasure were pros—the horn section was particularly hot—and Dan was a virtuoso guitar player; his songs combined Afro-Cuban melodies with lyrics that ranged from blistering political outcries to tender love songs. Nevertheless Dan's main source of income was not the band, but selling mason jars full of skunkweed.

Anne never was able to explain to me why she liked Dan so much. Maybe it was the outlaw musician thing or maybe he was just one of those people who are such misanthropic assholes that if they're nice to you at all, it makes you feel special. Their sweetness is so limited, like a honeysuckle with its single bead of nectar, that if you do manage to squeeze it out on your tongue it seems like one of the wonders of the world.

Dan was on his second marriage at that point; it was during his first, before Anne met Mark, that she and Dan had become involved romantically. This was one of the parts of the story I had forgotten until she sent me the excerpts from her old journals and I got to relive those times through her eyes.

The legend of Anne and Dan began on a stormy night at the Armadillo Beer Garden when lightning knocked out the sound system and Dan unplugged his big blond guitar and dedicated a solo acoustic number to her. She knew him only slightly at the time, but this romantic gesture, combined with some similarly dramatic late-night appearances at her apartment, got her attention. Once she was hooked, he went on to torture her with his bizarre concept of marital fidelity, according to which it was fine to write impassioned love songs for your other woman, fine to make out with her in between sets in front of your band, fine to lie in her bed all night till sunrise, all fine, as long as you didn't actually *do it*. So they didn't, in the most fifties technical sense.

Inspired by Dan's music, Anne wrote some performance

pieces to be presented in collaboration with the band. She re-cruited performers from the waitstaff of Les Amis, the university-area café where she worked, but needed at least one person with stage experience. She thought of the young mime who frequented the restaurant. He was only nineteen then, seven years younger than she, but carried himself with a mysteriously serene, self-contained poise.

Before long, late nights of peyote, sex, and readings from *The Tibetan Book of the Dead* had transformed Anne and Mark into a passionate twosome, and she bid adios to the convoluted atten-tions of Señor Del Santo.

Mark taught Anne to make life masks from plaster bandages, and they began selling them on the Drag. He found glass pieces behind a glassblower's shop and fashioned them into mobiles that he hung in front of their windows. He would pick up a piece of wire in the gutter and bend it with his fingers into a little clown, or a heart with an arrow through it for her.

And then they had their beautiful baby, Rose.

By the time I came on the scene, it was later in the day, a year and a half later to be specific. Rose was in the full flush of tod-dlerhood, and there was tension over money and parenting and responsibilities. Who forgot to put away the milk last night, who left the dirty diaper sitting there, who came home at two-thirty in the morning. Anne was overwhelmed and Mark was not much help. Often in a dark mood, he holed up in the attic, reading and smoking and scribbling in his journal.

Perhaps due to all this, Anne's connection with Dan had re-kindled not long before I met her. She started going to Dan's gigs more frequently, and he had given her the Great Dane puppy. He was in a fairly new second marriage, but I noticed when he called Anne at work, she took his calls with the door closed.

Anything good I felt about Dan came from seeing him perform. The Hole in the Wall's low stage backed up to a storefront window on the street, so we could see the band and hear the music while we waited to get in. Anne, honey! the guy at the door would say when he spotted her, and slip us through for free. The tables and bar were jammed, and people danced in the narrow aisles between them. We would wriggle in among them, whirling around, picking up each other's moves, waggling hips, clacking imaginary castanets, laughing into each other's eyes. Dan Del Santo looked on from under his Rasta hat in his inscrutable way, singing his low-down serenades and pitching his lugubrious woo.

Two of the best venues for an aspiring performance poet such as myself at the time were the Alamo Lounge, a dusty little bar in a decrepit brick hotel just west of downtown, and Spellman's, a crooked, dimly lit wooden shack in my neighborhood that sold beer and a good-sized bowl of beans and rice for ninety-five cents. Both were also havens for singer-songwriters—Townes Van Zandt and Butch Hancock were fixtures at the Alamo—as well as jazz players, depending on which night you came.

I was a regular at Spellman's on Open Mike Poetry Thursdays, where the audience was typically composed of (a) other poets waiting their turn, (b) people who only had ninety-five cents for dinner, and (c) singer-songwriters who couldn't remember which day of the week it was.

Though these performances were something anyone could

sign up for and were really no big deal, I thought of them as an early but indispensable phase of my campaign to build a following and become a national phenomenon. I dressed for my appearances in various getups, a fedora pulled low over my eyes and a black bustier or an ice hockey uniform, complete with pads and helmet. I often got a case of nerves before the show, and prepared for my appearance as I had seen Bette Midler do when she played the Janis Joplin character in *The Rose*, with a few swigs of whatever, often taking a drink with me onstage, and maybe a cigarette too.

For my debut appearance with the Nodotties, I planned a performance titled "Let's Go to Bed With Marion Winik on Valentine's Day." I would read the poems about men and relationships that were part of my forthcoming chapbook, dressed in red flannel feet pajamas and lying on a folding patio-lounger, countering the raw emotion of the poems with this absurd staging. It would be sexy and heartbreaking and funny and profound, a guided tour of attraction, passion, obsession, cruelty, squalor, pallor, debasement, abasement, defacement, fake sangfroid, helpless rage, brutal stupidity, and arctic loneliness. So said the posters I plastered all over town.

Though rehearsing with the Nodottie boys was fun, this show turned out to be the biggest disaster and embarrassment of my entire performance career. Though it did not stop me altogether from drinking before going onstage, I am sure I never performed that drunk again.

Oh, that fucking chaise longue. I'll never forget it. I couldn't get it to go flat at all: it was like a trick chair from a novelty store. The second you pushed the footrest down, the head popped up, and just as you flattened out the head, the foot would come flying.

When I finally did get it all straightened out, it collapsed on me the minute I sat down, and I had to crawl out from underneath it. The first time people were laughing. The second time people were still laughing. After that, most figured out this was not a planned element of the performance.

I forgot the words to the poems I knew by heart and couldn't find the poems I had typed up. I shuffled through piles of paper, spilling them on the floor, stopping and starting and stopping again when I realized I had the wrong poem. And all the while I was wearing red flannel feet pajamas with little lambies on them, God help me. Naturally the whole world was there to witness this debacle, thanks to my hundreds of xeroxed flyers. My housemates were there. People from work were there. Buck from the boot repair shop was there. Mark was there, of course, and Anne was there, though she left early to catch the end of Dan's show.

At this point I knew Anne was still in love with Dan, though she always said she was just a fan, they were just going for a walk, she was just going to pick up an ounce. But the way she acted about him was just not all that friend-like. She got a kind of lightness and girlishness about her when she talked to him or was going to see him. He was the good part, the respite, the emotional coffee break from the Sisyphean routines of her days and weeks. I knew that he often met her in the park when she walked Jude, and I noticed how regularly that dog needed to be walked.

Rose liked to go to the park too, and Anne took her often—but on these occasions she might leave Rose to spend time with their housemate Susie, who was a second mother to the little girl, or with Rose's daddy. Sometimes with her daddy and me, who had formed a kind of two-man support group, People Who Don't

Like Dan Del Santo As Much As Anne Does. In the process, our friendship deepened. If I visited late at night, I would wander up to the attic and find him, have him help me ask the *I Ching* a question. Or we would do a throw for him, which inevitably yielded a darker prognosis.

Look at this changing line, he said. Nine at the beginning. *You let your magic tortoise go, And look at me with the corners of your mouth drooping. Misfortune.*

Oh come on, it doesn't really say that.

It does, come look.

Hmmmm. Okay, so go chase down your magic tortoise.

Right, he agreed, how far could it have gone?

Though Anne was not completely candid with me at first— her relationship with Dan confused and disturbed her and I could hardly have looked like a font of wisdom—I soon realized they were in love and I was shocked. Aside from the fact that it was Dan, whom I just could not imagine being in love with, he was married, she was with Mark, and they had Rose. And anyone could see Mark knew. What the hell was she thinking?

But you know, after further consideration, I began to view the whole thing differently. Really, this was 1981, not 1891. Whatever was going on between them, it was something she needed. And if she didn't want Mark, and had somebody else, then maybe . . . well, obviously real-life arrangements between grown-ups were much more complex than I had previously imagined.

Late night at the castle, a few weeks after Valentine's Day. We're in the kitchen, just me and Mark, and I'm looking at the funny drawings in his sketchbook, inhaling his scent of Dr. Bronner's peppermint soap laced with boy sweat and a whiff of pot. Our legs are touching under the table, his painter's pants, my blue jeans.

How did you get your clown name? I ask him.

Olo? he says. Look at this. He gets a pen and writes *olo*. It's a cock and balls, see?

My mouth drops open. I grab the pen and turn it into eyes and nose and he says, Right, I see with my dick, and we are laughing.

We are younger than Anne, and we don't rhyme with Dan, and we are suddenly both starving. We eat a half a jar of jalapenos with our tuna fish.

In March, my book of poems, *nonstop*, with cover typography by Anne and illustrations by my best friend, Sandye, was produced at Speleo Press in Driftwood, Texas. The printer and his wife lived in a tree house out in the country; the press was in an old barn. In their fairytale kitchen in the air, Nancy taught me her recipe for eggplant parmigiana and Terry agreed to let me come down and watch the printing process.

Anne had wanted to take the tepee out in the country anyway, so she, Mark, and I made a plan to go together and pitch it at Speleo for a couple of nights. I was excited about the trip for a number of reasons. But Mark and Anne weren't getting along very well; he was depressed and she was agitated and cranky and I was certainly no help defusing the tension. In fact, I was smoldering like a tire, sending my own little smoke signal out the roof of the tepee.

Anne drove back to Austin one afternoon to do an errand and

left us there, watching Rose. Mark, sounding bitter and discouraged, told me he felt very alone all the time now. He wanted to get some drugs, asked me if I had any ideas.

I have an idea, I said.

What?

Nothing.

Really, what?

He knew what I was thinking and all I had to do was say it. But I didn't want to be the one. You go first, no you go first, no you.

That night in the dark in that tepee I was so aware of the positions of everyone's bodies it was as if I were watching a heat-sensitive display screen. When I finally fell asleep I dreamed that they were making love and then that we were making love and then I woke up, staring into the cricket-crazed blackness.

Anne must have slept poorly too; in the morning she was exhausted and sick of us. She told us if we were thinking of becoming lovers, we should just go ahead with it. These things can work, she said, if people are discreet and considerate.

That is how I remembered it, that she had given her permission, that she had seen what was coming more clearly than we had, and Anne agreed during the twenty-first-century Baltimore summit that it was true. Ah, but where was the discreet and considerate part, my dear? she asked, shaking her head.

Good question.

No more than a few days after we got back from Driftwood, I was giving Mark a ride home from Scottie's. Both of us had been hyper and talkative earlier in the evening, but in the car we were silent. We pulled into their driveway; tires crunching through the gravel. The house was dark. He reached over and turned off the engine. I swiveled toward him and with no further transition we were kissing hard. It was our first kiss, but there was no gentle prelude, no exploratory tongue, no thinking of how to seem, what tack to take. We skipped right past the usual advertisements for one's sensuality and technique.

Finally, I had my hands in his hair. Finally, my fingers traced the bones of the face and throat whose configuration I had studied so many times. Finally, his hands were on me, on my back, under my shirt, dragging me toward him. When the space between us, not to mention the gearshift, became unbearable, I hopped over it and straddled his lap, facing him.

The '78 Subaru station wagon was not a roomy car, and we soon outgrew it. So he opened the door on the passenger side, and we rolled out into the driveway in the moonlight.

A few minutes later, Jude started to bark. Someone let her out and suddenly the dog was staring down at us. She was not the only one. The light went on in Anne's bedroom, and I saw her outline in the window.

Oh, wow, I said. Look up.

He looked, then paused. Why don't you just go. I'll deal with her.

I'm not going, I said. She'll be happy for us. I mean, she said we could. She wanted us to.

This was a rather optimistic interpretation of Anne's frustrated just-go-ahead-and-do-it speech, for in fact she was furious. Most of her rage was concentrated on the complete outrageousness of us having done it in her driveway, of all the places in the world, and then parading in to tell her about it. This was not what I had in mind, she said quietly, sucking on her cigarette. Then she started screaming.

Anne, calm the fuck down, said Mark.

I guess I should go home, I said.

Yes, you should, said Anne. Stop and zip your jeans on the way out.

I tiptoed down the stairs and through the living room, where Jude was sleeping on the rug. She heard my footsteps, padded over, and nosed her head into my ribs, and I ran my hands over her smooth, soft fur. I wished I had my own dog. My own boyfriend, for that matter. But I didn't deserve either one because I was the biggest schmuck who ever lived.

As I went to the car, I imagined I could see a chalk line around the spot where we had been, like the outline of bodies at a crime scene. The warmth had evaporated off my skin and the night felt cold, my clothes clammy and sticky and full of stones.

Anne exiled me from her life and gave me the cold shoulder at work, passing me in the halls without a glance. I stayed away from Mark, too, and started hanging out at home again just in time for one of those galvanizing public moments that pulled our household together like the congregation at a current-events revival meeting. For on the afternoon of March 30, a twenty-five-year-old drifter, as reports incessantly put it, shot Ronald Reagan as he was arriving at the Washington Hilton to address a labor convention. The gunman stepped forward from a knot of television reporters and fired six times, his bullets striking the president and three others before he was arrested and taken into custody.

My housemate Jennifer watched in amazement as a picture of the glassy-eyed, disheveled would-be assassin was displayed on our TV screen. That's Johnny Hinckley, she said. He was a couple years ahead of me in school in Dallas.

For the next three days, as the story unfolded, we remained glued to the TV and the newspaper, as well as telephone reports on the Dallas reaction. (Such a nice boy! A member of the Rodeo Club!) It was soon revealed that the attempt on the president's life had no political purpose at all: Hinckley's sole motive was to get the attention of the actress Jodie Foster, then an undergraduate at Yale. A letter he had mailed to her that morning explained his plan, and his desire to prove his love and gain her respect by committing a historic act.

To us, this seemed a coda to the Lennon assassination, more hero worship gone mad, more death as the ultimate attention-getting device. And so appropriate for a person from Dallas, a city best known for the man murdered there in 1963.

The other thing that took my mind off my troubles with Mark and Anne was the imminent publication of my book. Sunday, April 26, was the day of my release party at the legendary, since-departed outdoor rock club Liberty Lunch. At the time, I believed with complete, naive conviction that it would be both the best day of my life and the closest thing I would ever have to a wedding. San-dye, the illustrator, flew down from New York for the event, and we got decked out in our vintage finery—I wore a wide-necked, powder-blue dress with white stitching and a twirly skirt. Sandye, my sister, Nancy, and I took some very good LSD that day. My publisher, David Yates, came into town from New Braunfels and sold several hundred copies of the book from a wooden picnic table, delighted by the free beer, the tripping girls, and everything else.

I hadn't expected Mark and Anne to come and they didn't; it was the weekend of both Anne's thirtieth and Rose's second birthdays and they had other things to do. I hadn't seen them in weeks and felt their absence keenly. To stay busy, I'd been going to double features, catching up on my neglected homework (yes, somehow amid all of this I was taking graduate classes at UT), and figuring out my taxes: it says in the yellow datebook I paid the IRS $103 that year. I went with Marguerite, our newest houseguest, to a reading by poet Denise Levertov. Marguerite was a breathy, blond seventeen-year-old from England, an aspiring poet herself. I had seemingly become her idol, but was impatient with it, not as nice as Anne once had been to me.

Though I halfheartedly attempted to breathe new life into a few improbable old crushes—a clean-cut young lawyer from work, a Hispanic guitarist from San Antonio, the guy from the boot repair store—I was still thinking about Mark all the time. My body was unmoved by my heart's regret, and I wrote a song about it I could sing right now.

> This morning I woke up dreamin
> But my dreams had told me a lie
> Those sweet dreams had me believin
> I would find you by my side

Well it's too early to start feeling guilty
And wicked, and misunderstood
Too early to face the somethin so bad
That came out of somethin so good

Don't tell me I'm late for work
The phone is ringin and the sky is blue
Don't tell me it's another morning
I got to wake up without you

I know you love me like a brother
Cause it's the only way that you can
How can you love me like a lover
When you're some other woman's man

I'm just the saxophone in the pawnshop
Your wife won't let you play
But come in tonight, we'll practice the tune
I hum to myself all day

Don't make me no cup of coffee
To drive this sweet dream out of my head
Cause really I think I would much rather
Go on back to bed.

Meanwhile, even as I made her the jealous wife of my narrative, I wasn't letting go of Anne either. It was somehow part of
a conversation with her, a way of keeping her in my head, that I

signed up for a weekend astrology seminar at the Women's Center, where I did all our charts, Mark's, Anne's, and mine. I knew we were all Tauruses but I was amazed to see Mark's moon in Capricorn and his Virgo rising. Just like me, he was triple earth. His Venus was in Gemini—the twins. Maybe that meant he could love both of us. And he had Mars in Cancer, signifying basic conflicts about home and family. But even more problematic, as my teacher pointed out, were that four of his planets were retrograde, not to mention the Finger of Yod formed by his Saturn and Neptune. Quicksand, she muttered, shaking her head. Spiritual quicksand.

Okay, but maybe I could help him out with my grand trines in earth and fire! The teacher called these a steamroller combination. With that energy, she said, nothing will stand in your way.

Anne had her sun, Mercury, and Mars all in Taurus, which was a major grounding in earth, but her Venus, like Mark's, was in Gemini. I shook my head. Obviously, I had fallen in with natural-born polygamists. My own Venus was in Aries. That's where I got my headstrong love and my orgasm-oriented sexuality.

As if I were playing with my Mark and Anne dolls, doing their charts made me feel on top of the situation.

When I asked the astrology teacher about my upcoming relocation to New York City, she checked some transits. Saturn was on the move, opposing my natal Venus. She said she had no choice but to predict some bumps in the road along the way. Plan carefully; she said. Start now. Travel as light as you can.

As soon as I got home, I followed her advice. I started a list of things to do and wrote on the first line, in bold capital letters,

YARD SALE. Traveling light was no problem. I would get rid of everything.

Shortly after the coincidence of my book party and her birthday, I couldn't take the distance between me and Anne anymore. I had been making overtures of friendship at work for weeks but she wasn't buying it—no lunch at Arby's, no laughing at my jokes, no nothing. Finally I decided I would just show up at her house, but first went by Folk Toy and bought Rose a bunch of small presents. When she found me on her doorstep with wrapped gifts in hand, Anne laughed with resignation and invited me in. We sat and ate a bowl of popcorn with butter and nutritional yeast, a flavor that still says Anne to me as powerfully as chilies recall Mark.

Years later, I read about her coming to forgive me in her wise, beautifully written journal: "Things I did not take into account: the enormity of Marion's need, how young she and Mark are, how slim an understanding of her power Marion has, how lovely it is in the springtime . . .

"I realized this afternoon how happily I responded to Marion in my life because I had been so lonely. It made me remember myself at her age, and how carelessly I moved in and out of lonely people's lives. In fact, I can remember quite well the revelation, when I realized how lonely most people are, and how tenderly they must be treated."

As minimal an understanding as I had of this at the time, as poor a friend as I had turned out to be, she missed me. After Rose went down for her nap, she began to tell me how difficult things had become with Mark. He was really beginning to scare her. He had been morose for weeks, distant and mean. He slept into the afternoon every day and haunted the house at night, drunk or high, throwing the *I Ching* over and over.

The night of her birthday, he had taken a pocketknife and scratched the faces off the mural in their bathroom. This was a painting she had made of the two of them in an Edenesque garden, Mark in his clown attire, chin on knee, the abstract Anne lying beside him, naked and smiling. Come look, she said, and the sight of those gouges filled me with dread and fear.

Have you seen Dan? I asked her.

A little, she said. She told me he was furious about Mark's behavior, very worried for her and Rose, and was now talking about leaving his wife so they could be together. But something about his power over her and her desire for him seemed scary to her too. She had dreamed a couple of nights earlier that he was a vampire. Now she was trying, with limited success, to keep him at arm's length.

My own twenty-third birthday was just a few days away, May 7, and I still have two presents given to me that day—a silver pocketknife in the shape of a fish from Marguerite, my unwanted groupie, and the *I Ching* from Anne.

When Anne handed me the yellow book and the silk purse with its three coins, just like hers, tears came to my eyes. I opened the cover and saw the inscription. *To Marion, delightful friend, beloved sister.*

I felt humbled by her generosity. I still do.

Four days after my birthday, I got home from work to find everyone crying. Marguerite, they told me, had been hit by a truck and instantly killed the evening before while riding her bike on Lamar Boulevard, near Whole Foods. It was too horrible to be true, yet it was true. We never learned all the details; it was a hit-and-run and the driver was never found. I felt paralyzed with guilt about the way I'd treated her. I felt I had failed to receive an important message, and now I would never know.

On May 14, I went to see Dan at the Hole in the Wall because I wanted to talk to Anne and I thought she would be there. She wasn't. I listened to him sing one of the love songs I knew he'd written for her, felt ill, and left. At home there was a message that a friend of Anne's I didn't know well, a man her age named Lee, had died suddenly that afternoon, probably of an aneurysm or heart failure, they weren't sure.

As all my New Age-y friends and my political friends felt by now, something was wrong with the time; the spring was as filled with death as it was with blossoms. It didn't seem to be just our group, or even just Austin—the day before, during Marguerite's memorial service, there had been an attempted assassination on the pope in Rome. Something brutal was going on, a grinding shift of massive gears, and people were getting crushed in it. These deaths were so unexpected and crazy, the whole world started to seem unsafe.

On May 16, I went to see the Nodotties as usual. The next day was Mark's birthday, his twenty-third as well, and I assumed Anne would be there. But I couldn't find her among the group milling around Scottie's that night, and when Mark came out before the show to set up the stage, he looked pale and far away.

Sallie, Anne's friend who had performed with Yoko Ono,

came up to me and told me Anne had been staying at Sallie's house for the past two nights. At *her* house? Why her fucking house? I felt jealous and excluded, especially as she went on to tell me new developments I thought I should have already known.

Don't tell anyone, she said dramatically, before explaining that the other day Mark had told Anne he'd turned on the gas jets in their bedroom for a while, then turned them off again. Just an experiment. She wasn't even sure if it was true, but if it was—can you imagine if she had come in with a cigarette? What if Rose had been home? Sallie whispered, clutching my arm. He's out of control; she can't stay there.

I went straight backstage and found Mark bent over his clown suitcase, putting on his makeup using the mirror in the lid.

Hi, I said.

He flashed me a wan substitute for a smile.

Are you okay? I asked.

I've been better.

I hear Anne is staying at Sallie's.

Yeah, she fucking left me. I'm thinking of going up to clown school in North Carolina for a while. I've got to get out of here. I want to take Rose with me, but Anne won't let me. I wonder what kind of father she thinks Dan is going to make.

I stared at him. What do you mean?

Look at this thing, he said, pulling the *I Ching* out of his clown suitcase. I crouched beside him as he showed me hexagram forty-four, Coming to Meet. *The principle of darkness*, he read, *after having been eliminated, furtively and unexpectedly obtrudes from within and below.* Dan Del Santo, wouldn't you say? *A bold girl lightly surrenders herself.*

To, I believe, Dan Del Santo. *The inferior man rises only because the superior man does not regard him as dangerous and so lends him power.* Why, it's the story of Mark Hutchison and Dan Del Santo, drug dealer, woman stealer, motherfucker par excellence.

Mark, forget the goddamn *I Ching*. It's not doing you any good.

Really? I feel like it's the only truth available at this point. Anne's so full of shit these days, I certainly can't rely on her. Which reminds me, she said you're leaving in two weeks. That's not right, is it?

No, it is. It's coming up fast. When will I see you? Come by my yard sale next Saturday. I'll just be sitting there all day, we can hang out.

He looked up and raised an eyebrow, flirting a little, which at this point seemed like a healthy sign. If you're good, I said, I'll throw you in the trunk and give you a ride to North Carolina.

Anne told me at work on Monday why she had left Mark.

A few days earlier, she and Dan had finally made love for the first time, but the long-awaited event had been a nightmare. The room at the Alamo Hotel was so haunted the walls whispered, she said, and it took her a half hour to put in her diaphragm and then it hurt like hell. Nothing was right, and all she could think about was Mark and Rose. How could I have left her with him? she thought. Out of habit, of course, but suddenly it seemed like a terrible idea.

Desperate with worry, she raced home as soon as they were done. There she found Mark high as a kite on peyote. Smiling and exuberant, he told her he had been sitting on top of the house, thinking about jumping, with Rose in his arms.

Despite the fact that it was the height of the yard sale season, my sale was a flop. People drove up, slowed down, then sped away, eyes averted, and even they were few and far between. It was a gray and humid day, with rain predicted for that afternoon, and those who came by saw my possessions looking even dingier than usual under a sunless sky. In any case, the intrinsic worthlessness of my stuff had already been noted by the professional garage sale vultures, who had circled by at 6:00 a.m. checking to see if I'd put out some French provincial furniture, a mink stole, or power tools in perfect working order.

By the time Mark rode up in the early afternoon, I was sitting on the front steps under threatening clouds with the majority of my earthly goods still surrounding me. In my lap was a diet soda and a cash box and on my head a battered Stetson I would sell if anyone asked.

I thought I might not see you, I said.

I couldn't let you go without saying goodbye. He spoke dully, as if half-asleep.

He dragged his bike onto the curb, leaned it against my futon platform (some slats broken, but only fifteen bucks), and sat down beside me. My bare leg touched the worn olive drab of his army pants, this action now our little code. For a while we just sat there in silence, looking through some old copies of literary journals I was trying to sell.

Remember the day we met? I said. It was just six months

ago. I told him how I remembered watching him coming into the kitchen with Rose on his hip.

It seems longer, he said.

How's Rose? I asked him, not wanting to bring up anything Anne had told me.

I haven't seen her in a couple of days, he said quietly, looking down. Anne hasn't been at the house and I've been in and out myself.

We sat there for a long time without talking. A couple drove up in a metallic blue Buick, paused, and drove away.

I'm not going to sell anything, I sighed. And it's gonna pour any minute. What am I going to do with all this shit?

I'm sorry, I'm not being a very good customer, Mark said. He got up and began to look around the yard. Okay, whaddya got? Books? I need books. Bras? Bandannas? Spatulas? I need spatulas. Record albums! Socks!

Then he picked up a brown porkpie hat and pulled it low over his eyebrows and leaned on the cane I used briefly when I had water on the knee. As he hunched over and hobbled toward me, he was transformed into a very old man. He slowly lowered himself to sit on the edge of a coffee table. There were so many things in my youth that I could not understand, he said in a quavering voice. I was a fool, and I had everyone convinced otherwise. I knew so much and could make sense out of nothing. Now I am an old man, and I look back on my life with many regrets.

So many regrets, he repeated, shaking his head sadly. He looked at me again, then rose slowly, unsteadily, on his cane and hobbled toward the road. Suddenly I realized he was about to climb on his bike and leave.

Wait! I called and started to run toward him. Don't go yet.

He paused for a moment, then tossed me the hat.

Bye, girl, he said. Come get me out of that pawnshop some time.

Why don't you just come with me, I said.

Would you really take me?

Would you really come?

We looked at each other. Well, that settles it, I guess, he said. He got on his bike. You be careful in that big city.

Come see me! You should! We can do a show up there!

I ran to him and hugged him, and he stood with his arms at his sides, letting me. Just as I was about to drop my arms, he reached around me and kissed me on the mouth. Then he put his hands on my shoulders and pushed me away.

Remember me, he said, and he jumped on his bike and started pedaling down the street.

Remember me, too, I said to the gray air.

A light rain began after he left and continued through Saturday evening, interfering with garage sales and outdoor weddings. Sunday was hot and sticky. Though the sun never came out, the rain tapered off by morning; organizers of a Frisbee golf tournament in Pease Park that afternoon were surprised but pleased not to have to cancel. However, unbeknownst to all but meteorologists, warm moist air from the Gulf of Mexico was moving rapidly into the area at middle levels of the atmosphere. Air closer to the earth was heated throughout the day, while an upper-level trough of low pressure arrived early in the evening. That did it. Cloud tops reached forty to forty-five thousand feet and remained in that range for more than seven hours.

Heavy rain began falling in Austin at about 9:30 p.m. Within hours, rain had fallen at intensities approaching the world record: six inches in one hour, ten inches in two and a half.

The effect of so much precipitation in such a short period was compounded by several factors. The ground was already saturated from Saturday's rain, and a typical urban concentration of impervious surfaces—streets, parking lots, sidewalks—had reduced absorption. North of the city, there were other problems. A few years earlier, this area had been nothing but fields. Then construction began in the late seventies. Because it was outside the corporate limits, developers were not hampered by flood-sensitive building codes, resulting in rural roads with flimsy, narrow bridges, low-water crossings, and no storm culverts.

By midnight, the water on Burnet Road, just a couple miles north of our house, reached nineteen and a half feet, and homes and businesses along Shoal Creek were being washed away by the wave as it moved south. It picked up heavy industrial equipment, large commercial trucks, and passenger cars, moving them miles from where it had found them.

When we awoke Monday morning, the Memorial Day flood had already claimed its victims; the first was a woman who had been driving over the new bridge on Duval Road when it collapsed. Helicopters buzzed overhead, checking the banks of the receding streams for bodies.

Our house was on a hill just a half mile from Lamar Boulevard, the major thoroughfare where Marguerite had been killed. Lamar ran all the way through town from north to south, and near Shoal Creek for most of its course. It was a low point, with roads running downhill into it on either side. These roads were closed and empty except for stranded, abandoned cars, as my housemates and I saw when we left our house to find out what was going on.

A river of water between two and three feet deep still ran through Lamar. Bobbing along the water's surface was detritus from the houses and stores upstream: shoes, cans of corn, broken planks, and huge shards of glass. I saw a set of measuring spoons, a brassiere, a child's piano, and several bloated books. The windows of the Whole Foods across the street had shattered and the turbulent water raced through the store clearing the shelves like a mad shopper; we were able to pluck out sealed bottles of vitamins and oranges as they floated past.

Around the corner, the Louis Shanks furniture store had lost its display windows, and now club chairs, ottomans, and end tables lay on the sidewalk, speckled with dirt and grass, or remained partially submerged in the street's deeper pools. I watched a woman inspect an olive-green, crushed-velvet lounger for damage, then call to her husband to help her hoist it into a little red wagon they'd brought to haul their booty home. Most bizarre were the car dealerships near the intersection of Sixth and Lamar. Cars had been lifted up by the big wave and stacked one on top of the other, four and five and six at a pop, and they remained in those piles now that the waters receded. One Toyota was actually in a tree, wedged in among the branches.

We wandered the area, picking our way through the downed trees and deeper pools. When we reached the parking lot of a bar called the Tavern, at Twelfth and Lamar, I stopped and caught my breath. Anne's red car was among the vehicles scattered every which way in the lot. It had obviously been underwater. I opened a back door. The flannel sheets and woven Mexican blankets Anne used to cover the torn upholstery were soaked, as were piles of paper, magazines, clothes. Then with a shock I recognized Mark's clown suitcase floating on the floorboards. It was splayed open, almost empty, a few pots of greasepaint bobbing in the filthy water along with one of Rose's dolls. I picked up the dripping little Navajo baby and ran home to call them.

Anne answered the phone.

Anne, Jesus Christ, are you all right?

Yes, it wasn't too bad down here, but how are you?

The garage apartment flooded, but we're all fine. But Anne, I just saw your car in the parking lot of the Tavern.

You did? Oh, fuck. Mark had it last night. I haven't heard from him yet. I've been worried sick.

Later that day, we talked again. Anne told me that Mark had been trying to drive home from Mike's, but the water was so deep on Lamar he had to leave the car in the Tavern parking lot and walk back to Mike's.

Why did he ever even leave? I asked.

He was on his way over here; he wanted to make sure we were okay. He tried to call, but the phones were out for a while. He finally made it on foot a couple hours ago.

What about the car?

Oh, who knows? I think we'll have to tow it out of there and find out. Best case, it dries off and runs like magic. Worst case, it's permanently fucked. He could have been killed. You know they've been pulling bodies out of the creek all day?

What?

Wait a minute, Anne said, and I heard her end of a shouted conversation. Where are you going? Why now? Okay, well, I need help with Rose, and the car, and—okay, bye! Don't forget to write!

For Christ's sake, she muttered. Sorry, Mark just left, I don't know where he's going and he's so upset about his clown suitcase and he's acting as bizarrely as I've ever seen him. This morning I asked him what he was going to do and he said, Either quit smoking or kill myself.

Do you think he's serious?

Well, I don't trust him, that's for sure. I don't know what to do. Are you still leaving on Thursday?

I was. And flood or no flood, I had to get ready to go. There were still lots of details to take care of—I hadn't yet filed a change of address at the post office or closed my bank account and I was supposedly leaving in forty-eight hours. As Austin continued to dry itself off, gather its broken branches, and count its losses, I was returning library books and renting a U-Haul.

I had come a long way into this move without stopping to feel sad about leaving but at the eleventh hour, the reality of departure finally kicked in. When I got home that evening, all I wanted to do was make the clock stop: sit in the living room and watch Kathy and Tim eating Marmite, listen to Bill and Jennifer argue about the *MacNeil/Lehrer Report*. But I had to get going. There was still a lot to accomplish. I kept telling myself this, but I couldn't seem to move. In the end, I watched as Jennifer finished packing my boxes, Kath labeled them in her funny British schoolgirl printing, and Bill and Tim did the heavy lifting as Barry White played in the background.

It was evening when my room was empty and the U-Haul was full and I called to have some pizza delivered. It didn't come and didn't come and that is why when the phone rang I was sure it would be the delivery boy asking for directions.

But it was Anne.

He hung himself with the hammock on the porch off our bedroom. Her voice was in shreds.

When?

I found him about a half hour ago. The police just got here.

What happened?

Oh, God, she sobbed. I came home this afternoon because I was worried about him. He was fooling around up in the attic so Rose and I went to take a nap in our bedroom. At some point he came and woke me and asked me if I wanted to make love and I said no and I fell back asleep. Her voice was too choked to go on; she put down the phone to get a tissue. I could hear a police radio in the background, footsteps, other voices. I must have slept for hours, I don't know. When we found him—her voice caught and dropped to almost nothing—he was so cold, Marion, so hard and so cold.

I felt like I was turning to stone myself. Oh my God, Anne. Rose was with you?

Yes, she wailed.

I'm coming right now, I said.

She said, Yes, come soon, and we hung up. I stood there with the phone in my hand. In my brain there was a cascade of glass, black sleet, static like on a TV with no reception. I turned slowly and looked around at my friends, all of whom were staring at me. Mark killed himself.

Looks of stunned horror. Sharp intakes of breath. Questions anyone would ask. I continued standing there. It seemed to be all I could manage.

Do you want me to drive you over? Jennifer asked.

Yes, I said. That would be good.

As we left, I noticed the pizza delivery boy across the street with his pile of flat white boxes. He was going to the wrong house. I didn't do anything about it. I guessed he would figure it out. But among the other details I remember from the rest of that crazy night, the terrible angle of Mark's head and the thick white hammock roped around his neck, somebody saying Rose should have something on besides a diaper, somebody saying, Put all this pot away while the cops are here, people tromping through the house, smoking cigarettes in the living room, murmuring in the tepee, Anne's friend Susie lighting candles and incense everywhere and Rose three steps behind her blowing them out, the cops talking about cutting him down, using the phrase over and over until I thought I would scream, and, right when I first got there, Anne hugging me hard, so hard, and ranting aloud as if she were talking to Mark, Oh baby it wasn't that bad, it wasn't that bad, Mike and Myke taking turns following her around all night like a tag team of bodyguards, gentle Jude barking, barking at the police, barking at the paramedics, barking till we had to lock her in the shed, among all these details that hang askew in my memory like a wall of crooked photographs, I also remember how the pizza never came.

It was another few weeks before I left Austin for good, and it was September before I stopped moving, stopped driving my car in

pointless arcs through the United States and Canada. It was a
good while after that when I finally decided that drinking too
much and having one-night stands were not particularly useful
ways of dealing with grief. By the next winter, in my apartment
in New York City, I had about two dozen drafts of a poem called
"Waiting for the Pizza" and no more understanding of how this
could have happened than I did before. Around then I stopped
thinking about it so much, and worked on making new bad things
happen to me until this one was buried like a whole civilization at
the bottom of an archaeological site.

From a vantage point two decades later, even a death as un-
natural and untimely as Mark's takes on the quality of a fore-
gone conclusion, the simple incontrovertibility of historical fact.
Because it did happen, and thus became a part of the chain of
causation of everything that came after it, you begin to forget
that it didn't have to happen at all. At the time, it was the opposite. Half the time, we couldn't even believe it *had* happened, and
had to keep convincing ourselves that it had, accepting it all over
again. The questions of why and how it had come about created a
fog of rumors and speculation that hung over all of us.

For the last few weeks, he'd been taking pills and going to gay
bars, Sallie confided. When I reported her remarks to Anne in a
scornful way, she shrugged. She said actually Mark had had some
homosexual encounters along the way and there was every possibility he'd been going to gay bars and taking Quaaludes, though
she hardly thought of them as causes of death.

He was losing everything, said Myke. The car was gone, the
clown suitcase was gone, Anne was on her way out with Rose.
Of course, the simple soap opera explanation, that he had killed

himself because Anne was leaving him and taking Rose and he couldn't bear it, makes sense—except instead of just having to live separately from his little girl, he gave her up completely, forever, and he stole himself from her, too. In this light, it was the usual senseless teenage-type suicide, one that says, Okay, *now* you'll pay attention. *Now* you'll see how much you've hurt me. *Now* you'll know how bad I feel. One that wounds the survivors far more intensely and permanently than the dead person, who can't quite imagine that he or she won't be around to harvest the remorse, ever intended.

Some of Mark's relatives, who really knew nothing about him except that he was a good boy and Anne was seven years his senior, thought she had trapped him into fatherhood too young, though how this led to suicide was kind of unclear to me. I got wind of this explanation at the funeral in his hometown in North Texas, not far from Oklahoma.

Alongside Mark's pale, bewildered family, Anne and I picked at Jell-O with fruit hanging in it. They could make no better sense of us than we of them. This was particularly clear when I went with Anne to meet with the minister who performed the service and we tried to tell him something about Mark's life. One detail—his clown shows at birthday parties—got through, and in the eulogy we heard a lot about how Mark loved to entertain children. Of them all, only his dark-haired, serious older sister seemed like someone who might have been related to him, seemed like she had known the same person we had. She and Anne and I went through photo albums one day; they gave me a picture of Mark at five blowing out candles on his birthday cake.

Anne was just barely keeping it together. Her gray eyes were cloudy and swollen and her hair a wild wreck. She literally had not changed her clothes since the day Mark died, as though that might stop time, and we had to coax her out of those jeans and into a skirt for the funeral. She barely ate and stayed up night after night smoking cigarettes and drinking the liquor I had to drive over to a different county to buy for her. The night of Mark's death she'd been wailing and half-babbling, but by this time she'd grown very quiet. I think she didn't know whom to trust. At the time, there seemed to be so many layers of truth, so many different stories, so many different groups of people privy to different information, it was hard to know who was safe and what was real.

Until we saw Mark in his casket. That was real. The pancake makeup was troweled over the bruises on his neck and made a mask of his still features. It would have been more natural to see him in his familiar white greasepaint than in that orangey North Texas funeral home flesh color, dressed in a white suit with his hair parted and slicked down to the side.

In talking about Mark's suicide, people often mentioned Marguerite, Lee, the thirteen people in the flood: there was a feeling these deaths had somehow normalized dying, made it seem a more ordinary possibility than usual, something any of us might do in the course of a rough afternoon. It *was* starting to feel like death was in the air, living close among us. It's a good thing it went no further, especially among the more fragile and dramatic characters we knew.

There's a way of dancing with death when you're young that Mark was an extreme example of, and I have seen it in lesser and similar degrees in others since. This type of person loves death, death imagery, death music, death theater, the poetry of death, *The Tibetan Book of the Dead.* All their heroes are dead, and every kind of intoxication—sex, drugs, cigarettes, mysticism, even the self-sweet fog of depression—is an attempt to spring open death's locket or drink death's juice. Death is invited to every occasion, but always with a certain cynical insouciance, as if death wouldn't possibly accept, and with a complete inability to imagine what it means if it does. Like day-trippers at the River Styx, they think they can stop in at Hades's snack bar and come right back.

In retrospect, it seems kind of crazy that no one called a suicide hotline. We had every symptom and sign, threats, gas jets, dry runs, even an announcement. I think it was because he had made death such a part of his persona that we never knew when the line was crossed, when it was suddenly the kind of death that ends your life instead of being an accessory to it.

Anne always maintained that Mark had a mean streak; the cruel circumstances of his suicide certainly proved it. He did nothing to stop her from blaming herself—in fact, just about everything to ensure it. You don't want to have sex with me? Okay, that's it. A load of guilt, anger, and sorrow so huge it was almost mythic collapsed on Anne's shoulders. I'm sure a weaker person would have been buried. The strength of her own instinct for survival, her love and absolute sense of responsibility for Rose— she would walk through hell before repeating her own mother's disappearance—and what I feel justified in describing as the dark power of Dan Del Santo over her: these were her lifelines.

I remember us worrying so much at the time about Rose having seen Mark's body, a terrible image whose effects we could hardly imagine. But two years old was too young, or just young enough: with no language or frame for the thing, it floated out of any conscious grasp. In a letter I got from her recently, she sounds happy and clearheaded. She has been working with home- less teenagers for the last six years, lives with her boyfriend and her brother, hopes to finish college with a degree in nursing. She wrote of her gratitude and respect for her mother, her dreams of travel, a vision of settling down and having children. "I don't have the devastating feelings someone might have if their parent died when they were older," she said, "but sometimes I feel a little void in the back of my head, like something's missing and I can't put my finger on it."

Anne told me recently that Rose makes mobiles.

Rose's letter made me sorry I had missed twenty years of her life. For a couple of weeks after Mark's death, I stuck to her and her mother like glue and tried hard, as many people did, to help. I remember Sallie and her boyfriend took Rose to the zoo in San Antonio and were back hours after they said they would be. Anne was insane with worry. They had a terrible fight and were never friends again. One way or another, Anne parted company with most of the people who had been in her circle during the time she and Mark had lived in the castle. It seems that once a crisis is over, people succumb to the urge to flee. In Anne's ease the phenome- non was compounded by her increasing moodiness and temper— plenty of people, like Sallie, she just plain drove off. Others drifted away, especially after she married Dan.

I was neither driven nor drifted; in fact, our story never had an official ending. When I finally left Austin in my U-Haul, I stopped in Virginia, where Anne had gone to stay with her family. We hung out with her old best friend DiAnne, a gentle, bookish young woman with owl-round glasses and a dry Southern wit, and Anne came back to herself a little. The three of us talked for hours, easing into it with local gossip and news of their old friends, finally getting to some of what Anne had endured in the past months. Yet in that conversation and in those that followed, on walks through the countryside or on the couch in DiAnne's living room over cigarettes and wine, there was one thing we never talked about, one thing that never came up before I drove on to New York.

We never once talked about or acknowledged what had happened between me and Mark, between the three of us, in fact. It seemed inappropriate, supposedly unimportant yet actually dangerous. It became a nonissue to the point that I feel out of line bringing it up even now. But this shoving under the rug has not been without consequences.

At the time, I felt weirdly robbed of my loss. Everyone thought of me as Anne's friend; not many knew about my thing with Mark. "Thing" is about the best word I can think of for it; it wasn't even an affair. Even if people did know about it, I doubt they planned to send me sympathy cards. Sorry for the Loss of Your Best Friend's Man Who You Fucked in Her Driveway. There was no other way to describe what he was to me, and I didn't have the right to mourn him as any version of widow. So I never did.

At the time of Mark's death, Anne had repressed a great deal of anger to let me back into her life. After the suicide, the feelings went even deeper underground. Meanwhile, she married Dan and had a daughter and a son with him, and though I loved those kids and her, I could never feel comfortable in their house on my return visits to town. When I moved back to Austin in 1983, we both thought we would resume our friendship, but it never quite clicked. The conversation we needed to have did not occur until I saw her in Baltimore in 2001.

By then, Anne had not seen Dan in almost ten years. He was busted by the DEA in 1992 and jumped bail a few weeks after his arrest, leaving her with three small children and more chaos and debt than many of us see in a lifetime. A couple months after our reunion, Dan died in Oaxaca, Mexico, of an overdose of painkillers.

By that time we had lost so many people. The man who published my book of poems, and a boy who lived with us in that house on Pressler Street, and my father, and Jennifer's father, and I won't even try to list all the people who died after that, but there are no losses exactly like that of a twenty-three-year-old suicide.

Perhaps the most piercing thing I've read about suicide comes from G. K. Chesterton, who pointed out that while a person who commits murder kills just one person, the person who commits suicide kills the whole world.

Well, that's the idea, isn't it? But then the world struggles back to life without them. Twenty years later, two women meet in Baltimore, one all gray, one getting there, and none of the differences between them are as clear as their primary similarity, their survival. The anger is gone, the reasons are gone, the buzz of speculation, gossip, and news is gone, the last of the bathwater long swirled down the drain with the long-gone baby. What is left now is only what started the whole thing in the first place: the spark in the heart when you meet someone you love.

V

Later

THE THINGS
THEY GOOGLED

If they were young, they googled the things they didn't know. Some were things they were supposed to know for school, like the habits of the hammerhead shark, the list of perfect squares under a hundred, the phrase "rite of passage." When they got bored, they googled images of peace signs, photographs of rainbows, a video of a girl singing about Friday, and another of a baby laughing and laughing. They googled Anne Hathaway. If they were boys, they googled how to build a bomb. If they could get on the computer when their parents weren't home, they googled things they weren't supposed to know about, things like "sodomy" and "lesbian." Then they cleared the search history and googled "hammerhead shark."

If they were old, they googled the things they had forgotten: names of actors and movies and hurricanes, old sports scores, the vice president under Carter, the ingredients in a Manhattan, the hours of the liquor store, "liquor stores open Sunday," directions. They googled things that had escaped them: the definition of feckless, a synonym for regime, most of the answers to the Sunday crossword puzzle. They googled remedies for burns and bee stings.

If they were lonely, they googled "sex." They googled "sex xxx." They googled long-lost lab partners, old boyfriends, their ex-husband's new girlfriend. They googled cute pictures of baby koalas. They googled the word "lonely." They googled "distended stomach," "nosebleed that won't stop," "numbness," "insomnia," and "cancer symptoms."

The things they googled were determined by forgetfulness, by need, by desire, by curiosity, and by the endless availability of information. In fact, there was no point in remembering anything except how to google. They didn't even have to remember what they were googling: as soon as they'd typed "When does g—", just that much, Google already knew the question was when *Glee* season three would begin. When they googled "pleonism," Google politely looked up "pleonasm." Google never made them feel bad for not knowing.

So they googled how to lose weight and pictures of psoriasis and checklists for diagnosing attention-deficit disorder. If they were pregnant, there was no end to their googling. Others googled when it would rain and how much it would rain and when to plant their gardens. They googled the tides and the seasons. They googled sunrise and sunset. They googled births and deaths. They googled themselves, which was sometimes unsettling, turning up Boston Marathon times and class reunions and obituaries not their own.

How did they live before Google, they wondered. How did anyone know anything? How did anyone remember, while driving through Mohnton, Pennsylvania, the name of the young blond actress in the movie *Witness* who was from that town?

When they were hungry, they googled "recipe chard cannellini beans," "recipe apple gingersnap," or "recipe rice noodle salad." How to freeze tomatoes. How to peel and seed tomatoes. Whether you can add grated zucchini to cornbread mix. How to tell if an egg is rotten, and if one egg is rotten, are all the others rotten too? "Best no-egg cornbread." "Best no-egg omelette." "Best restaurant brunch."

Plagued by the familiarity of an essay they had read, they googled "The Things They Googled," and again Google was there before they'd finished typing. It was a reference to the short story "The Things They Carried," of course, the beautiful Vietnam War story by Tim O'Brien. Google showed them where to read it online, and some dove in right away, while others ordered used copies of the collection for ninety-nine cents plus shipping, and still others reserved a copy at their local libraries.

But after all the searching and finding, all the slapped foreheads and the *ahas*, after all of it, there was still something missing. It was the size of a gingersnap, a two-week-old koala, a liquor store. It looked a bit like Kelly McGillis or Walter Mondale. It was excellent for soothing burns and heartaches. It was not in their computer or their phone or on any file server anywhere. Older search engines would be required.

WHAT IF YOU
WERE RIGHT?

What if you were twenty-two, and there was a boy at your office, a Jewish studies major from Harvard who did a Big Bird impression? And after you got through ignoring him because he was such a nerd, stooping over your carrel in his white button-down shirt, you realized he was the love of your life. Who can say what kind of tarty getups you would wear to work, what enthusiasm you would develop for Franz Kafka and Milan Kundera, what vistas of eternity would open up between rumpled sheets in a narrow bed on the Upper West Side?

What if three months later that boy suddenly startled and bolted, and not one word you could say, not one self-destructive, melodramatic crisis you could stage, would bring him back? You could lie down in the hallway outside his apartment all night, and he would not open the door.

Something like this can really mess you up, you know? You

could spend quite a while feeling bad and acting worse. You could hitch up a train of bad poems and lost weekends and therapy sessions, and *whoosh*—there goes 1982.

But let's say you eventually get off your personal locomotive of doom, move to Texas, get married, have children. The mystery of how this boy could have stopped loving you remains a cold case for more than ten years. To regain your balance, you develop the essential ironic distance. You tell the story with scorn and pity for yourself, apologies for him. You tell it often.

But get this. What if one day Big Bird is on a cross-country trip, and he stops to see you in the pink-granite office building in Austin, Texas, where you now write manuals for a software company? You talk to him in the parking lot out front because he has only a minute. He just wants to say, after all this time, that you were right. He loved you. Of course he loved you, and he should have kept loving you, but you were too scary back then. You and your friends were doing hard drugs, for God's sake, and he was a Jewish studies major who was seeing a psychiatrist three times a week. It felt like electricity but also a little like electrocution. He can say this now at last. Which is why he has stopped by.

This conversation permanently qualifies as one of the best things that has ever happened to you. It actually changes you. Some part of you that has been sitting on death row for a decade hears that there were procedural mistakes during the trial and is let out of jail. She walks the streets again. The missing piece is in place, and it's not that he was gay, or in love with another girl, or suffering from a secret illness, or even that he never loved you at all. At last the story has an end: a godsend.

So you can finally get over him. More or less.

THE BOOK OF JOB: A QUIZ

These fill-in-the-blank review questions follow the chapter on Job in A Child's Bible: Lessons from the Prophets and Writings, *by Seymour Rossel. I ran into this book after I came up with the idea of writing a series of personal essays based on biblical incidents. First, of course, I had to read the Bible. But the Bible and I did not hit it off, so I revised my plan. I would read collections of Bible stories aimed at children. Children's Bibles proved to be more my speed, and Rossel's version—with its review questions, word search puzzles, and colored illustrations like those I remembered from Hebrew school long ago—perfectly addressed my case of spiritual arrested development.*

1. Oh, dry bones! God will breathe life into you, said _____.

   If the prophet Ezekiel comes to my house, I will show him my home mausoleum, located on top of the bookshelf in my living room. Look, Ezekiel, here's my mother in the silver ice bucket that she won with my dad in the 1965 Husband and Wife Tournament at Hollywood Golf Club in Deal, New Jersey. I would have mixed a little of my father in there with her, but robbers stole him, in his hermetically sealed brown plastic box, out of my mother's jewelry drawer back in the eighties. I also have my first husband, Tony, and our stillborn son, whom we called Peewee.

Originally each was in a red, covered urn with a heart-like shape, a big one and a little one, but Peewee's was smashed when my second husband threw a ball for the dog. I tracked down the young potter, who was older by then, and he kindly made a replacement. It was much larger than the first, as if the ashes might have grown by age seventeen.

2. All your children are dead, said _____.

All ten of Job's kids, seven boys and three girls, whom he worried about constantly, were having dinner at his oldest son's house when it was hit by a tornado. Four years ago, my friend Ellen received a similar message about her sixteen-year-old daughter, Audrey: a car accident in a thunderstorm on the way to a birthday party. Every day Ellen wakes up and gets this news again. Audrey's dogs, Mocha and Cookie, are still waiting for her to walk in the door.

None of my children are dead, except Peewee, and I have let him go. I could not hold on to a sadness that size for very long. Now it is absorbed in the bones and the fluids of my body. I have three other children, who have all survived their lives so far, and I have my dachshund, who is exactly the size of a baby. In the morning, when we are rolling around and nosing each other, he puts his paw—big for such a short leg, with roughened pads and curved black nails—on my cheek as gently as if it were a hand.

3. Do you still believe in God? said _____.

Job's wife is a nudnik renegade, at the end of her rope after watching her husband's reaction to the loss of their children, their possessions, and his livelihood. He just sits there on the floor, scratching his oozing sores with broken shards of pottery. What happens to her after that is not totally clear. It seems she sticks with him.

I have a tattoo of my second husband's initials on my right shoulder blade. It turns out I made a more permanent decision when I got the tattoo than I did when I married him. We were able to undo our marriage, but the tattoo has been absorbed into the tissues of my body. After considering having layers of my skin removed by laser, or having the tattoo hidden by a larger tattoo, I had a brief affair with my ex, then made my peace with it.

4. People should be happy when God punishes them for doing wrong, said _____.

When I started having health problems and had to quit drinking, my fantasies of indulgence became more and more extravagant. I wanted to stay up all night doing cocaine and drinking Veuve Clicquot. Or have carloads of OxyContin delivered from pharmacies in Canada and wash it down with hits of ecstasy and tumblers of gin and grapefruit juice. I think this is approximately what Job feels, although he expresses it somewhat differently—at least in the King James Version. But instead of being allowed to climb back up into his mother's womb and sleep forever, or even wash himself clean with snow water, what he gets is a parade of moronic friends like Elihu coming over to make insensitive comments. Which just shows you how realistic the Bible can be.

5. If you were really good, God would answer your prayers, said _____.

6. You are being punished even less than you deserve, said _____.

7. God's justice is always straight, said _____.

Why do we always want to make people's suffering their own fault? He was drinking. She was careless. He refused the operation. They were not wearing seat belts. Enough, pals. Find someone else to torture with your theories and your chitchat. Job, did you think of getting a dog?

8. I am nothing. Forgive me, said _____.

Of course, he would have said anything at that point. Apparently it all worked out well for him. He got a new house and new kids and patched things up with the wife. His boils healed, and he lived 140 more years. What I think is, he just could not hold on to a sadness that size for very long. That is the one gift we have against all this trouble: our weakness. Things go wrong, people are dopes, your body is fragile, the ones you love can't help you, even your children are crushed in the unfeeling vise of time. But if you don't kill yourself or become a hopeless addict or die some other way, you go on, and more things happen. Eventually, some of them are good things. Ask the Jews. Ask anyone. Someday, when we are 140 years old, I will ask my friend Ellen.

WHAT IF YOU WERE WRONG?

The other day I received an email from a woman named Marjorie, who'd just read a short memoir I wrote, set in Austin back in 1981. She, too, had vivid recollections of the period and people described—a serious flood, a piano in a tree, a dog the size of a pony, a jazz musician the size of a Volkswagen, a suicide. Her letter was a surprise to receive and interesting to read but there were two sentences in particular that knocked me over.

"Once Mark and I were talking about women and weight and body types and he told me that you had a twenty-inch waist and that he found you so beautiful. I remember that you looked like the Shaktis in my Far Eastern art history book."

This was like getting thirty-two-year-old news from Mars. I could not take it in. I don't mean the twenty-inch waist, I know I had a decent waist, though this number sounds like it was rounded down somewhere along the way.

The impossible thing, the radioactive space rock, was the idea that at some point in history two people sat around talking about the beauty of women's bodies and I was the example.

That the dark, ethereal boy, who was my good friend's neglected boyfriend, who took me in his arms one night in the car, who with the terrible shortsightedness of youth and torment hung himself with the rope from a hammock later that spring, said he found me so beautiful.

That Marjorie, who apparently rode her bike from Minnesota and lived in the big house with Mark and the others for four months, and of whom I have no memory at all, said I looked like the Shaktis in her Far Eastern art history book. I picture them as concupiscent hourglasses: bounteous bosoms and tapered waists, brimming hips and jingling ankles, their third eyes radiating tantra into the hypnotized cosmos.

Just like me!

There are two kinds of praise. The kind you take lightly because you already know it is true, and the kind you ignore because it cannot get through your resistance to this information. For example, my friend Kim, a doe-eyed Italian beauty, is also very bright. You tell her she's beautiful and she just smiles: she's heard it before. Then you tell her, after she's beaten you once again at Scrabble, that she is smart. She snorts. Come on, I'm a hairdresser.

Are we all impermeable to the thing we most need to know?

Some ancient turning away, some shrug, some no that still echoes off the walls of your skull. Your heart. What you wouldn't have done to make them see. Who, you don't even know, it was so long ago. These days almost everyone is very kind and complimentary. They love your smile. You look great in those pants. Your jokes! Hilarious. You are quick as quicksilver. You kill at Scrabble. The biggest bully left is the one in your own head.

The other day, in my mid-fifties, I got that email. Mark said he found me so beautiful, Marjorie saw me on the wall of a Hindu temple. Is it too late to be a Shakti, do you think? What if my waist is twenty-eight inches now, or thirty-four? What if I wear bright blue reading glasses that make my daughter laugh? What if some sort of farm implement has rolled a trail over my skin?

So beautiful. I have been carrying those words around like pebbles, like chips of the rock from Mars. I keep them in the pocket of my Shakti pantaloons. What I want to do is hand them out to everyone.

THE PLACE
OF THINGS

⌣

Oh, no, said my mother, who had come out onto the lawn to survey the items stacked along the curb from the mailbox to the driveway. We can't throw this away. She put her hand on an oversized cherry cabinet with a woven wood-grain pattern on its front.

Why not? I replied.

It's much too nice to dump in the street, she said.

But what is it? I asked.

Well, said my mother, it could be a bar.

A bar? I echoed, and bent to inspect it more closely. I was certain it came from the street in the first place, one of many quasi-treasures rescued by my brother-in-law, Steve, from other people's curbside piles in the 1970s and '80s. Steve was quite the trash-picker. I had been throwing out his stuff all morning.

My mother lived for about thirty years alone in the house where my sister and I grew up, where my father died in the mid-eighties. All in all, there were about fifty years of shoving things in the upstairs room and its large, attic-like closet. However, when a friend of hers moved to a small apartment from a house also lived in for decades, disgorging truckloads of possessions in the process, my mother was inspired to lighten up. She had only to mention to me the idea of cleaning out the upstairs and I sped to suburban New Jersey to get the job underway. Better now than later. (My sister, my partner in the tear-filled cleaning of this house that occurred two years later, got a bye on this round, since she is an accountant and it was late in tax season.)

Though some might have spent the day sifting dreamily through scrapbooks and wardrobes, my mother and I took a more utilitarian approach. She helped me with the schlepping until a trash bag we were carrying to the curb burst and the magazines that popped out smacked her in the face and skinned her nose. This was my fault for overloading the trash bag, so I didn't object when she quit helping after that, sitting at her desk smoking cigarettes, talking on the phone. Just stay away from the computer, I thought, having solved enough confounding mysteries of America Online for one day.

On I went, carrying everything to the curb or to the giveaway pile, including a few potentially sentimental items like my father's old Super Bowl party decorations and Steve's art portfolio from Cooper Union. No one has looked at any of this stuff in decades, I told myself, and though I have missed Steve bitterly since he died of AIDS in the mid-nineties, I was not the sort of person for whom reclaiming his possessions would make a difference.

You didn't throw out Daddy's Marine Corps medals, did you?

my mother asked when I was done and came in for a Bloody Mary and a tuna sandwich.

No, I assured her. Close call.

What about my black tote bag? The one I told you I wanted to keep.

Um, I said, casting about. I think I did accidentally chuck it. Don't worry, I can find it.

As she followed me out to the yard, I knew the tote bag would not be the end of the recall. Something else would have to come back in. It was the mystery cabinet, of course, the heaviest thing of all. My friend Sandye had had to be enlisted to help me carry it down the stairs.

A bar, huh. I opened the door of the cabinet. Apparently, I'd had it standing sideways, because when I tilted my head I saw that it did contain some built-in drawers and what could have been a wine rack. See, said my mother, I think it was a wall-mounted bar in one of the apartments Daddy and I lived in before you were born.

I still didn't believe her. I'm going to end up carrying that damn thing out of here again, I said.

I bet one of the boys will want it, she said.

They better, I replied. I fantasized aloud about how I was going to go around the house after her funeral, cornering each grandson in turn. *Noah*, I'd say. *Nana left something very special just for you. She wanted you to have it. Come upstairs, let me show it to you.*

My mother saw nothing wrong with this joke, because black humor is what Nana is leaving just for me. It will be sad when there's no one around to enjoy our favorite story, about the thieves who ransacked her dresser looking for jewelry and made off instead with a sealed box that contained my father's ashes.

Sandye came over again to help me get the cabinet back upstairs. She had just moved her increasingly feeble grandmother out of a Florida condominium and was familiar with both the process and the emotional dynamics of our situation. I told her guiltily about throwing away all Steve's stuff. But that's how it is, she said comfortingly. You live, you die, your stuff goes out to the curb.

The problem is that it's not always in that order. For a massive disruption of the natural sequence, take New Orleans after Katrina. When people were finally able to return to their flooded houses, they had to gut them and drag all the soggy stuff inside out to the street. This was the only chance for saving the structures. According to my friend Sue, the piles of sad household items stayed for weeks, and then it was all hauled to multiblock dumpsites, where it rested for another spell. Months later you would be walking down the street, she said, and spot a Barbie sticking out of the mud next to the sidewalk, or a soup ladle, or a tortoiseshell comb.

Sue and Jack live in Lakeview, the neighborhood immediately adjacent to the Seventeenth Street Canal breach. I went down to visit them during the first postdisaster Mardi Gras in February 2006. On the way to their house from the airport, we drove past the long line of hollowed-out houses on Canal Boulevard, their ruined walls spray-painted with initials and dates by would-be rescuers. Across house after house, for mile after mile, ran the waterline, a wide brown stripe hitting the upper part of the front door.

Now you see why so many people are not coming back, Sue said, cruising through yet another nonoperational traffic light.

When we arrived at her place, we saw the weird miracle she and Jack had told us about. Though their roof had been damaged by the hurricane, the floodwaters had literally stopped in their front yard.

Staying in their unchanged house, chock full of paintings and furniture and rugs and books, in the middle of a silent neighborhood—every shop, gas station, church, and restaurant closed—was an eerie experience. I could understand why Jack said he wasn't leaving, but I could also see why Sue talked about wanting to move. Maybe to an apartment uptown, she was thinking. Or to North Carolina. What will we do with all this stuff, though? she said, gesturing helplessly around.

You'll have a yard sale, I said. People who have lost everything need new things, right?

It's strange, she said, but you can't even give stuff away here now.

Maybe it's not that strange. Maybe it's like when a kid loses her teddy bear and you think you're going to solve the problem by handing her a new one. She throws it on the ground. She doesn't want that teddy bear, or any other one you might come up with. She wants the one that's gone. (And what if she accepts the new bear? She risks losing it again. Forget bears; they only break your heart.)

What is it, after all, that makes a place home? Is it the physical location or the objects inside it? The place or the things? The refugees from destroyed villages in Eastern Europe or Central America who feel homeless forever; Jack and other New Orleanians who won't leave no matter how hard it gets—these are Place People. Their home is a piece of Earth, a longitude and latitude.

Things People have addresses too, but they can make themselves at home in different spots as long as they have their familiar possessions with them. These objects contain their history, the history of their family. An embroidered cloth, a framed picture, a chest of drawers. A teddy bear. Their problem is that if they lose those things, they can never go home again.

Though it's maybe a little presumptuous to imagine you know how you'd feel in the face of such a loss, I'm pretty sure I'm not a Things Person. If I lost everything in my house but my family was fine and I got out with my laptop and a few photo albums, I could get over the rest. But if my home is a place, I'm not sure where it is. Here in Baltimore, where I've lived for less than five years? I don't think so. New York, New Jersey, Texas, Pennsylvania? I had an apartment in the French Quarter once. It's still there. I checked.

Thinking back, when I felt incredibly homesick after spending months in Europe, I found I missed the U.S. highway system more than anything else. I just wanted to see an American road. Of course I was only twenty then, and didn't even have a place to live. All my stuff was in postcollege storage in my mother's attic. Where it remained for thirty years, until that spring morning two years before my mother's death when it all went to the curb.

Not long after my mother died, I moved from a rural Pennsylvania farmhouse to a skinny row home in Baltimore. My sister and I had just completed the final purging of my mother's possessions and the sale of our childhood home. With this experience fresh in my mind, I was ruthless in my downsizing. I put whole rooms of furniture on Craigslist; I had huge barrels of trash at the curb every week. I could just see my sons, years in the future, opening the half-dozen big blue Rubbermaid boxes that contained my "literary archives" and saying, Gosh, I wonder why Mom kept all these back issues of airline magazines.

I set a bonfire in the field out back and burned them.

All this being said, there are things I have not given up. I love using the little cutting board my first husband, Tony, had when I moved in with him in that French Quarter apartment in 1983, and his sons still have a few of his T-shirts. My mother's old coffee mug and steel ruler are on my desk as I write, along with a leather box with compartments for cufflinks and change that has PUT IT HERE, HY embossed in gold letters on the lid.

Every night I sleep on the king-size mattress on which my second son was born, and on which Tony died four years later. It rests on a headboard and frame that belonged to my parents, and both of them died in bed. A bridge into and out of life, crossed by four of my most beloved, a yacht I sail every night into the sea of dreams.

Here is where my insouciant approach to possessions stops altogether. It would take no less than a hurricane, I think, to get it away from me.

LOVE, LOSS, AND WHAT I COOKED

I knew I was falling in love when I broke an egg into my coffee while trying to make a man an omelet. I stared at the submerged yolk poaching in my java and thought: Girl, you are gone. Just then the butter began to burn and the smoke alarm agreed: *we are on fire.*

Almost every day I scald myself or cut myself or find avocado in my hair because I cook with my whole body and sometimes drink too much wine in the process. My cookbook is five tattered manila folders filled with stained clippings and splattered scraps of hand-writing. A history of pans of hot oil and blenders full of ice, written in spilled salt, drizzled honey, and crushed tomatoes.

My mother was a golfer, not a cook. She made London broil with Adolph's meat tenderizer and pot roast sauced in ketchup and Lipton's Onion Soup Mix. Of course I became a vegetarian. At twelve, I developed a disgusting recipe that involved frying up every vegetable we had in the house— celery, carrots, and onions—then adding curry powder, raisins, and tomato sauce. I ate it proudly every day.

At college I lived in a vegetarian co-op with twenty-two like-minded souls. A shelf in our high-ceilinged, pale yellow kitchen housed copies of *The Vegetarian Epicure* and *The Moosewood Cookbook*. As I took my turn making vats of bean soup and flats of cornbread tamale pie, the fundamentals of meatless cooking took hold. The fundamentals of psychedelic drugs, Marxism, and astrology also took hold, though none held my attention as long as the way to make chili from bulgur wheat and V8 juice.

My early twenties were years of experimentation: I lived in a lot of places, knew a lot of people, imbibed a lot of substances. Then I settled down with a bartender I'd met at Mardi Gras. The barbecued shrimp of our New Orleans courtship was followed by a gold mine of Italian recipes from my new mother-in-law. Stromboli with thin-sliced salami; marinara with hot Italian sausage and meatballs; steak layered with provolone, sprinkled with garlic, and rolled into *braciola*, according to instructions in her slanting Catholic-school penmanship.

My first pregnancy was an unexplained full-term stillbirth. Afterward, I lay in the dark thinking I would never get up again until a woman I barely knew brought a Styrofoam box of food I could not recognize. It was yellow, dark green, tan, and orange. It could have been a blue plate special from the planet Venus.

She sat there staring at me until I ate it. And I felt a surge of un-expected strength and well-being. I was not macrobiotic for very long, but I formed a relationship with brown rice, miso, and col-lards that lasts to this day.

After Tony died of AIDS when our sons were four and six, soaking adzuki beans was too much trouble. I barely had the time or will to open a box of Jell-O, much less make fruit-juice kanten. Though my boys had been raised on lentil burgers and organic chicken nuggets, they seemed more than happy with our new friends, Hamburger Helper and ramen. I added tofu to the soup for old times' sake.

For five years I dated a man who was both an excellent chef and a restaurant critic, which led to a fattening, cooking-free life-style. One night early on, I made him a big *zuppa di* clams accord-ing to my mother's friend Lois Altschul's recipe, which I'd found on a yellow index card in my Seafood folder. I dropped the platter on the floor on the way to the table. In retrospect, it was a sign.

After the big guy and I broke up, I met a skinny philosopher who ate mostly trail mix. I married him and moved to rural Central Pennsylvania. I had a hard time getting used to my new environment, a meat-and-potatoes kind of place with restaurant choices ranging from Wendy's to Arby's and grocery stores rang-ing from Walmart to Shurfine. This situation, combined with my lack of friends and activities, led to an intense phase of renewal in my cooking. I had all the time in the world to learn to bake bread, can tomatoes, and make pies from scratch with apples from the orchard down the road or raspberries the kids brought in from the backyard. If I wanted Mexican or Thai or even decent Jewish rye, I had to make it myself.

In Baltimore, I shop for groceries constantly. I have five lists going at once: Giant, Trader Joe's, Trinacria, Asia Food, and Wells Discount Liquors, and usually have to stop at Eddie's anyway for one last thing when I pick up Jane from school. Just a bunch of parsley or a tin of cashews. Plus a nice pack of Berger cookies for the girl. No matter how much money I take to Waverly Farmers Market, I spend it all. I visit Whole Foods only on my birthday.

Strangers on the internet teach me their tomatillo salsa, rosewater crème brûlée, Hangtown fry, and coconut curry mussels—I try not to spill shiraz on my laptop. From my old folders I make pasta with fresh tuna and oil-cured olives, buttery pilaf with vermicelli, Moroccan *harira* soup from an eighties-era *Cooking Light*. My younger son graduated from college in New Orleans with a degree in jambalaya and crawfish. The kid fries eggs like a genius.

When I miss my mother, I make her London broil. These days we eat it over spring greens with mint and cilantro and a dressing made from fish sauce and limes, but the secret of its tenderness has not changed.

NEWFOUNDLAND

Recently, my friend Sandye and I were drinking some local microbrew in Fells Point, and she reminded me of the time we were in Newfoundland and met these guys who served us delicious beer they had made in their garage. It was the first time we ever had homemade beer, remember? Sandye said. And it was the first time I truly liked, even loved, beer.

I put down my glass, pressed my lips together, and squinted into the middle distance. We were in Newfoundland? I finally said.

I think it is exactly because of my terrible memory that I have become a memoirist. If I don't write it down, I'm sure to forget it. Even writing it down is no guarantee. Sometimes I read about my past in old books of mine and I have the same reaction other readers do. I did that? Are you kidding me?

While other memoirists seem to have unlimited drilling rights in the rich territory of childhood, I am largely reduced to the re-tailing of the immediate past. Memoirs of the Month, as it were. My childhood is a lighted button in an elevator, a metal milk box, a parquet floor. All overused and worn out by now. If only I could remember one thing I haven't already dug up, one brand-new memory never handled, never pulled apart and tatted into lace.

Even if one is not facing senescence, as is your humble re-porter, neural storage isn't as permanent or as reliable as one might hope. Everyone is forgetting everything all the time.

Fortunately, it seems the government is about to spend a great deal of money on mapping the brain, as they have previously done with the human genome. Surely, they will be able to pinpoint the location of the secret warehouse where all the missing memories are stockpiled.

It will be on a flat, empty highway under a low gray sky, a cinderblock building with tumbleweeds cartwheeling past.

It turns out that quite a bit is already known about the subject of forgetting, as I read in an excellent book called *The Seven Sins of Memory* by Daniel Schacter. The author, who is a professor of psychology at Harvard, offers a breakdown of the various types of forgetting and misremembering, which I can share with you only because I took notes:

The Sin of Transience. This is the forgetting that occurs over time in people of all ages. For example, in the days after your father's funeral, you had a pretty clear idea of what leftovers were in the fridge, and even what shelves they were stored on. Now you only know there was so, so much food.

The Sin of Absentmindedness. The forgetting caused by not pay-ing attention in the first place. You were out on the sidewalk saying goodbye to some relatives when the neighbor who brought the sloppy joes arrived, and that is why you don't remember which neighbor it was.

The Sin of Blocking. It was what's-her-name, the one whose husband had a carpet store. It's on the tip of your tongue. It begins with a *k*. Kerouac? Kardashian? It will come to you in a couple of days.

The Sin of Misattribution. Your memory of the scene in your mother's dining room looks like something from a Woody Allen movie because you're actually remembering a scene from *Annie Hall*.

The Sin of Suggestibility. Somebody said it was Karasic. So it must be Karasic, right?

The Sin of Bias. Decades earlier, Mrs. Karasic called pet control on your bloodthirsty wire-haired fox terrier, Kukla, so you don't think of her as the nice lady who brought food after Daddy's funeral.

The Sin of Persistence. If only you could forget the way your father looked in his coffin. If only you had never seen it. The drawn cheeks, the closed eyelids, the awkward yarmulke. The so-not-him.

My hilarious, hard-headed, and noisy father fell silent for good on April 4, 1985. I was remembering the date as March 5, but then so much about this period, including the obnoxious food-fest that followed it, is unclear. I was able to look up the date in a manuscript stored on the hard drive of this computer, and so stand corrected. I will have to call my sister, Nancy, and tell her; we spent fifteen minutes earlier this morning recalling the beautiful Steuben vase my mother won in a golf tournament. It was smashed by the cat when she jumped on the table and batted at a plastic drinking straw someone had stuck in it. I don't remember this as clearly as Nancy does, though as we spoke it started to come back: perhaps, she suggests, because it was she who left the straw? She says we were terribly rude to Mommy about the loss. Mothers now ourselves, we hate to think of this. On the other hand, this is one of those brand-new, never-before-remembered memories I so enjoy. A lovely fluted crystal vase rising straight out of the neural muck.

Disk storage, camera phones, search engines, sisters—all sweet blessings to the aging brain.

According to Dr. Schacter, the seven sins may cause us problems but they play a positive role as well, preventing us from becoming overwhelmed with useless information. One certainly doesn't need a blueprint of the inside of the refrigerator in April 1985, and perhaps it and all succeeding ones had to go to make way for the current layout, specific down to a tiny Tupperware containing garlic aioli, wedged at the back of a shelf.

Let me get that for you, maybe with some carrot sticks.

Despite its sometimes frustrating and unreliable operation, memory creates identity. Even what we misremember is part of who we are, the gaps filled in artfully by a web of guesswork.

Perhaps it is no surprise that I was wrong about even the missing Canadian memories mentioned earlier. We were not in Newfoundland; we were in Nova Scotia. *The Sin of Beer* is missing from Schacter's list. If the fates allow it, Sandye and I will celebrate the sixtieth year of our friendship in 2026. All sins will be in play. It will be unforgettable.

THE GETAWAY

When I had only two children and they were small, I spent a few days in a cabin in the woods at a retreat for artists and writers. I remember standing in the grocery store in Georgia, befuddled. What did I like to eat? I had no idea. I was pretty sure it wasn't Hot Pockets or sliced orange cheese. Eventually, I put in my cart a bag of rice, a bottle of Tabasco, and one can each of beans and mustard greens, chosen for their endearing Southern brand names and labels.

Oh, coffee. And a bottle of wine, and a peach.

A mother can forget what she likes. She can even forget what she is like.

Wherever you go, there you are, say the Buddhists: but so are they. The fruit of your loins, in their Fruit of the Looms. Buy them, clean them, fold them, fix them, hunt them, buy some more. Eventually, you run out of memory, like a computer running too many applications. Before you were the finder of socks, the maker of sandwiches, the driver of carpools, the kisser of boo-boos, the full-service factotum of family life, you were a person who filled whole days with something. What was it? Who were you? There is only one way to find out.

Though it is difficult to abandon those who count on you for their very undergarments, if you play your cards right, distant obligations arise. A business trip. Personal duty. An obligatory invitation. Really, you must go. If only to pry yourself loose from your pathetic martyrdom and see what is left. Goodbye! Back soon! Just microwave them for two minutes on high!

To gaze at the ocean. To meditate on a mountaintop. To steam in lavender and eucalyptus. To this list must be added what I have found to be an equally restorative experience of spiritual solitude: to sit in the airport terminal. There are few things more stressful than being in an airport with a horde of children, but when you travel alone, the place is transformed. In its airy, comfortable reaches, wholly devoted to sitting, reading, and snacking, you are resurrected as an individual.

One person, one seat, one ticket, one will. No arguments.

Whatever automatic reaction people have to you when you appear in public with your family—pity or amusement, aesthetic appreciation or concern—when you are alone, those reactions are nowhere in evidence. Nor is the presumption that, because you are with children, such reactions may be displayed with impunity. No, instead of conducting your private life on a public stage with generally humiliating results, you will be as untroubled as if wrapped in a cocoon, free to read *The New York Times* and drink Starbucks coffee. How could aromatherapy on Big Sur be better than this?

And you never know, perhaps they will announce a delay. When traveling with children, your powerlessness over such things is a problem, a violation of natural law that must be explained and re-explained, even to teenagers. When solo, powerlessness is the dharma. The fact is, you will have to sit there, accomplishing nothing, for many hours.

Try to adjust. You have packed three books, and even now someone has discarded a copy of the *New Yorker* containing a fifteen-thousand-word article by Janet Malcolm or Diane Middlebrook. This may be your only chance in the next decade to get through these articles.

After a while, you might even stop looking up every time a small voice utters, "Mommy." Or maybe you won't. Either way, you will soon remember what you like to eat.

You might think a hotel room a more luxurious experience of solitude than a terminal gate, and it has its points, but it lacks the invigorating friction of a public setting. It is the presence of strangers combined with the act of transit that resets one's sense of self. See: suddenly, you are a woman in black jeans sitting in a chair reading a fifteen-thousand-word magazine article. A compact, self-contained organism. If someone speaks to you, they do so politely, and if they look at you, they do so covertly, because that's all that's allowed. Your boundaries, under continual assault by the condition of motherhood, start to firm up. You are mutating into that least maternal and most impermeable of beings, a stranger.

My first experience of this occurred years before my pathetic martyrdom, when I took a trip at eighteen. I flew to Taos for a yoga retreat, first staying overnight in Albuquerque in a Holiday Inn, then caught a bus the next day to the mountains. I had a sense of who I was during that wheezy journey. I know this only because I wrote about it excitedly in my journal: girlness is separated from airness by red flannel shirtness. (Sorry, it was 1975 and, as I said, I was eighteen.) I filled pages with the bubbly chronicle of my experiences, including my purchase of a bright green Navajo blanket the day before. I leaned against the yellowed window of the bus, that blanket in my lap, as small, dusty Southwestern towns went by outside, populated by ethnic groups I had never seen before.

No one knew a thing about me. I could tell them my name was Kitty or that I was an orphan. I could tell them nothing and let them wonder. After so much adolescent self-loathing, I almost had a crush on myself.

In maturity, auto-romantic opportunities are rare; also endangered are the crushes on strangers that were a standard feature of my younger travels. Not that I can't still fall in love with someone on the basis of a ten-minute conversation. I can, but my adult life tends to be overpopulated. Nowadays, most people I meet remind me so much of someone I already know that I just get confused. In any case, if I talk to someone, I won't be able to read my book. Or make my lists, for the other urge that comes over me shortly after liberating myself from my schedules and responsibilities is the compulsion to make lists of things to do when I return. Even on car trips I do this, scribbling messy columns of verb phrases in a notebook open on the passenger seat. It is hard to write in the car, but I always remember a slightly dotty, doe-eyed poet I used to know named Sandra Lynn who said she wrote her poems while driving. If Sandra Lynn can do it, so can I.

Lists of things to do are poems of a kind. The free verse of a vast and efficient future, in which cars are inspected, birthday presents wrapped, videos returned, boxes of books packed up and sent off to young nephews. What a beautiful life I'm going to have when I get home. And yet, despite the bright promise of the lists, and the refreshed quality of my identity, I have never once managed a smooth homecoming. Two seconds into reentry, the traveling me has vanished, my self-possession left at baggage claim.

I walk in the door, and all the things and people I am responsible for seem to fly toward me, neglected and furious. Everything is wrong, and crooked, and left out on the counter. My husband, who has done everything a person possibly could to keep life running smoothly at home, is annoyed in advance, knowing I will be a bitch. So how was it? he asks.

Oh God, it was great, I say.

Already, in the other room, they are shouting for me. Mom!

They never stopped the whole time you were gone, my husband says wearily. So what did you do?

Nothing, I say, dropping my suitcase and moving swiftly toward a jar of peanut butter with the lid off, which is also shouting my name. Nothing.

AUGUST IN PARIS

⁓

The term "family travel" is an oxymoron. What you see if you visit Chichen Itza with your children in tow is the same thing you see in Ocho Rios or Epcot Center: the exotic crushed relentlessly under the heel of the mundane. For example, the only reason I found to stay up past midnight in Paris during our infamous family trip of 2005 was the same as at home—where the hell are the kids? And while it is true that I had spent much of the month wishing my family would fall into the Seine, after I actually lost two of the children, I changed my tune.

On the way home from dinner, seventeen-year-old Emma and fifteen-year-old Vince had jumped off the subway at the nasty Châtelet stop to find a club Emma had read about on the internet. Had we actually given permission for this? Be back by midnight! I called.

At 1:15, the phone rang. It was Emma, calling from a pay

phone to say that they had missed the last train. Her younger brother Sam answered the call and by the time I got there, she had hung up. I chided Sam about this, as if he could have prevented it, and the poor boy was beside himself.

An hour later, I was standing outside our small borrowed apartment, heart pounding and mind racing. The rue de la Tombe-Issoire was as silent and motionless as a hyperrealist painting, every shuttered pastry shop, every glowing street lamp, every parked scooter pulsing with ominous portent. On the corner, the red digital marquee of a closed-up drugstore ticked off the minutes. 2:11. 2:12.

At what point should I wake my husband, Crispin? When would we have to call his ex-wife in Baltimore and tell her we had lost her daughter? When to go to the police? I gingerly began to imagine what could have gone wrong. They weren't dead, of that I was fairly certain, but they could be with bad people. Bad people with cheap vodka and bad drugs. Bad people in bad apartments with no furniture, with smelly mattresses and uncircumcised penises, with larcenous hearts and false assurances.

Vince was tall and sort of imposing-looking, but he was only fifteen. Emma was small and vulnerable and, though less reckless than Vince, no wizard of circumspection. But part of my panic that night was that I assumed the two of them wouldn't do this on purpose. Something had to have happened to them.

At 3:21, a white police van pulled up right in front of me and three young officers, two male and one female, leapt out. Le Mod Squad. I rushed up to them shouting in broken French. *Les enfants! Ils sont disparus!*

They looked at me like I was nuts and said to go the main

police station and file a missing persons report. Then they went into the alley with flashlights, executed *la mission*, rushed back to the car, and sped away.

Practicing for the post-August crime rush, perhaps.

Around 4:00, I went inside to pee. Are they not back yet? my mother-in-law, Joyce, whispered down from the loft. It turned out that both she and her friend Sallie had been awake all night, woken by the 1:15 phone call. She tiptoed down the narrow wooden staircase to join the vigil, a tiny white-haired woman in a flannel bathrobe. Life is tough, people are weak, Marx was right—these are the building blocks of my mother-in-law's worldview. Much in the world does not pass her exacting muster. Lucky for me, when I met her for the first time, a couple of months into my relationship with her son, a forty-year-old woman in horrifically short cutoffs (that detail haunts me), floating into her living room like a Macy's parade balloon of midlife romantic happiness, she took to me right away. Having been hated by my previous mother-in-law, I cherished my good fortune. In fact, this whole trip to Paris had its inception when I said something dreamy about wanting to spend some time there, and Joyce sighed, I've never been. And now I'll probably never go.

My own mother hadn't been either, I realized. And though each of these elderly widows needed little help in most areas, it seemed Paris was my department. I had been several times, I speak a little French, I know a few people.

If I had planned a trip for just the three of us . . . but this simple, civilized approach never crossed my mind. I never thought of leaving my husband, or the five kids we had between us, aged five to seventeen, or my best friend Sandye and her four-year-old, and now both of our mothers were coming, and pretty soon Joyce decided she couldn't leave her best friend either . . . and so we were twelve.

I emailed a Paris-based contact to see if he had any leads on lodging. He offered me his place, because he, like everyone else, was leaving for the month. Though he had only one toilet and two bedrooms, there was a daybed in the kitchen. Of course we would fit! I arranged two shifts of travel, so we'd never be more than eight at once.

Unsurprisingly, Joyce took a dark view of the missing-children situation. I told her I had spoken with the police earlier and they said I had to go to the station.

So go, she said.

Wearily I trudged back out to the alley and pushed open the iron gate. I was only halfway down the next block when I felt so cold and tired that I wondered if I mightn't wait until morning. I should get Crispin's opinion, I decided, and turned around.

Crispin, I whispered, kneeling by the bed. One blue eye opened under its gingery eyebrow. The kids never came home.

He pushed himself up on one elbow. What the hell, he said grimly. Like his mother, he was quite certain that I should go to the police station immediately—even though we had no idea where it was, and it was the middle of the night.

Other husbands might have objected—but this is the problem with always acting like you are the most capable person around and don't want or need any help at all. People will take you right up on it.

I arrived at the precinct around 5 a.m. Outside at a guard booth were a pair of cops, male and female, both smoking. I

looked longingly at their Gauloises but felt that bumming a cigarette might not be best opening move.

Inside was a large, dirty reception area with three more gen-
darmes lounging behind a long counter. One was fat, one had a
moustache, one was fat and had a moustache. They heard my
tale—*les enfants ne rentraient jamais!*—but were unimpressed. First
of all, said the moustache, there was nothing they could do right
away—no phone call to make, no database to check. A missing
persons report was a *grande procedure* and I should come back with
our passports around 7:00 and plan to spend most of the day.

However, he continued, *les enfants* would probably be home by
the time I got there, because the trains and buses started running
again at 5:30. I searched their faces, hoping for something more.
Au revoir, madame, they said. The one with the moustache threw in
a Gallic shrug.

Back at the ranch, Crispin and Joyce were at the table sipping
coffee. Once I had weakly responded to all their questions, we fell
silent. Outside, the sky paled to gray.

The Depression-era song "April in Paris" was written by Yip
Harburg, also the lyricist of "Over the Rainbow." Frankly, the lyrics are uninspired—blossoming chestnuts, singing hearts, etc.—
but apparently, the mere thought of April in Paris was enough to
lift the spirits of New Yorkers in breadlines to the extent that the
song lived on for all time as a symbol of romance.

Our family, unfortunately, missed April by a season and a
half. Instead, we had August, the month when those who live in
Paris leave and lend their apartments to others. One by one, the
shops close, the window-gates are pulled shut, the chairs and tables are hauled in. Only the museums staunchly hold wide their

portals as the city is given over to throngs of tourists. These are the people of August, people who dare not speak its name, because they cannot. What kind of word has three vowels and one diacritical mark before you ever get a consonant? *Août*. Really.

On our trip so far:

Vince had fallen ill—his throat swollen, his lungs congested. Never a stalwart sort, he lay moaning on the kitchen daybed as if on a Civil War battlefield. His illness was a poignant throwback to other family vacations: Hayes's horrific diarrhea in Mexico at eighteen months, Sam's ear infection in Jamaica, Emma's impacted tooth in San Francisco, the headaches and digestive problems that tend to follow Crispin around the globe and can escalate to crisis proportions if one of us happens to leave the Tylenol at home.

The interpersonal tensions of the group had been steadily rising. One evening, just before we went out to dinner, we had a gloves-off brawl about the location of a particular Italian restaurant. It was me against them—Crispin, Hayes, and Vince—and I was right in the end, but that didn't help. The meta-arguments, as usual, were the killer: This is your worst trait! Vince said darkly, meaning that I argue so hard, which seemed a low blow considering they were all 100 percent incorrect, but by then Hayes had done the typical Hayes thing of changing what he had been saying so he was actually not wrong, which is *his* worst trait, and this move destroyed the fragile alliance between him and Crispin. Vince at one point tried to smooth things over, saying everyone has bad traits, but Hayes shouted him down.

These people are not very nice to me, I sadly concluded (again). And though we were not at home, I continued in my domestic enslavement to them, their clothes, their meals, their dishes, their rumpled beds. And all of this was my fault, of course, since the ultimate horribleness of one's horrible children is that one has only oneself to blame.

Hayes was at an age when a trip to Paris with his mother and her entourage was far from an appealing prospect. He had insisted on bringing his golf clubs, despite my increasingly hysterical explanations that there were no golf courses in Paris. Now he sat morosely in the tiny apartment, staring at his golf bag. One day, we took three subway lines to the outskirts of the city so he could hit balls on a driving range set up in the middle of a racetrack. This did not make either of us feel any better.

My mother, on the other hand, was no trouble at all. During the Italian restaurant imbroglio and most others, she repaired to a table in the alley with her martini, her cigarette, and one of the seven books she had imported from her public library. Having passed on the task of driving me insane to the younger generation, she could now relax. By the time the kids disappeared, she and Hayes had taken their flight home.

Around 5:45 a.m., the front gate clanged shut; Joyce, Crispin, and I all heard it. We looked up from our mugs into each other's eyes. Then we heard the soft chatter, the familiar voices, and raced out onto the stoop.

When the two of them saw the three of us lined up like that, shrimpy and exhausted, their jaws dropped. They'd had no idea how much worry they had caused us and had only even begun meandering their way home in the last couple of hours, my midnight curfew apparently forgotten. Meanwhile, we grown-ups filled them in on exactly what we had been through in their protracted absence.

While Vince, who has been my son all his life, didn't seem too concerned about the worry he had caused—just another drop in the bucket—my stepdaughter, Emma, felt very badly. It was rather refreshing for me to see the forlorn, anxious, apologetic look on her face. I don't think my boys ever learned to make that face.

Perhaps more time would have been devoted to the aftermath of this crisis if another hadn't broken in its wake. I received a phone call from my mother in which she used the f-word at least fifteen times, explaining that she and Hayes had been delayed overnight in Boston, then flown to Washington instead of Baltimore, and had arrived at BWI thirty-six hours behind schedule only to find that Hayes had lost my mother's car keys.

By this time, stress had sandblasted every synapse in my brain. I could imagine getting into this sort of situation with my mother, and my primary reaction was, better him than me.

For our last day, I pulled myself together and planned a three-stop outing: the famous Deyrolle taxidermy shop, a restaurant with a view, a carnival in the Tuileries. We set out gamely enough but hit the Paris-in-August trifecta. All three places were closed, despite the assurances in my guidebooks. At the sight of the carnies taking down the Ferris wheel, the youngest members of our party burst into tears.

Good thing we're leaving tomorrow, said Vince, before they roll up the streets.

At that point, believe it or not, it started to rain.

Ah well. Soon it would be September, and we would be back home in Glen Rock, Pennsylvania, where the fact that everything was open for business and we had four toilets in our house would not make us as happy as you might think.

OUR BIG FAT
NEW ORLEANS
GRADUATION

Though I have neither superpowers nor a signature form-fitting costume, I do have something in common with comic book heroes. I have a historic nemesis. Mine is a seventy-two-year-old Italian lady from Philadelphia, my first husband's mother.

This defender of decency, aka "Grandma Grace," has strong opinions and she sticks by them. Mickey Mouse, Marriott hotels, Jesus, and Coca-Cola are in. Barack Obama, Pepsi, and Marion Winik are out. Also on the blacklist, I learned during our trip to New Orleans for Vince's college graduation, is that ancient symbol of the French monarchy, the fleur-de-lis. I was admiring one in an abstract assemblage by one of the artists who hang work on the iron gates of Jackson Square. What a cool painting, I said.

I hate that floor de less! she retorted in her squeaky, somewhat Marge Simpson–ish voice. And look! It's everywhere!

But it always has been, I told her. It's, like, the official symbol of New Orleans.

Only since 2004! she replied heatedly.

Grandma Grace and I got along for about a half hour in the mid-nineties, both stoned on grief and somewhat delusional after the death of the young man who was her son and my husband. Before that and ever since, she has found little to appreciate in my character. Perhaps I seem to her to be a nasty cross between a controlling Jewish American princess and a self-indulgent smarty-pants. Perhaps I am. Still, you might think the fact that I produced and raised her darling grandsons would redeem me.

On the contrary, she has tried to protect them from me as best she can.

In recent years, as the boys have grown up, our rendezvous are fewer and further between. The last was at Hayes's graduation from Georgetown in 2010, for which she came down on a bus from her home in the Poconos. The ceremony went smoothly enough, but Grandma Grace does not enjoy celebrations of the chaotic, alcoholic sort my offspring and I go in for. She spent most of Hayes's graduation party in the basement reminiscing about Catholic school with a guest who unwittingly admitted having attended one. When I returned her to the Greyhound terminal, she literally leapt from my car with her roller bag and fled.

The stressfulness of this occasion was a chilling preview of what would go down in 2012, when Vince would graduate from Loyola in New Orleans. He would walk across the stage with his best friend since age three, Sam Shahin, whose parents have played a major supporting role in our lives. They were the family I wanted to be with—the family that likes me, for God's sake.

The significance of this graduation was even greater because New Orleans was the city where I had met the boys' father. My encouraging Vince to go to college there had been a way of strengthening our bond to a place I loved. From the moment I arrived at Mardi Gras in 1983, I had recognized this tropical mutant of a city, this mecca of Sodomites and Gomorrans, as my spiritual hometown. Among the misogynist gay guys, the drunken yet genteel Southerners, the skinny black people in kitchens, the fat white people on porches, the characters out of Tennessee Williams and Ellen Gilchrist and Anne Rice, I somehow fit right in.

Of course, that was in the years before the accursed fleur-de-lis took hold.

Ever since Hayes's swan song at Georgetown, I have been strategizing the final Big Easy commencement. I had to accept, finally, that my usual approach to Grandma Grace—saccharine toadying punctuated by flashes of rage—would be as successful as it had ever had been, which is to say, not very. I would do better if I had any idea *how* to do better (at least I think I would), and I have no doubt that our difficulties are as much my fault as hers. In fact, I've noticed that whenever I've written about our troubles, readers are just as likely to take her side as mine. She herself has no interest in reading anything I write, which is probably for the best.

The good news about Vince's graduation was that some of her other family members would attend with her, making arrangements, sharing flights and hotels. This was excellent. I could rent my own car and stay with my friends, swooping in only for key events. To further increase my chances of emotional survival, I decided to take not only my children, Hayes and Jane, but our dog Beau. (Ever since Southwest started letting small pets travel in the cabin for $75, I have become that nutty old lady who won't go anywhere without her dachshund.)

Vince's graduation was held in the Superdome, now the pimped-out Mercedes-Benz Superdome, having put its 2005 nightmare of semi-televised raping and thirst in the past. When I arrived with children and cousins in tow, I learned both the Shahins and the Grandma group had saved us seats.

What to do? Well, my eleven-year-old daughter Jane and I had joined Grace at the baccalaureate mass the day before, the only ones who had. I could tell by the faint smile that hovered briefly on her lips that she was glad to see us. And what if she was annoyed now? How much more annoyed could she be? I sat with my old friends, who had been through so many of the joys and trials of the last twenty years with me, and we launched into the nostalgia and boohooing.

Little Loyola New Orleans put on quite an extravaganza, complete with a medieval-castle stage set, jumbotrons, confetti explosions, and a jazz band. I couldn't help teasing Hayes about the contrast between this and the commencement at Georgetown, which had been of the high-school gymnasium variety. The only diversion from the name-droning was provided by the school's mascot, a bulldog, who lounged onstage during the proceedings.

After the ceremony, I met Grace in the aisle. That was amazing, I effused, wasn't it? No, she told me. Hayes's was way better!

I don't think the cake and champagne on the plaza convinced her either. But if things had ended at that point, I would have had the moral victory of keeping a smile on my face no matter what.

Alas.

Since it happened to be Mother's Day, the kids suggested we celebrate with brunch at Café du Monde. As the hour approached, I was still driving around town trying to scoop up all the sleeping partiers, and I put in a call to Grace. Yeah, Mar, she said grimly by way of hello. Her use of this nickname never seems affectionate, but perhaps it is—I can hardly claim to understand her.

Finally, we were assembled: the nine of us clustered around pushed-together tables at the crowded café, waiting. It occurred to me to try to organize our order in advance. Since the beignets come three to a plate, I could figure out how many orders and simplify the process. Like an idiot, I asked Grace and her group what they wanted.

We each want one, she said.

One beignet or one order of beignets? I said. They come three to an order.

We know that, Grace told me. We were here yesterday! We each want one.

One. One what? Now the aunt and uncle joined her, pointing to the table and chiming in. Perhaps I should have been able to understand that they each wanted their own order, but I could not. I snapped my head in the other direction and stared into the napkin holder, breathing heavily. My children watched me with trepidation.

Just in time, the elderly Polish waitress arrived to circumvent the violence. In a matter of hours, we would all be fleeing with our roller bags.

Goodbye, dear New Orleans, goodbye. I take with me my college-educated, Tabasco-swillin', bass-playin', crawfish-addicted Saints fan. I take with me two large plastic cups, once brimming with the finest of Bloody Marys. I take as well my Mother's Day gift, purchased by the kids from an artist in Jackson Square. The fleur-de-lis would have been good, but they found something better still: a painting of google-eyed aliens with the motto IT COULD BE WORSE lettered across it.

As they say in New Orleans: Yeah you right.

PARTY TIME IN THE LOST CITY

This is the first in a series of 134 articles about the Atlantis resort I will be writing to fund my upcoming Visa bill.

Family vacations are all about creating magical memories, and here's one we Winiks will treasure from our four-day visit to the Bahamas back in the summer of 2011.

It was 11:00 a.m., Day Two of our trip. Hayes and Vince, my twenty-four and twenty-two-year-old sons, were chillaxing on our eleventh-floor balcony. Fragrant smoke wafted through the railing over a phantasmagoric vista: mangrove and hibiscus, vast freeform pools surrounded by flotillas of lounges, a DJ in a gazebo spinning Usher for the midmorning mojito crowd, and beyond all that, the turquoise sea. In the other direction, we could see right into what we had dubbed "The Factory," a complex of loading docks and warehouses through which trucks and workers streamed continuously. Our Terrace View Room, as the reservation agent described it, was just $500/night on summer special.

Inside, twelve-year-old Jane had finished reviewing the map of the water park that is the centerpiece of the Atlantis resort (and you don't pay anything extra for it, which is a phrase I will be using only once today). Let's go! our energetic leader shouted at her slowpoke troop. Meanwhile, Vince's girlfriend Shannon was trying to determine which of her bikinis was most likely to survive the Leap of Faith.

Suddenly, on a whim, I slipped out to the terrace. My sons watched me curiously, as the last time I'd taken a hit of pot, in the early 2000s, I spent the next nine hours locked in my bedroom considering institutionalization as my New Year's party rolled on without me.

FAQ: How do you buy drugs at Atlantis?

Easy, dude, it's right on the beach! Find one of the freelance jet-ski rental guys the notice in your hotel room warns you not to have any dealings with. Vince recommends Mr. Pointy Tooth, who is the kingpin of the operation.

So, yeah. Whoa. I was really, really wasted. Sternly I ordered myself to remain calm.

Come on, Mommy! You said you would go on the slide today! Jane said, and if I could say no to that sweet, beautiful youngest child of mine, we wouldn't have been at Atlantis in the first place. I have never been to a resort in my life, never wanted to go to one, have always been the Paris-on-$10-a-day type of traveler. In August. But somehow we started hanging out with these rich friends who were all Atlantis this, Atlantis that, and Jane was hooked. I thought, what the hell, we'll do it once.

Once is right.

I trailed my group through acres of resort landscaping, which shamelessly combined real vegetation, birds, and sea creatures (a manta ray the size of my Yaris) with faux caves and waterfalls, all of it nestled among turreted pink hotels and seahorse monuments. It was sort of Mesoamerican, sort of Egyptian, sort of Greek, sort of Gothic—an Epcot Center of ancient civilization! Bizarrely, it also featured giant blowups of the trippy characters of Cartoon Network's *Adventure Time*, like Finn the Human, Jake the Dog, Lady Rainicorn, and the Lumpy Space Princess.

Do you think they paid *Adventure Time* or *Adventure Time* paid them? Jane wondered.

I think everybody pays them. The 2,900 hotel guests, at least one of whom, in the Royal Tower Bridge Suite, is in for $25,000 per night; the day-trippers at the water attractions, the gamblers at the casino, the revelers at the nightclubs, the yacht crowd at the marina, all of us.

At last we plopped our tubes into the Current, a mile-long river ride. As we bobbed dreamily beneath the palm fronds and buff Bahamian lifeguards, my head, initially propped on my hand in a jaunty pose, sank toward the pillowy tube. Mmmm. The lovely soporific effect was way better than marijuana psychosis.

Wake up, Mom, I heard Jane say, and I opened my eyes. I was turned backward, facing Hayes, who was laughing evilly. Our tubes were inching up some sort of conveyor belt.

Mom! We're about to go over the falls! Jane said, trying to spin me around.

What? I clapped my hand over my sunglasses. Was this the vertical two-hundred-foot drop off the peak of the Mayan pyramid into the shark tank?

Jane spent the next three days imitating my pitiful scream as I went over the edge—less a "woo-hoo!" than the sort of plea for mercy once heard at the Spanish Inquisition.

Mom! Wasn't that great? said Jane, dragging me onward to the Abyss, a body slide entered from a platform tucked beneath five-story-high yellow tulips that somehow recalled the Hunger Games. But no time for literary musings. I had to stay with my family.

Of course, I eventually took the wrong fork and ended up in a watery cavern alone. Just as I caught sight of Jane in the distance, scouting around for me, I accidentally slid down a chute into a pool. I sat dumbfounded until my hero came bounding around a curve.

Mom, said Jane, I think you might be taking too much of your medication.

Cheapness and generosity run side by side in me. Atlantis kicked those warring impulses into full-on battle. After just a couple of days of $12 cocktails and $40 entrées and $7 bottles of water (all charged with cartoon-character plastic room keys), I began to lose my grip. It seemed like a bargain when dinner at the Bobby Flay restaurant was only $323, compared with the $453 I'd dropped at Nobu or $466 at the Jean-Georges little hut on the beach. Though I'd never had much sympathy for people who run up credit card bills in the tens of thousands, suddenly I understood how it could happen. When you're so out of your league, it all becomes Monopoly money. And you have to eat. Once the fam had whipped through the mountain of trail mix, beef jerky, and energy bars

I'd imported from Trader Joe's, what could we do but hit the $25 breakfast buffet? Twenty-five dollars—you forget what that can buy in the real world. Anyway, I think it was only $20 for Jane. I ordered myself a cup of coffee and sneaked bites off Shannon's plate (even though the waiter promptly removed my silverware to prevent just this).

That night, I got a little cranky on the ten-mile walk back to the room through the medieval passages, underwater ruins, and Bulgari-store jetways. The big kids were racing ahead to get ready for their night out, and Jane was peering curiously into the video game arcade. She asked me if she could buy something, I believe; anyway, there was some request that involved money. I was feeling overspent and underappreciated. In fact, I was feeling like my mother, who for all her many virtues was a lifelong lousy tipper.

Basically, it had been a long day of intoxication and constipation. So I yelled at Jane and she got huffy and stomped off.

And there I was, crossing the torch-lit Hunger Games lagoon by myself. Should I make a left at Chichen Itza or head straight to the barracudas?

Then I saw Jane, lurking up ahead in a stand of palms. Mad as she was, she wasn't going to let me get lost. She continued this tiptoe surveillance procedure all the way back to the hotel, where we quickly made up. After all, we had our dolphin swim ($264 for two) the very next morning!

Jane and I cuddled in bed and watched the Food Network, while the others ran off to get wasted and throw their money away. I had given the boys my mother's blackjack system, a creased and yellowed photocopy with ragged edges and penciled notations.

After a half century of avid gambling, my mother died in the black. Yet even with the secret paper, her young descendants lost more than $700 in a couple of nights.

Hayes, I heard, dropped $300 worth of chips in the sand during a party with some girls who had flown in by private jet. Unbelievably, he later found them—then lost the stack on a single bet. Vince, on the other hand, found an unspent $20 on the dresser one morning and ran back to the casino before coffee. When he returned without it, he nonetheless seemed to believe that because he had been up $60 the night before, he had won, despite the fact that his activities had bankrupted his newly founded music production company.

On our last day, as the losses were totted up, Jane surveyed her brothers coldly: unshaven, hungover specimens of fiscal irresponsibility. She shrugged. I've lost all respect for you, she said.

For me, she suggested a day at the spa and swimming laps, as well as a break from my "self-absorbed" fixation on reading the comments people post on my columns.

Meanwhile, there was so much of Atlantis we had not yet seen. We'd missed at least three expensive restaurants, and I had just learned you could snorkel in the aquarium. I never got over to the yacht marina to check out the so-called "millionaire Starbucks." At least we got to spend some quality time with Jackie, a thirty-eight-year-old dolphin mother of three. Jackie had an amazing story: she'd been cooped up in some off-brand fish park in Mississippi until it was wrecked by Hurricane Katrina. After months swimming around the debris-filled Gulf, her whole posse had been rescued and relocated to Atlantis. Honeymoon heaven! Three of them got pregnant the first year.

For me, it was back home to Baltimore, where we arrived to

find my hot, sticky house overrun by mice and fleas. Within seconds of our arrival, we were all vacuuming, scrubbing, and spraying, transformed from pampered travelers to embittered custodial staff.

We're in the Factory, said Jane sadly.

And so we will be until next year, when I plan to take our vacation at an eco-resort in the jungle with twelve-step meetings.

CRIME REPORT: ROBBED IN PERU

Policia Nacional del Peru—Policia de Turismo Cusco Date: 23 June 2013; hour: 12:10 p.m.

In the city of Cusco in the Office of the Tourist Police, the tourist MARION LISA WINIK (55), a U.S. national, single, a teacher, presented herself without personal documents or papers of transit through the city. The aforementioned tourist had suffered the loss of her brown handbag in a cafeteria . . .

Mallmanya Inn—Date: 23 June 2013; hour: 6:10 a.m.

In the unheated breakfast room of our hotel, I was writing a journal entry titled "Cranky in Cusco." Though earlier I'd been having a pretty good time on my educational tour of Peru with twenty-five seventh graders, their teachers, and some of their parents, Day Six found me in a snit. I'd broken a fifty-five-year ban on organized travel to take this tour with my daughter, Jane, and I'd begun to remember why I might not like such a trip. I also remembered that I was not all that interested in ruins or the brutish ancient civilizations behind them.

Machu Picchu, I admitted, was the best of the bunch. If you like mountain scenery. Which I don't. Hoping to get the ill humor out of my system, I journaled at length about the smelly hotel, the boring food, the effects of the endless walking on my arthritic knees.

When Jane came down with a group of six girls for breakfast, I suggested we skip the daily rolls and margarine and try our luck elsewhere. A few blocks away, we came upon a fancy pastry shop where I was only slightly surprised to find almost all the other members of our tour group already dining. Things were looking up, I felt. So much so that I pulled out my journal to note that fact. La Valeriana. Good quiche.

When I put my journal back into my bag, I saw I had a text message from the short-lived boyfriend who had broken up with me on the eve of this journey. I had just begun to reply, stabbing at the touchscreen keyboard, when the waitress brought our bill. I reached down for my purse, which had been wedged between me and the girl beside me on the bench. It wasn't there. It wasn't on the other side of me, or on the floor.

Since none of us had even seen anyone approach the table, this was clearly the work of a magician.

So much for "Cranky in Cusco"—the journal was now history, along with my money, credit cards, ID, and the novel I was reading. Jane's iPhone was in there, too, but thanks to that texting ex, mine was not. Worst, I had lost my passport.

During the time I was at the police station filing my report, four other robbery victims came in. Officer Juvenal Zerceda Vasquez regretfully explained that this was the weekend of the Festival of the Sun, when professional thieves come to Cusco from all over the country. I pictured a chartered bus, *Ocean's 11* on the DVD player, and umbrella drinks.

He proceeded to type up a detailed description of every item in the purse, then printed the report using a dot-matrix printer and a sheet of carbon paper. My wrinkled copy is all that remains of the *estuche multicolor conteniendo lapiceros y maquillaje* ("multicolored pouch containing pens and makeup"), the *cuadernillo personal* ("personal journal"), and the *billetera floreado* ("flowered wallet"). Actually, it was polka-dot, but I couldn't get that across.

Next, he let me use the phone to call the U.S. Embassy. The woman who answered brusquely informed me that I would need to change my flight to Lima, get passport photos, fill out the DS-11 and DS-64 online, and by the way, the Peruvian immigration office closes at noon. Since all this would cost a pretty penny, I should immediately message my contacts in the United States to explain my plight and ask for money. (God, I thought, are some of those emails for real?)

When are you supposed to fly home? she asked. Tuesday evening, I said. It was Sunday.

It'll be tight, she said grimly. Tomorrow is a national holiday.

And there's nothing you can do for me?

No, she said firmly. Nothing.

I returned to the hotel in a police cruiser. Too depressed to remain conscious, I fell into a deep sleep of many hours. When I awoke, any complaints I may have had about organized tourism were forgotten, for it had become my fairy godmother.

The director of our tour group had been on the phone to the head office in Boston.

They had changed my flight from Cusco to Lima and arranged for a local to meet me at the plane. I was handed a Xerox copy of my old passport and an envelope of cash for cabs and fees. In the meantime, I was advised to relax and enjoy the national holiday.

Believe it or not, I did.

My escort, Martin, turned out to be an ex-skateboarder whose band had once played the Warped Tour. With his help, I was able to negotiate taxi fees, maneuver through traffic, fill out forms, get photos, swear I told the truth and nothing but the truth, then race across town with my brand-new passport to the Peruvian immigration office, which as you know closes at noon, but where the line to find out what line to wait in is a mile long, where armed guards are charged with preventing you from asking questions, where you need two copies and a receipt for your payment from the bank, where at 11:45 a fat man puts everybody's passport in a pile and gets on the phone to order lunch.

Having been in a state of extreme stress for eight hours, I was starting to lose it. I slumped to the floor in exhaustion, wondering vaguely where I would sleep that night, what would happen to Jane when she got home if I was unable to rejoin the group before they left the country.

Martin was a mild sort, but he rose to the occasion. Braving the guard, he stormed the counter and got my passport back. At which point the fat man returned everyone else's passports, too, so that we walked out of there like Olympic heroes.

Then we returned to the airport and met up with my tour group, and we all came home.

There is a reason these things happen to me and not other people, people who lock their doors and use fanny packs when abroad and don't take their passports out of the hotel. My son Vince has kindly called it an "aura of vulnerability."

May it fail to kill me and continue to provide amusement for us all.

THE END OF THE
WORLD AS WE
KNOW IT

My daughter Jane, born on the summer solstice of the millennium, was excited by the prospect that the year 2012 would be the end of the world, according to the predictions of the Mayan calendar, the *I Ching*, and *The New York Times* Styles section. In her opinion, nothing could be more awesome than to bear witness to this cataclysmic, presumably pyrotechnic spectacle and its unimaginable blockbuster aftermath.

As Jane seems to suspect, as she herself has taught me, even the end of the world won't be the end of the world.

For example, about fifteen years ago, I was at my ob-gyn's office getting a Pap smear. You still have the IUD, she remembered, her head between my legs, no doubt staring the thing in its shiny eye.

Yep, I replied, in the laconic way of one in stirrups.

And you turn forty this year, right?

Yep.

Well, if you're thinking of having any more kids, you'd better get a move on.

What?! I squawked. Are you crazy? If it weren't physically impossible at that moment, my knees would have snapped together for emphasis.

With my sons aged ten and eight, was I going to have another baby? I don't think so! With my single life running smoothly, would I get married again? Hell, no. Would I sell my beloved house in my home of more than twenty years, Austin, Texas, and move 1,700 miles across the country? Double-triple no freaking way. Would I perhaps choose to live in a rural area in Central Pennsylvania? Had I even heard of Central Pennsylvania? OK, stop now, you're killing me.

Of course I did every one of these things.

When I first started changing my whole life, just a few months after that doctor visit, it was easy. I was as corny as Kansas in August and as high as a flag on the Fourth of July: in love, in love, in love with a wonderful guy. Emotionally, I was already gone, with each visit during our year of long-distance romance ratcheting the intensity up a notch. Logistically, I was catching up fast. Breaking the news to my sons, putting my house on the market, calling movers, saying goodbye to my friends—no problem.

As a self-employed widow, I had no job and no ex-spouse to hold me back. I knew there were things I would miss from my life in Austin, but I didn't care. I had always looked for the wild card in the deck, and I had definitely drawn it this time. I threw a big party, shoved my cats and kids in the car, and got on the interstate.

Three days later, Memorial Day weekend 1999, I arrived at my giant new house in the middle of nowhere and burst into tears. It was very, very hot, much hotter than it had been during the January reconnaissance visit when I first fell in love with the airy rooms and wood-plank floors, and there was no air-conditioning. With those beautiful floors completely covered by mountains of unpacked moving boxes, I suddenly noticed the ugly wallpaper in the dining room.

After a brief, tasteful meltdown, I pulled myself together. I had to. I had a houseful of dislocated, riled-up children, and the wedding to my second husband was in a couple of weeks. Definitely no time for a full-bore collapse.

By fall, I had overcome the immediate hurdles and was pregnant to boot. Though my new husband and I were thrilled about it, both our mothers were dubious. Shit! said my mother-in-law, a one-time population-control activist. Jesus Christ! commented my mother, who told people both my sister and I were "idiots" for having additional children in our forties.

No matter how I'd reacted to my ob-gyn's question just a year earlier, now I wanted a baby: a new person from all this newness, a concrete expression of us.

Nevertheless, I had a tough time during that pregnancy, which burgeoned over the course of my first winter and spring in Pennsylvania. With my sons back in school and my new husband busy at the college where he taught, it dawned on me what I had done.

I was completely alone. I had not one friend, no doctor, no

dentist, no place to get my hair cut or my nails done or buy nutritional yeast. Where was my running trail, my Mexican restaurant? As the snow fell outside my window, the pain of losing everything and everyone I had left finally hit me. Meanwhile, the house had some flaws, my husband was sometimes distant, my children and stepchildren were becoming surly preteenagers. Soon I was as big as a young whale and wearing the same gray sweatpants every day.

On the plus side, my doctor assured me you could take Zoloft while pregnant.

Perhaps you have not seen *Bride of Chucky*, a rather undistinguished horror film featuring a scar-faced baby doll and his glass-eyed, ratty-tressed little tramp of a wife. My favorite scene is the final one in the graveyard, wherein both Chucky and Mrs. Chucky are brought low. But as the crusty detective bends over Mrs. Chucky's charred corpse, prodding her tiny torso with an inquisitive finger, something stirs beneath her clothes. He recoils, but not fast enough. A glob of blood and mucus shoots out from under her skirt into his face, and a few heaves later, Baby Chucky pops out behind it and immediately sets on the detective with his pointed teeth.

You know, that cannot have been her first baby. They just don't come out like that when they have to blaze the trail. Once you've got a well-worn path, it's another story. In fact, the birth of my daughter Jane in June 2000, though distinct in many other details, proceeded with some of the same *éclat* as Mrs. Chucky's delivery. Ouch, ouch, ouch, whoosh. Alas, poor Mrs. Chucky's eyelids fluttered shut for the last time after splattering the detective with her offspring. I, on the other hand, felt immediately reborn, as if I would float right up off the delivery table with joy. It was over: the pregnancy, the labor, the peeing every five minutes, the whole damn thing!

Then my first daughter, my second-marriage, premenopause bonus, was placed in my arms, and I wafted gently back to Earth.

For the next year or so, I had the daily joy of watching my baby girl wake up in the morning. The dark fringe of lashes fluttered against her rosy cheek. Her blueberry eyes, dancing with light. And the first thing she saw—the ceiling fan, the kitty, or, if we were lucky, one of her family—was the recipient of a brilliant, wide, toothless, guileless smile. And then they just kept coming, those smiles, like a stream of bubbles from the mouth of a carnival fish. Sometimes I had to wonder if wasn't all that Zoloft I took when I was pregnant.

For Jane the infant, every day was a fresh start, one she met merrily and head-on, with none but the most cheerful expectations. Very similar to the way she later, at eleven and a half, living in Baltimore with her divorced mom, faced the prospect of total world destruction by every astronomical, astrological, and supra-historical means.

In small ways, the world is ending all the time, and for a mother this is particularly true, as raising kids invites a constant onslaught of milestones, game-changing developments, and sudden, unexpected new realities. Sometimes these new realities arrive with a burst of joy and inspiration, and other times they feel more like colliding with the asteroid Nibiru as the sun aligns with Sagittarius at the center of the universe. Sometimes it is a bad dream that won't end. Other times, it is a reverie you hope to bask in indefinitely.

Either way, get ready for the end of the world.

A MOTHER OF A
CERTAIN AGE

When people learn that I had a baby in my forties, they often comment, I bet that keeps you young. I gather they are referring to the age-defying effects of chasing children around the backyard and watching *Teletubbies*. But I wasn't young when I had Jane. I already had two boys who were putting gray in my hair, and I added two stepchildren when I married the man who would become Jane's father. So keeping me young was really not possible, nor has reinvigoration been the gist since.

A couple of Wednesdays ago, for example, at about 8:30 in the evening, I started a bath for Jane and her two friends, the Bacha sisters, who were at our house for a sleepover because all are attending basketball camp together. Once they were situated in their bubbles, I went downstairs to call my sixteen-year-old son, Vince, on his cell phone, since he had not come home after getting off work at the pool.

Vince walked in just as I hit the kitchen. Since he had been in the house less than five minutes since school let out, I suggested that he stay in for the night. No way, he said; he was only here to pick up his stepbrother, Sam, fifteen, so they could go "chill" at Trav's.

What exactly is involved in chilling at Trav's I will leave to your imagination—God knows, it's had a vivid dramatic life in mine. In any case, feeling that enough chilling at Trav's had gone on of late, I denied permission for the excursion. Shock, outrage, and furious debate ensued. The main arguments offered were that they are teenagers, it is summer, and I am stupid.

I had to interrupt the showdown to go upstairs, get the girls out of the bath, and deliver them to my husband for bedtime reading. Then back downstairs to continue ruining teenage lives. Disgruntled, Sam and Vince filed to the basement to play electric guitars and mess around on the internet.

Meanwhile, in the living room, my oldest son, Hayes, and his girlfriend, Dana, were home from college and entwined on the couch watching *Law and Order SVU*. It was a delightful episode in which a necrophiliac is suspected of raping a girl in a coma. I was not finished folding the laundry to this stimulating accompaniment when my husband appeared to tell me that the girls could not fall asleep and were now in our bed.

I dashed upstairs to move them and sing "Somewhere over the Rainbow." Though this song offers serious challenges to a person of such limited vocal talents as myself, I find its plaintive, desperate vision of a happier future in a more welcoming place often fits my mood at this time of the evening. However, I had to cut off in the middle of the lemon drops because I thought I heard the front door creak open and shut. But no, when I got downstairs all the prisoners were still in their cellblocks.

I tried to stay awake to keep things under control, but at 10:45 I crawled into bed beside my sleeping husband, Jane, the Bachas, and our miniature dachshund. About an hour later, something woke me. I rushed downstairs and the TV-watching son confirmed my suspicions: They just rolled, he said.

Indeed, my car was gone from the driveway.

The next half hour was devoted to reeling them back in by cell phone and confiscating car keys. Brief curses and imprecations were exchanged, with plans to continue disciplinary action on the morrow.

If you think a perimenopausal woman goes right back to sleep when awoken at midnight, you are quite mistaken. I finally dozed off at around 3:00, when again something woke me.

Dammit, Vince, I growled. But it was little Jane, half-asleep and weeping with embarrassment, having uncharacteristically wet the bed. I dragged myself up to help and comfort her. Fortunately, the Bacha sisters slept through this phase of the action.

Back in bed, now with husband, dachshund, and daughter, I began to worry about getting up at 6:30 to get the girls to camp. My husband, wide awake at this point, went down to lower the volume on the video game being played in the basement, which somehow thumps directly into our mattress.

A couple of hours later the alarm indeed went off, and I started making pancakes and finding shoes and fixing ponytails for wacky hair day. Though there was little danger of seeing Vince and Sam before noon, I meditated on the details of their punishment (inevitably less draconian than it should have been; I am notorious for the lameness of my penalties). I fed the dog and the cats and helped Hayes cook his organic steel-cut oat groats, because it's not just teenage girls on fad diets anymore. I filled the girls' water bottles and sent them out to the car. Then I tossed back a couple of Aleves with the last of my coffee and started out on another day of rejuvenation.

INVISIBLE INK

One of the few times I have felt like a hero of any kind was the day fifteen-year-old Vince found the decomposing body of our long-lost cat in a creek near our house. We'll have to just leave him there, said Vince. He was therefore pretty impressed when I managed to get what used to be Pudge off the rock, out of the water, and into double Hefty bags.

Certain tasks of parenting have a mythic quality, and over time you may take your demigod status for granted. You give life, you administer justice, you heal, you bestow, you redeem. You bury the dead cat. But in fact, your authority is far from ultimate: not only there are sorrows that cannot be managed and children who will not be managed either, but as I have recently learned, you rule only at the pleasure of strangers at the county courthouse.

Not long after Pudge's funeral, I sat beside Vince in a courtroom. Two years earlier, when he was in eighth grade, he and three other boys guzzled some booze and committed an act of vandalism involving thirty-two headstones and ninety-nine bananas, leaving the graveyard a wreck a week before Easter. I knew nothing about it for quite some time. Then one day the cops showed up at our house and Vince confessed. I was horrified and shocked, and of course swung into disciplinary action: I punished him, I lectured him, I took him to counseling. He wanted to help pay for the damages or even help fix them himself, but suddenly the police stopped returning our calls.

What I didn't understand was that we were past the point when a phone call would help, past the apologize-and-help-clean-up phase. I finally got it two years later when the system worked its way around to our case and the real authorities arrived on the scene.

The affable public defender, the young probation officer in jeans, the obviously decent judge in his black robes. He seemed to hear his words afresh each of the four times he repeated the series of questions designed to make the boys think twice before confirming their guilt. The felony charges they faced were very serious.

I'm sorry, said the first boy; I'm sorry, said the second and third; I'm sorry, said my boy in his baggy suit and fresh haircut, my boy a foot taller than I am, and I waited in all my smallness for the judge to pronounce his sentence. For the probation officer to make her assessment, for the drug-and-alcohol evaluator to come back with a report.

We're not going to recommend a placement, they reassured me—meaning they wouldn't be taking my son away to live somewhere else. Great, I thought, still sick to my stomach.

Instead, it was ninety hours of community service, weekly drug testing at the courthouse, and an after-school victim-awareness course held in a reform school in a nasty part of town. My son emerged pie-eyed each week, half-ambling, half-scurrying across the parking lot to my car. I would turn off NPR and hear his stories of baby-scalding and clerk-knifing, and think dark thoughts about the juvenile justice system. But in the end I believe the whole ordeal made him a little more cautious about choosing his place on the criminal spectrum.

And they let him do the community service at a local organic farm run by benevolent, hardworking old hippies.

We were lucky, but I was not reassured. I had seen a glimpse of what can happen. What a shock when the great and powerful Mommy tumbles from her throne, her phone calls not taken, her school notes carried off in the breeze, her boo-boo bunny melting on the floor. You know the boo-boo bunny, right, a plastic-sheathed cube of ice dressed in fuzzy rabbit ears, used to soothe the cries of mildly injured toddlers. It works like a charm—until the day it doesn't. Like time-outs and pet funerals and curfews, like so much of what we do as parents, it is a kind of make-believe. Our empires are provisional, our authority temporary, stamped with an expiration date in invisible ink.

You do the best you can until you can't anymore. Then you take a deep breath and join the mortals.

WHICH HURTS
WORSE?

~

When you send a child to college, you may feel a little sensitive about the imminent outsourcing or termination of most of your parental duties. However, if your nest is not truly empty, you will not be the only person affected by the upcoming changes. For example, since all four of her half-siblings moved out by the time she was eight, my daughter Jane has been raised as an only child. The darling of the entire family, she will never experience the ruthless machinations of a fully operational sibling regime. Our own began to crumble in 2006 when the children of my family lost their dynastic leader, my older son Hayes.

When Hayes departed for college a few states south, it took two cars to fit all his stuff, so his brother Vince chauffeured me and little Jane in my car and King Hayes followed in his Jeep. Vince was so excited about his learner's permit. It was exciting for me, too, especially when he did things like darting into the left lane on the DC beltway when traffic was so thick Hayes couldn't follow us.

What are you doing, Vince? I cried, and a few minutes later, when Hayes still hadn't reappeared, I called him on the cell phone to make sure he knew the name of our exit. He answered me with a stream of recriminations, though he knew I was not driving and what had just happened was out of my control.

Soon afterward, Vince got annoyed by my direction-giving and began shouting that I was crazy and he would never drive anywhere with me again. Right then, Jane began whining from the backseat that she needed to go the bathroom. Now! I have to go now! she insisted.

A gas station appeared on the right and our maddened group swerved into it, Hayes somehow suddenly right behind us. The boys got out of their respective cars.

Dude! said Vince to his older sibling. I'm so sorry about what happened back there!

Dude, said Hayes magnanimously, clapping his back, it was cool. I wasn't mad.

God, Mom is such a freak!

For real! Let's go in and get some beef jerky.

In disbelief, I watched them start to head into the gas station.

I'm hungry, too, said Jane. Her main man Hayes turned around and tossed her up on his shoulders. I'll get you a snack, babe, he said.

Didn't you have to go to the bathroom? I called after her. Damn kids.

In the weeks after we left Hayes in his dorm, things were weird and sad. Certainly, ganging up on Mom wasn't the same.

A two-man junta, particularly if one of the corps is Cindy Lou Who, is very different than three against one, or five against one if stepsibling reservists are on tap. And the house was just so quiet without the beatings and roughhousing, without Hayes's famous game, "Which Hurts Worse?"

Meanwhile, I kept staring wistfully at the leftovers piling up in the fridge; I couldn't seem to adjust the quantities I cooked for dinner, and Hayes was the only one who ate leftovers anyway. Not only did Vince revile anything encased in tinfoil, Saran, or Tupperware, he was always at band practice at dinnertime and favored pretzels dipped in Tabasco sauce when he returned. Jane, on the other hand, ate pasta with butter and cheese. She also ate pasta with butter and cheese.

One day I ran into Vince's guidance counselor in the high school parking lot. Vince seems so different this year, she told me.

Really? I said. Like how?

She thought a minute. Well, the other day I saw him in the hall, and he gave me a smile and said, Hello, Mrs. Dzwonczyk. He never did that before!

Wow, I thought. That *is* hard to believe.

When I reported this conversation to a friend who was in a similar situation, she suggested that some sort of gravitational shift was underway in our families. She had never realized how exclusively her family's dinner conversation focused on her older son until he left, and they started to talk to the younger one. Dungeons & Dragons is so interesting, once you understand it, she gushed, aglow with her new crush.

How far can this go? I wondered as I stared at a plate of left-over homemade sushi rolls in the refrigerator. Vince, I said, isn't sushi one of your favorite foods?

He thought a minute. Yeah, he said, give me that, then settled down beside Jane to watch *The Fairly OddParents*. Well, well, well. It seemed Vince had begun to notice a few job openings around here: eater of leftovers, friend of little sisters, greeter of guidance counselors.

So it goes every fall. The parents go around whining about their emptying nests while the little brothers and sisters move up a peg in the pecking order, unable to believe at first that no one's swatting them down.

Do you miss Hayes? I asked Vince one day while we were watching a movie on television. It was exciting for both of us to learn that our television received channels other than ESPN, the official network of the Hayes administration.

Well, he said. He hasn't been gone that long.

But you lived with him every day of your life for sixteen years, and then he just disappeared.

Vince looked around at the wide-open plain of the living room, vacant of rampaging bison and marauding tribal leaders. Yeah, he said. That's what I mean.

These days, the boys are thirty-one and twenty-nine. One is in private equity, the other is a music producer and tours with a rock band. When they do get together, they mostly just drink and carouse, old friends rather than ruler and subject, or even rivals. I believe they have an argument or two for old times' sake, late at night after most of the beer is gone.

They are both much nicer to me than they used to be, though they still answer each other's phone calls when they won't answer mine. Perhaps I could change my name from "Mom" to something more compelling.

I keep a black-and-white picture on my dresser of Vince in a swimming pool at about age five, wailing into the camera with scrunched eyes and wide-open mouth. For a long time I didn't even notice that Hayes was lurking behind him in the background, smirking evilly, until Hayes himself pointed it out. When I showed Vince, he seemed filled with nostalgia.

That's it, he said, grinning. That was our childhood.

THE EVOLUTION
OF US

~

After I left home for college at seventeen, I never lived in my hometown in New Jersey again, and at the time of my mother's death I
was a three-and-a-half-hour drive away. But in those last months,
the distance between us evaporated. We were in a hospital room,
me sleeping on the floor beside her bed; we were in her bathroom,
me sitting on the closed toilet to make sure she didn't fall in the
shower; we were in her car, me behind the wheel, off to Costco to
pick up the many pills, shots, and syrups it took to keep her going.

Cast in the roles of seventy-nine-year-old woman with lung
cancer and her devoted fifty-year-old daughter, you could hardly
see the relationship we once had or the people we once were.
But roll back the clock to 1975 or so. She was a golfing, bridge-
playing, stock-market-investing conservative. I was a bohemian in
training, a poet, a hitchhiking vegetarian. Our hairstyles alone—

her bouffant waves set weekly at the salon, my ratty mess brushed about as often—said it all.

I saw her as the emblem of what I would never be. In fact, I figured out what I wanted to be by saying, Not that. Not every teenager is quite as determined to diverge 180 degrees from her nearest role model as I was, but for all my dedication to nonconformism, I was following a rather well-worn path. So, if a person rebels against her parents, then her own child rebels against her—what do you think happens?

Not long after he could talk, my son Hayes expressed his desire to wear designer clothes, play football and golf, and sell junk bonds. As soon as he could understand what kind of people were in his immediate circle—a free-thinking writer mom, a hairdresser dad, their artsy, progressive friends—he began to wonder if there had been a mix-up in the hospital. But then he got to know my mother, of whose company he was somewhat deprived since we lived in Texas and she was still in Jersey. Once she drove him to his first golf lesson in her Lexus, the matter of his lineage was cleared up. You had only to see them hunkered down in the halfway house in their polo shirts, sipping Snapple and discussing the NFL draft, to see exactly how much can skip a generation.

If I was Hayes's version of "not that," my mother was "all that"—at eleven, he listed her as his hero on his Myspace page. Most of the time, I found the situation rather charming. Looking back at my own upbringing, I saw how wisely my mother had handled my choices—tolerating them in a way that communicated both disagreement and acceptance, a way that kept her in my life and in my head. When I made mistakes she forgave me. She showed up at every poetry reading I invited her to, and she enjoyed them. No longer cast as my opponent, she was the de facto president of my fan club.

Then, as a junior in high school, Hayes announced his intention to shoot for a nomination to the U.S. Naval Academy in Annapolis. My mother was thrilled. For me, it was a bit of a shock.

As I talked it over with friends, I saw that Hayes was typical of a whole slice of his generation, rebelling against their Deadhead parents by becoming clean-cut, upstanding members of the establishment. Bankers. Military recruits. Born-again Wall Street traders. If there's one thing we flower-power people had to notice, it was the fact that our kids were doing just what we did—i.e., whatever would most horrify their elders.

And so, as Hayes embarked on the arduous process of securing a nomination to the Academy, I followed my mother's example and hung in there with him. He filled out applications, wrote letters, took physical exams, and made long drives to see congressmen around the state; I proofread and took his suit to the cleaners. Then the two of us went to Annapolis with my mother and great-uncle, an alum who attended in the fifties, for the Navy–Rice game. As the cadets marched onto the football field in full dress uniform with the band playing "Over There," my mother had tears on her cheeks. Hayes was rapt.

A few months later, we got word that he had received the senator's nomination.

But right on its heels came a phone call—he was medically disqualified due to his scoliosis, a minor condition that had not required treatment nor stopped him from playing varsity football. In fact, it was I who had insisted he mention it on the physical history form. Now it looked like I had sabotaged his dream.

However, by then Hayes had spent a weekend on campus among the plebes, who passed both Friday and Saturday nights sitting on their geometrically-tucked-in beds playing video games. The scales of military life had begun to fall from his eyes. He was surprisingly quick to forgive me.

On my mother's last Christmas among us, Hayes and I drove to New Jersey together to pick her up so she wouldn't spend the holidays alone. But by the time we got her back to our house, I wasn't sure we'd done the right thing—she was too weak to do anything but lie on the living room couch, draped in blankets and a post-chemo turban.

Thankfully, she perked up on Christmas morning, first watching her seven-year-old namesake open a parade of individually wrapped Webkinz, then becoming quite enchanted with Hayes's present to me: a brown tweed skirt and crisp white blouse. I lifted the garments from the tissue paper and held them in the air, a bit nonplussed. I live on a farm, I work at home . . . does anything about me say "tweed skirt?"

My mother, however, could not say enough about the "terrific outfit." She snatched the skirt from me and examined the label, exclaiming approvingly. Then she began to brainstorm all the many occasions to which I might wear these items. Meetings! she suggested. Don't you go to meetings?

I just kept smiling. I knew Hayes would forgive me when I exchanged the gift.

My mother and I had forgiven each other long ago.

GRAND THEFT
LITHO

In case you think your mother's death is going to put a stop to her always being right about everything and your coming up always just short of the mark, I draw your attention to the Case of the Missing Calder.

During the nine months of my mother's illness in 2007 and 2008, my sister Nancy and I spent as much time as we had since we were kids in our childhood home, a ranch house in a fifty-year-old development in Monmouth County, New Jersey. It was an hour and a half for Nancy from Suffern, New York, and three hours for me from Glen Rock, Pennsylvania, but we came as often as we could. It was surely one of my mother's last pleasures—as golf, bridge, theater, books, and finally even *Jeopardy!* were taken from her—to see us mutate into the Winik Girls again.

As Nancy and I spelled each other at doctor's appointments, in the hospital, and at her bedside, our mother gradually turned over to us not just medical and household decisions but the management of the intricate, ruthlessly organized empire we referred to as Jane Winik Incorporated. My CPA sister was appointed treasurer and I, the writer, became secretary. Actually, the division of labor occurred after my approach to record-keeping of bill payments and bank deposits was deemed inadequate.

In general and as always, both of us were killing ourselves to please our mother and we mostly succeeded, but there were a few things she didn't quite trust us on, and it turned out she was right.

Even before the days of handing over safe deposit box keys and signing powers of attorney, my mother feared that my sister and I did not fully appreciate the value of the small number of artists' prints and oil paintings she and my late father had collected. For one thing, she knew that this art was not to either of our taste. There was the depressing modernist cityscape, the twirling, impastoed tango dancers, the "cubist" snow-roofed barn, the obligatory Don Quixote in the powder room. But, she would point out, the Vasarely certainly is worth something! And the Calder!

My mother's Alexander Calder print, which hung in a place of honor in the living room under its own art lamp, was (as my sister has just read me from the authentication) a red, blue, and yellow abstract lithograph titled Caracol, number sixty-five of seventy-five, bought by my parents in 1980. On the day of the home sale at which we hoped to sell my mother's remaining furniture and possessions (we'd already given thirty-seven bags of perfectly kept, size six-petite suits, dresses, and golf attire to Jewish Family and

Children's Services), both it and the Vasarely were stowed in my old bedroom with other items not for sale.

The sale was to begin at nine on a Saturday, and neither my sister nor I made it there in time. When the real estate agent who was selling the house for us got there at 8:30, there were a dozen people waiting, and when he unlocked the door they poured in in a frenzy. By the time I arrived at 10:30, my sister was on the front lawn with one of my mother's lifelong best friends, discussing the theft of the entire set of my grandmother's silver flatware. (It was in the drawer of a highboy, also not for sale.) I walked in, went straight to the back bedroom, and determined that the Calder also was gone.

The rest of the day was a blur. The poor flummoxed real estate agent thought he might have sold a painting tagged at $5 to a blond lady who worked at Home Depot—he had only seen it from the rear, while conducting another transaction. However, when we tracked her down, the blond lady assured us she had purchased the Toulouse-Lautrec knockoff and there had been no Calder in the house by the time she got there. She surely would have known. Meanwhile, she asked, were we definitely not interested in selling the Vasarely?

By this time we felt we loved the obnoxious op-art Vasarely as much as anything we'd ever seen and would no more part with it than we would our own children.

By the end of the day, rehashing the mysterious thefts over and over with the New Jersey home sale habitués, we found ourselves deep into a sort of Agatha Christie-meets-Danny DeVito scenario. There were helpful neighbors picking through a tray of earrings, a ridiculously young cop scribbling on a notepad, a handsome, graying junk dealer hauling out the living room set. Everybody had a different opinion, another line of speculation. Meanwhile my mother's size-six petite ghost floated in the background, fingering the discolored rectangle on the wood paneling beneath the disconnected art lamp.

By that time, so much had happened since my mother's death in April that she would have hated. Some of it was Wall Street's fault, some of it was the government's, but some of it, Nancy and I knew, was ours. Of course she would have forgiven us—our mother couldn't hold a grudge long enough to smoke two cigarettes—but it's different when you have to imagine your own pardon.

Not to mention your Calder, as red and blue and yellow and egregiously wiggly as ever, God knows where, God knows where, God knows where.

UNBLENDING

The day Crispin and I got married in 1999, not one but nine new relationships were created. Or maybe ten, if you count mine with Crispin's ex-wife. She did not participate in the wedding, needless to say, but all four of our children were pressed into service, some less enthusiastically than others. Hayes had been bearing up well with all the changes in his life until then, but that day his appearance as best man involved trudging along with his head down, scowling, making eye contact with no one.

The word "blending" is used—perhaps wishfully—to describe what happens when families do this, as if you pushed the blender button and had a delicious smoothie ten seconds later. Not quite. It's slow, it's complicated, it's radically inconsistent—even when the blender's been running for ten years, there are still chunks of ice and globs of strawberry left. While some pairings thrive, others are plagued with resentments, and every one of them affects every other one.

For example, while Emma and I hit it off instantly, Hayes and Emma did not, and it didn't help when Hayes noticed that his unwanted older sister was Mommy's new best friend. Little Sam was terrified that I was stealing his father and worked so hard at monopolizing Crispin's attention when he came out each weekend that I began to give him the same dirty looks he gave me. Meanwhile, he worshipped Vince, who was awful to him.

It was a mess, but much of it smoothed out over time. Much credit for this goes to Jane, who came along about a year into the action to glue the family together with her beauty, her joie de vivre, and her equal relationship to one and all.

While Jane was working her magic, everyone else was growing up. About the time he hit adolescence, Sam and I began to get along fine, and Vince and Sam became serious bros. Hayes and Crispin, who had a classic oldest son–new stepdad competition going, found at least some respite watching televised sports. Emma and I remained in love, even as she put her real mom through the typical teenage-girl gauntlet.

And then Crispin and I began to fall apart as a couple, and we did not do it discreetly or decently, to both of our eternal regret and shame. We clashed over everything from the credit card statement to the bottles and cans in the recycling bin, and we sacrificed every bit of trust we had to these vicious arguments. Both of our older children got dragged into the drama and the conflicting loyalties, while Vince and Sam desperately tried to pretend that everything was OK for as long as possible; maybe if they didn't rock the boat it would stop rocking.

Well, it didn't. Shipwreck ensued. By the time Crispin moved out in December of 2008, even Jane knew her parents had to get away from each other. Worried about how she was taking it all, I delicately asked one night in the bathtub if she felt bad that Daddy didn't live with us anymore.

She considered a moment, her head lowered as if deeply concentrating on soaping her leg. Well, I'm really sad not to live with Daddy, she said, and then she lifted her head and looked me full in the eyes. But it's better, isn't it?

Jane adjusted to the situation quicker than anyone else. Six months out, my boys were still mad at Crispin, Emma worried about both of us, and Sam, after having had the hardest time making his place in the family, mourned it most of anyone. He finally got his driver's license so he could come up to visit whenever he wanted, but where? Dad's house? Marion's house? And where's Vince? (Chilling at Trav's, no doubt.) Then Emma went to college in New York, Hayes to Washington, Vince to New Orleans, Sam to Boulder. And that was just the first round. Crispin moved deeper into rural Pennsylvania; Jane and I set up in Baltimore.

Once you make the smoothie, you can't get back your strawberries and your milk and your ice. Whatever we had after our family unblended, it was not exactly what we started with. The strongest relationships stuck—Vince and Sam, me and Crispin's mom—but many were abandoned. What does it mean to be someone's ex-stepmother?

Not much, really, and I often feel a little embarrassed by this, like I broke a promise. I think Crispin does, too.

At least we have Jane. And she has all of us.

UNBROKEN CHAIN

Have you heard of Car Seat Headrest? Neutral Milk Hotel? Nilüfer Yanya? Tay-K? Alt-J? Milo, the rapper who references Nabokov and Aristotle, rhyming "axis" with "praxis"? These are some of the musicians my daughter and I listened to in the car coming home from a Taylor Swift concert in Washington, DC, one night in July 2018. Jane, who turned eighteen in June and got a tattoo and a vape to celebrate, is a big girl now. As I write this, she will only be living at home for another twenty-eight days and then she will be off to the Catskills to attend a school that advertises itself as "a place to think." She is ready for that. She acquired her notebooks even before her shower caddy and extra-long twin sheets.

Like her notebook connoisseurship, Jane's musical knowledge comes from the internet. Thanks to its brilliantly pulsing and ever-proliferating threads, she is forever discovering new artists who have no corporate connections, no advertising, no presence in the mainstream media. This Car Seat Headrest of whom I speak—this is one guy, a gay man in his twenties, who recorded his first four albums in the back seat of a car using GarageBand on his laptop. He has transcended playlist status: Jane's boyfriend gave her the vinyl version of his first album for Valentine's Day, then our deejay neighbor brought over a turntable.

To me, Mr. Headrest sounds a little like Jonathan Richman or the Velvet Underground. I like him very much. He's much better than the harsh rap music Jane also loves: Brockhampton, for example, a dozen rappers and producers who met on a Kanye West fan forum and moved into a group house in San Marcos, Texas. Or Rico Nasty, whose name says it all. Or "Poop, poop, scoop-diddy-whoop," a timeless new lyric from Kanye himself.

Just when you think you are living in a science fiction novel, a stray strand of the fabric of the old world pokes through. One evening I heard the unspeakably lovely opening guitar riff of "Unbroken Chain," from the Grateful Dead's *Live at the Mars Hotel*, coming from somewhere in the distance. I had not heard it in years. Moved almost to tears, I wandered into the hall and realized that it was coming from Jane's bedroom. Isn't this the most beautiful song, she said.

She is, after all, my daughter. She is starting to like hot sauce, she says the word "fuck" too much, she strongly feels that no matter what she ends up doing in life, it certainly will not be what her mother does. Thank God, she cries fervently whenever she hears good news, though she doesn't have the faintest bit of religious feeling. Like me, she has a scary talent for mishaps. She managed to lose her iPhone on the way into the concert last night—we had to keep running back and forth to the parking lot as we were told first that no purses, then no cameras, then no nothing was allowed inside. But when we called her number, a girl answered excitedly. I have your phone!

I knew the people at this concert would be awesome, said Jane, after we rendezvoused with our savior in front of the Redskins sign.

It was Taylor Swift's Reputation Stadium Tour, a stadium extravaganza with plumes of flame blasting heat and light into the night sky, golden-scaled serpents rearing two stories into the air, a segmented video display to rival Times Square, the singer flying around in fantastical baskets and cages, then being dropped off on a stage at the back, where she played old songs on an emerald-green acoustic guitar to the delight of my daughter and the two girls behind us, with whom she had bonded instantly. All were wearing previous tour T-shirts and cutoffs. We are the same person! she whispered to me. Taylor addressed all of her remarks directly to them, the zillion-bodied single person that they are, in a rambling declaration of love that went on through the night.

You guys have always been there for me, she said. When I had to go away for a while, you guys were there when I got back.

Jane was fifteen the last time we saw a Taylor Swift concert. Both she and Taylor, now twenty-eight, have changed a lot since then. Taylor doesn't write about crushes in the bleachers and teardrops on her guitar anymore; she mostly writes about being famous, a phase all pop stars seem to go through.

In the early days of Jane's fandom, I remember feeling awed at how utterly and abjectly she worshipped Taylor Swift, and I wondered if that sort of obsession would carry through once she started dating. Truth be told, I was worried, having gone through many unhappy such episodes in my younger years. These days Jane does have a boyfriend. But for her, no one will ever be Taylor Swift. Not even Mr. Headrest. It is clear that Taylor Swift is well aware of this phenomenon; this is what last night was all about. Eighty-two thousand of them, madly in love.

Surrounded by all this youth and passion, I felt a little fragile. Was I the oldest person there? Maybe. I danced a bit, but slid into my seat and started to yawn during the final set of songs and fireworks. After we found the car, Jane drove home (she drove down too; I've been officially retired as lead driver). On the way, she waxed philosophical.

I've been thinking, she said, moving into the left lane on 295, Ms. Yanya crooning in the background. As Ravens stadium glowed purple on the horizon, we were still traveling in the same fleet of cars in which we had left the concert, Baltimore fans returning home. Our lives are just so simple, and sweet, she finished.

I was struck dumb for a moment. We had just been talking about climate change, and this is pretty much the last thing I think about our lives. But to hear that this is how my daughter, freshly eighteen, about to leave home, feels about her life: thank God, as I have taught her to say.

MORNING
TRAFFIC ON
A STRANGE
PLANET

Tell me if this ever happens to you.

You are sitting at a red light in morning traffic, half-listening to the news on the radio, half-trying to decide how to juggle the elements of an ordinary day: the meetings, the appointments, the overscheduled children, the dirty house, the dreaded phone calls, the insurance company, the plumber, the cable provider. Which to do first, which second, which can be put off, which to axe entirely—oh wait, you need some cash and there's an ATM in the next block, should you stop now or get cash at the grocery store later—and click, something shifts.

The sun comes from behind a cloud, or slips behind a cloud, or the light doesn't change at all but your perspective somehow slips a notch out of alignment, and suddenly, the personality and situation that is so continually and thoroughly *you* seems arbitrary: separate from who you actually are. The mundane decisions that are the fabric of your day and your life seem like choosing between entrees for dinner on Mars.

What is this thing you call an insurance company?

You look around at the cars and the construction crew and the trees, and not just the things in your line of sight, it's all flooding in, language, books, cars, families, food allergies, massacres in distant lands, all the suffering in the world and all the babies born into it, and also the sweetness of nature and the possibility of joy, and you think, how did this happen? How did I end up a mote of consciousness at this particular intersection of the million strands?

Is it endorphins from your workout? Is it a flashback of some sort? Didn't the Talking Heads write a song about this?

For a moment you can see how the world will be when you are not in it, when you are just a misremembered character in the dreams of your grandchildren, when everyone you ever knew is gone. There will be mornings, there will be cars, and there will be decisions, and none of them will be yours. It's almost as if, for a microsecond, you have visited that you-less place.

Wait, you think, am I now an enlightened being? Is this cosmic consciousness, the goal of meditation and yoga, here at the corner of North Charles Street and Towsontown Boulevard? Or did I just forget to order decaf?

Before you can go home and write your inspirational book and start your cult, it is gone. And you've driven right past the ATM.

Then all the rest of it is back in a flash: the decisions, the errands, the to-do list and the schedule, the internal soundtrack of unfinished arguments and replayed conversations, of things you cannot believe you said that you must now agonize over for days or weeks, misunderstandings that can never be perfectly corrected. Plans, fears, dreams, wicked urges, vows of self-improvement. Everything that makes you you, more than half of which goes on below the surface, known only to you, and half of that so neurotic you can hardly put up with it.

Your body moving constantly into the future while your mind sorts endlessly through the past, a paranoid old lady reading discarded sections of yesterday's newspaper.

Be happy, you tell yourself. Be grateful. You have this car, you have this family, you have this grocery list and this ATM card. Some of the bad things that have happened to you are over and are not hurting you anymore. What more can you want?

But, you say, how can I be happy in this royal court of unfair destiny, this mad Sun King world of Shake Shacks and heated seats and bachelor parties in Jamaica, when three miles away from here there is broken glass and rat-a-tat and yellow tape, a high-pitched wail. On the other hand, how can I be sad when I have no right to be anything but happy? How can I stop worrying so much about how I feel?

The moments of respite tend to be random, and often come in traffic, though you once felt something similar in a very old convent you visited in France, and also upon waking up after anesthesia. Which is not to say you haven't tried a lot of other approaches, but transcendence often hides when you chase it.

Here comes the sun.

UNEXPECTED THINGS

after *The Pillow Book* by Sei Shōnagon

I return to my small gray Toyota just in time to see a huge SUV back into my front end before pulling away. At first I am horrified, then relieved to find that no damage has been done. After driving home, I get a second surprise: the silver Toyota logo was jarred loose by the impact and has fallen off the hood somewhere en route. A depressing black oval remains.

A lovely looming plant with hot-pink flowers edged in spiky white fringe—possibly dianthus—appears in the backyard in spring. It is like a gift with no card, unexpected.

At sixty-one I live alone with a cat and a dog: unexpected but actually just fine.

I cry so easily now. I've always been somewhat thin-skinned, but this is a new development. An editor I've worked with for many years calls to say he is moving to a different job; he certainly does not expect to hear choked sniffling on the other end of the line. And now my daughter has come home from college for the summer; she is angered by my unexpected tears, and easily causes them.

The vegetable stir-fry I threw together was okay, nothing special, but then I put an egg fried sunny-side up in very hot peanut oil on top of it. The crispy white and the silky yolk, the squiggle of sriracha, the sweet-salty vegetables and nutty brown rice—unbelievable!

When your ex-mother-in-law loves you so steadfastly that the relationship lasts many years after your marriage is over, that is unexpected. But even more unexpected is that, after decades of this happy connection, she changes her mind. She cuts you off completely, stops answering your emails, tells others you have said terrible things to her. You have no idea what these things are. You would have thought this impossible.

A notorious buffoon is elected to the highest office in the land. He lies, cheats, connives, and endangers the planet and all its inhabitants. Did anyone expect this?

A former college classmate, a Pulitzer Prize–winning journalist and author of many excellent nonfiction books, drops dead while taking a walk near his home in Chevy Chase, Maryland. "Last week I saw my cardiologist. He told me I drink too much," he wrote in an op-ed in *The New York Times* about a month ago. He surely did not expect this to be quoted in his obituary one month later.

As one might expect, the internet offers up a list of the fifty most unexpected discoveries. A royal-blue crawfish, a bubble-gum-pink grasshopper, a quarter intricately carved to show George Washington smoking reefer. A nest full of chicks in a barbecue grill, opened for the first time that season. Someone's dad found the red-laced hiking boot Reese Witherspoon threw over the cliff in the film version of *Wild*. A fisherman found a lumpy, luminous seventy-five-pound pearl and kept it for years as a good-luck charm, unaware that it was worth $100 million.

There are single earrings and many other pieces of jewelry I've mislaid and do not expect to find—particularly the gold dolphin pendant I loved so much, lost during a trip to Florida, perhaps in the trunk of the rental car. Nor do I think I will recover the abalone bracelet my old friend Kathy brought me from England, or the turquoise-and-silver one my children bought me to replace it, though I suspect those are in hiding nearby.

And what is this? The cat, who has been kept inside for the first three years of her life, is standing outside the back door waiting to come in. I will have to adjust.

Getting married and having babies. Being widowed, being divorced, being alone. Continually one has experiences one never expected to have, and things one could not live without keep falling away. Eventually one's certainties are few indeed. At this point one is recognized as a repository of great wisdom, called on frequently to dispense advice.

You swim joyfully in cold water for many years, then one day cannot bear it for even a second. Otherwise menopause is not so bad.

I often hear stories about people who get together with their long-lost true love from high school or college and live out their days in conjugal contentment. I can imagine the delight of this, especially because I am too tired and antisocial to meet new people, or to make a decent impression on them when I do. I visit with old boyfriends in my dreams but do not expect to see them anywhere else.

Once your memory starts to go, unexpected things are much more frequent. You start to put away a bottle of spicy V8 and, lo, there are two already in the cupboard. Whoever keeps buying the V8 must have also invited your neighbor for lunch: here she comes, carrying a bunch of mint from her garden.

One season after another, there are surprises: the sun breaking through a summer storm, the wicked orange bonfire of fall, winter branches coated in ice so they look like crystal, the brave crocuses of February and the explosion of cherry blossoms on the avenue in May. That's the thing about beauty—no matter how many times you see it, it is unexpected.

MARION WINIK is the author of *First Comes Love, The Big Book of the Dead,* and nine other books. She writes the Bohemian Rhapsody column at *Baltimore Fishbowl* and is the host of Baltimore WYPR's *The Weekly Reader.* She reviews books for *Newsday, People,* and *Kirkus Reviews* and teaches in the MFA program at the University of Baltimore. Find out more at marionwinik.com.

Printed in the United States
by Baker & Taylor Publisher Services